STRANGE IS THE NIGHT

S.P. MISKOWSKI

TREPIDATIO
PUBLISHING

This is a work of fiction. All of the characters, names, incidents, organizations, and dialogue in this novel are either the products of the author's imagination or are used fictitiously.

Trepidatio books may be ordered through booksellers or by contacting:
Trepidatio Publishing, an imprint of JournalStone
www.trepidatio.com
www.journalstone.com

The views expressed in this work are solely those of the authors and do not necessarily reflect the views of the publisher, and the publisher hereby disclaims any responsibility for them.

ISBN: 978-1-945373-74-9 (sc)
ISBN: 978-1-945373-75-6 (ebook)

Trepidatio Publishing rev. date: October 13, 2017

Library of Congress Control Number: 2017948075

Printed in the United States of America

Cover Design: kellydid/99designs
Cover Image: Katarina Blazhievskaya/Shutterstock.com
Edited by: Jess Landry

To Cory, with love

ACKNOWLEDGMENTS

A writer is nothing without a good editor. Thank you to the editors who accepted and improved these stories, and made this book possible: Jess Landry, David Longhorn, James Everington, Dan Howarth, Kate Jonez, Joe Pulver, John Marshall, Sam Cowan, Andy Cox, Robert Morrish, Richard Chizmar, and Mike Davis.

STRANGE IS
THE NIGHT

A.G.A.

"So, what do you call this thing?"

"Call it?"

"Yeah. Doesn't it have a name?"

The lounge was less than half full on a Tuesday night. All of the one- and two-cocktail drinkers had gone home at a reasonable hour. Besides Ed and Phil, only the diehard regulars, a few couples, and the occasional stray alcoholic remained.

"No," Ed replied. "It doesn't have a name."

"But…" Phil caught the waitress' eye and touched his glass to let her know they wanted another round of martinis. "How about when you summon it, when you 'call it forth,' you know?"

Ed drained his glass. He squinted at Phil.

"This is what I'm telling you," he said. "I don't summon it, or call it. I don't even know what it is."

"But you said it's a…"

"Yeah. I know what I said, but…"

"It sounds like some kind of superhero. Or anti-superhero. Is that the idea?"

"No." Ed leaned forward. "Look. I want you to know, I never asked for this thing to happen. I could have lived my whole life and it would never have occurred to me, right? So, I don't light candles. I don't send a message with a what-do-you-call-it, Ouija board. It isn't like that."

"Right," said Phil. "But you said it was a what, exactly?"

"Not me. Betsy. She's the one who acted like it was some kind of entity. She labeled it, gave it a category, whatever 'it' is. She was the one with the imagination, not me."

"Okay, and what did she label it, again?"

"Betsy called it my 'avenging guardian angel,'" Ed said in monotone. "Those are the words that she used. Not me."

The men went silent when the waitress arrived with fresh martinis. Phil gave the blonde a generous tip and a wink before she moved on.

"I thought you and Betsy were…"

"Over," Ed admitted. "Yeah. She packed up her knives and moved back to New York."

"You could follow her, nothing stopping you. Betsy's a Brooklyn girl at heart. Everybody knows that. You might like New York, too."

"I like what I do for a living, Phil. Senior management jobs in this game are not that easy to come by. Betsy could've worked anywhere. A chef can always find work, any city. She worked here, didn't she?"

"So…"

"She didn't want to stay. She didn't want to be with me. End of story."

"Sorry, man," Phil said. "Hey. Hey, cheers!"

They raised their glasses.

"Fuck women," said Phil. "And if you can't fuck 'em, to hell with 'em. Right?"

Ed sipped his martini. Across the room in the dusky half-light, their waitress leaned against the bar, poised and ready to start another round. The only window in the place was beveled at the edges, and too small to reveal more than figures rushing past on the busy street outside. Rain gave the shadowed bodies a sleek surface. They dashed by, coats shining like the dark feathers of nocturnal birds.

"Never mind about Betsy," Phil said. "Sorry. I only mentioned her because of this thing we're talking about. She called it an 'avenging angel'? She really said that? I mean, guardian angels, that's so…"

"Woo-woo?"

"Yeah. No disrespect to the lady. But, yeah."

"No, you're right," Ed told him. "Most people didn't realize she was into that bullshit. Tarot, spirit guides, even astral projection. She was talking to a psychic when she decided to move back to New York. Said it was her destiny."

"What a bitch. Uh, the psychic, not Betsy."

"Wasn't a woman, it was this guy with a shop on 1st Avenue, near the market."

"No kidding! What the hell's he doing telling another guy's girlfriend to leave him?"

"Destiny, remember? You can't fight it, apparently."

"But look, Ed, telling another guy's girl, practically a fiancée, almost his wife, to move to another city…"

"Yeah. I know. You're right. Yeah."

"I mean it's the lowest. Right?"

"I don't know," Ed said. "I can think of worse things."

"So this was the same guy who told her about the what's it, the A.G.A.? That's what I'm calling it. Sounds less loony."

Ed grinned. He set his martini on the table and sat staring down at it.

"No," he said. "It was just one of those things. We were, you know, we were in bed one Sunday. If you can picture what I'm saying."

"Okay. Yeah."

"Just, you know, watching something stupid on TV. Cartoons. I don't remember. Joking around. A nice day."

"Right," said Phil.

"And I was saying something about Ted Donovan…"

"The designer you told me about, right, from Portland?"

"Yeah. I was just letting off steam, nothing serious: the way the guy keeps asking questions about basic stuff, and the way he sucks up to people at work. He's too old to be there, really, and he ought to know it. That kind of thing."

"Sure," Phil said. "Sure."

"All of a sudden Betsy gets this look and she says: 'You better stop now.' I thought she was sick of hearing about the office, the politics, the backstabbing. It was all pretty standard. I talked about it the same way she talked about the waiters at Chez Marlene. But she gave me this strange look."

"Strange, like…?"

"I don't know. Scared."

"Scared?"

"Okay, maybe not scared. Concerned. Worried."

"But she doesn't even know the guy, right?"

"Right. Then, out of the blue, she says: 'Do you realize every person you've talked about like this ended up having something bad happen to them?'"

Phil laughed. Ed gave him a sheepish grin.

"I know," Ed said. "I know. It's a crazy thing to say, right? So, it was a Sunday. Raining as usual. We drank a glass of wine with breakfast, smoked a little. It was that kind of day. Also, I knew Betsy was seeing this psychic once a month, so I thought that was where it came from, the woo-woo talk. I laughed. I called her on it and she said no, this wasn't from the psychic, and it wasn't funny. This was something she had been thinking about for a while."

"How long is a while?"

"She said it was the reason she went to the psychic in the first place."

"What the hell does that mean?" Phil asked.

Ed held his glass and swirled the gin with his plastic tooth-pick and olive. He took a sip before he answered.

"She said she'd compiled a list, one day."

"A list. Of…?"

"People I'd dropped. You know, not just unfriended online but actually stopped seeing or maybe started avoiding. I had reasons. Some of these people were jerks. They were people who, you know, trashed me in some way or screwed me over. People I disliked and bitched about."

"Everybody could make a list like that," said Phil. "Anybody."

"Yeah," Ed said. He hesitated. "Now, you have to understand, this is what Betsy pointed out to me. This is how she described what I think of as ordinary life events."

"Granted. Sure. Grain of salt."

"Right, but…"

Ed surveyed the dim room with its assortment of ragged salesmen, silent couples, and drunks. The waitress at the bar shifted her weight, ready to bring another round at the smallest signal.

"The thing is," Ed said. "Every person on the list was somehow—messed up."

"You mean they were mentally ill?"

"No," Ed told him. "Not only that." He leaned forward again. "Like my ex-girlfriend, Jasmine."

"Oh boy," Phil said. "Buddy, I'm sorry to criticize your taste but that bitch was bat-shit insane, okay? Anybody who uses her ex's credit card number to buy flowers for his new girlfriend with a note saying you made her have an abortion…Jesus!"

"I know," Ed said. "Yeah, I know."

"So?"

"The thing is, Jasmine's in the hospital now."

"Oh, wow. Sorry. For what?" Phil asked.

"Cancer."

"No shit!"

"It's bad." Ed told him. "Stage four. You know, I got a voice message from her mom a while back. She said Jasmine's dying. It's in her glands; it's in her brain. She's not going to make it."

"Christ," said Phil. "Sorry. I…"

"No, it's okay. You didn't know. I didn't know until her mom called. Then I was going to send her flowers, but…"

"Yeah, that seems weird after the prank she pulled."

"I know," said Ed. "I didn't want to imply anything with the flowers, like I was getting even. So I just sent her a card."

"Jesus. Bad luck."

"Betsy didn't think it was luck. Well, she did when we first heard the news, but not after she wrote the list."

"No? Oh. Right. The 'avenging guardian angel.'" Phil laughed. Then he shook his head. "Women are crazy. Not all the time. They go crazy, then they normal out. It's all about the estrogen. I read an article. Maybe she was at one of those points in her cycle…"

"Maybe," said Ed. "I told her she was being silly and she let it slide. But the next morning, over coffee, she started telling me more about the list."

"The list? Oh yeah, the people who…"

"Screwed me over. Yeah. There was Jack, this guy I knew at Fontana, the company where I worked before?"

"Okay."

"Jack was this real truculent douchebag, broad, sharp looking, great suits, tossed the corporate lingo around and dropped names like nobody's business."

"Yeah?"

"Thing is, he acted like we were best friends. Not just co-workers but really tight, like we were college buddies or something, him and me 'against the world' kind of crap. Right up to the minute he told the people who interviewed me…"

"At the place where you work now, right? Big City?"

"Yeah. I used Jack as a reference because he insisted. He kept talking about how he had my back no matter what. Then he told

HR at Big City I had personal issues."

"Issues…"

"Vague yet insinuating. He didn't come right out and commit slander, is what I'm saying. He was smooth about it, like he didn't want to say anything, but he felt he ought to mention it. He felt an 'obligation' to warn them."

"How do you know this?"

"What do you think? The head of HR told me."

"That was lucky."

"No doubt. I could have missed the job of a lifetime. I would never have known Jack was trashing me behind my back except I knew the gal in HR. I bought her lunch, and she let me read the email exchange. We had mutual friends. She knew Jack was lying. She just couldn't figure out why."

"Compulsive?"

"I don't know, but I cursed that son of a bitch. I deleted him from my friend list as soon as I changed jobs. When I heard he was still talking about me, back at Fontana, I went ballistic."

"Should have punched the guy," Phil said quietly.

"I didn't have to. I didn't have a chance. A week later he drove his car off the South End Bridge into the bay."

Phil gave Ed a wide-eyed look. Then he closed his mouth. The two men exchanged a solemn expression.

"He…?"

"Died. Drowned. Or, I guess he was dead before he hit the water. Hell, who knows? Maybe he was wide awake, screaming all the way down."

Ed drained his glass. Phil followed, and then signaled the waitress.

"That's…"

"Yeah," said Ed.

"Did you know about it?"

"Well, sure. But, you know, people die, accidents happen, right? I didn't think any more about it. I was sorry somebody I knew had to bite it like that, but I wasn't going to his funeral after what he did. We were never really friends anyway. The guy was such a liar."

"Yeah," said Phil. "I hear you."

The waitress delivered two fresh drinks and collected the empty glasses. She gave Phil a little smile when she picked up the bills and he told her to keep the change.

"You're tipping on every round," Ed said after the waitress left.

"Yeah," Phil said, following the blonde with his gaze. "She's worth it, don't you think? Look at her, anticipating our every whim. This is outstanding service."

They laughed lightly and lifted their glasses. Phil turned his attention back to Ed's story.

"Okay, so two people you know came to a bad end. Okay, look, I can top that. Most people can."

"There was also the barista at Café Carafe, the one who never got my order right."

"Killing offense."

"Go ahead and laugh," Ed told him. "The guy's in a coma."

"What?"

Across the room the waitress picked up a new tray of drinks intended for another table. She whispered something to the bartender, who glanced at Phil and Ed before busying himself by wiping down the bar.

"He was on his bicycle when it happened. That day I told Betsy I was definitely going to complain to the manager because I was fed up. All I wanted was a mocha Frappuccino with soy, right? Same order, every time. He never got it right. Milk, vanilla, always something wrong. The person ahead of me never failed to get what he wanted, and the person after. Not me."

"I would've quit going there," Phil said. "It's bullshit, getting personal behind a fucking espresso counter. Who does he think he is?"

The bartender was looking at them. Phil gave him a smile, but the guy stared without acknowledging it while he wiped the bar with a wet rag, making slow, even circles.

"Café Carafe is right across the street from the office," Ed explained. "Everybody goes there. Betsy knew people who worked there. The next coffee shop is two blocks away. And I kept thinking the guy would get fired. Anyway. The last time I went there I was with my boss. We were in crunch mode, again. I was working twelve-, fourteen-hour days for three weeks straight. And I was trying to impress my boss. I invited him out for coffee, so I could get chummy with him and find out how I was doing. But then, just like all the other times, the barista screwed up the order."

"At least he was consistent."

"What can I say?" Ed stared down at his drink. "I lost it. Right there in the coffee shop, I just exploded. I started screaming at this moron at the top of my lungs. I call him about ten different highly inappropriate things. And I look over at my boss and he's shaking his head at me. He starts telling me to calm down, you know, it's okay, it's just *coffee*." Ed looked at Phil. "That was it, the limit. That made it, like, ten times worse. If the fucking barista had been on my side of that counter, I would have taken his head off. Here's my boss thinking I'm unstable or something, and how do you explain a thing like that?"

They sat in silence for a moment. Phil took a drink. Ed watched him.

"See?"

"See what?" Phil asked.

"You're thinking it, too: I over-reacted. You think I was wrong. It was just a bad week."

Phil was silent.

"Anyway," Ed told him. "We got out of there, and I was going to call the manager to complain and get this guy fired. That was my plan. But the next day I saw his picture in the paper. One of those cheerful headshots where you know something terrible happened. I read the story over a shot of vodka at the kitchen sink.

"It was raining when his shift ended. The barista was heading northeast on his bike toward Montlake when he hit a puddle. Turned out to be a pothole without a lid. Flipped his bike and he went flying into the tail end of a FedEx truck."

"Shit."

"That's what I said."

"I mean… Shit. Shit! That's just… That sucks."

There was a flurry of movement outside the beveled window, a flash of something exquisitely dark and shimmering in the rain. Phil flinched.

"Sorry," he told Ed. "For a second I thought somebody was running at the glass."

Ed grinned and nodded. Phil took another sip of his drink.

"And then there was my boss…" Ed began.

"Your boss? Don't tell me he's in a coma, too."

"No," said Ed. "Turned out I was right. He really thought I was losing it that day in the coffee shop. We had a couple of talks about it, and he told me to enroll in this anger management program."

"For yelling at a barista?"

"I know. That's so lame, right? But he was serious. Okay, he also wanted to bring in a couple of his friends from a company on the east side. He kept talking these guys up and telling me about the projects they worked on, and how they'd all spent two years in Shanghai with this other bastard he likes. I figured he was looking around the office for two people he could kick out. Ordinarily, I wouldn't be concerned."

"You said you knew the gal in HR."

"Yeah, well, I meant I was doing a great job. But now the boss had tagged me with this anger management bullshit, I was a target. It was a control thing, too. Next time I raised my voice there would be *consequences*."

"Jesus."

"Right," Ed agreed. "I was in a hell of a mood that weekend. Spent two days griping to Betsy, who did not want to hear it, okay? I went to work Monday expecting bad news. As soon as I get there, my boss' boss stops by my cubicle to have a little chat. We leave the building and take a walk around the block. He buys me coffee at Café Carafe, and the new barista gets my mocha Frappuccino with soy on the first try. We share a couple of jokes, and the boss' boss tells me they're adding a few more duties to my job description, plus a pay increase and a bonus for my hard work."

"Wow. Because…"

Ed failed to suppress a smile.

"My boss got caught on a security video banging a nineteen-year-old intern. The company's giving this girl a cash incentive to sign a non-disclosure agreement and go away."

"No shit!"

"Right."

"But this guy, your boss, he's alive?"

"If you want to call it that," said Ed. "He'll never get a recommendation for another job like that one. He's over. He's probably working the night shift at McDonald's."

"Fries and nineteen-year-olds."

"Yeah. And the gal in HR says he caught something from the intern, but she wouldn't say what, so you know it's bad. All in all, a very expensive ten-minute fuck."

They sat quietly for a moment. Then Phil asked, "How many…? Um, how many names were there, exactly…?"

"On Betsy's list?"

"Yeah."

"Eleven."

Phil's mouth stayed open for several seconds.

"Eleven?"

"Well, she went all the way back to middle school. Obsessive with details, my Betsy."

"Christ," said Phil. "What happened in middle school?"

"Nothing," Ed told him. "Really. It's nothing. This is a part of it that gets highly speculative, in my opinion."

"Isn't all of it speculative?"

"Sure, sure. You can believe this stuff or not. You can call it crazy."

There was another swift, oblique movement beyond the window. Phil blinked when a spray of water hit the glass.

"So, in middle school…" Phil prompted.

Ed rolled his eyes. He gazed at the window and said, "There was a kid named Swan. Arnie Swan, perfect name for a geek. Right? He took plenty of shit for it. He sat behind me in two classes, and he was always copying my work. Nobody else noticed, but I knew he was there, every day, stealing the answers, copying everything I did. He was this gawky little chicken neck, and nobody liked him. I didn't like him. He followed me around. I'd see him there, kind of hovering like a shadow. So I told him one day: 'Watch out on your way home, dummy.' Not that I planned anything. I wasn't a bully. I just wanted him to worry about it a little bit. I thought maybe it would keep him off my back."

"Don't tell me somebody beat him up on his way home."

"Nobody knows. Nobody ever saw the kid again. It was on the news and stuff, and the police asked around. They came to school and gave us a lecture on personal safety."

"You didn't say anything?"

"Like what? 'Hey officer, I told Swanny to watch his back the same day he disappeared…' Phil, why would I say anything? Kids run away. Kids disappear. Happens every day. The first time I thought of it again was years later. I told Betsy the story, and you see what she came up with. If she hadn't made a list, it would never have crossed my mind again."

Phil was quiet for a moment.

"You said there were eleven names. Eleven people."

"Right, but why go into it? Sure, sure. The high school Algebra teacher who flunked me was murdered by her husband, and the girl who turned me down for the prom was gang raped that night. The list goes on, but, like I said, shit happens all the time. It's eleven if you include the guy who went to HR and demanded my parking space because he had a limp and said he needed a spot closer to the ramp."

"You yelled at the guy?"

"No," said Ed with a sneer. "Of course not. I mean, not really. I said he was a freak and he was in my way. I only said that to Betsy."

"What did she say?"

"She said it made her feel sad."

"Huh."

"She didn't even know the guy. He was slow, he had trouble talking, and he had a terrible temper. You wouldn't expect that, in a disabled person. They're supposed to be so positive and 'rise above it all,' right? But this guy would get frustrated because he couldn't get the right words out or something, and he'd be furious! His face would turn red and his arms would shake. It was kind of funny."

"Was he a programmer?" Phil asked.

"No. Hell, no! He was on some special work contract. He sorted mail and delivered it and he ran the copy machine. Can you believe it? The copy machine operator wanted my parking space!"

Phil studied Ed's face for a moment. Then he asked, "So, what happened to him?"

Ed grinned. He tapped the rim of his martini glass with his toothpick.

"He choked to death on a bagel in the cafeteria."

Ed slurped down the last of his drink. Phil watched him and then scanned the room. The bartender was staring in their direction again.

"He choked to death, like, right there?" Phil asked. "Didn't that seem strange?"

"Definitely. People choke. It's a given. Anybody in food service ought to know the Heimlich maneuver, don't you think?"

"Yeah," said Phil. "I guess so, but what I meant was…"

"Don't you like your drink?" Ed asked.

Phil took a final sip. He nodded. "Great," he said. "Great martinis here."

"You want another round?"

"Oh boy, you know," said Phil. "I should actually be getting home."

"No."

"Yeah, I know. It sucks. I've got this presentation tomorrow…"

"Hey."

"Yeah?"

"Don't let it get to you," Ed said. His brow was furrowed and he gazed at Phil over the dregs of their last drink.

"What do you mean?" Phil said. He smiled but the corners of his mouth quivered ever so briefly. Outside the window, on the darkened street, the rain was coming down in torrents.

"I should buy one last round," said Ed. "Come on."

"No. Don't worry about it."

They looked away from one another.

"Well, if that's how it is. Thanks for listening. Ever since Betsy left, I've been spending too much time alone. Thinking too much."

"That's natural."

"Thinking stupid thoughts. Going through stuff."

"It's normal," Phil said. "Everybody does that."

"I mean her stuff."

Phil looked up from the bills he had fanned out across the tabletop as a final tip for the waitress.

"Her stuff?"

"Yeah," said Ed. "She forgot her cell phone."

"Ha! Women!" Phil laughed. It was an abrupt, barking sound. He wasn't smiling.

"Actually," Ed said. "I stole it before she left for the airport."

Phil counted the money and put his wallet away. "Why?" he asked with his eyes averted. "Why would you do that?"

"So I could see who she was screwing."

Ed's eyes glistened like beetles in the half-light. Phil considered Ed's face and then the table. Condensation dripped from the martini glasses, forming tiny pools on each side of the bills he had laid down.

"You're going through a rough time," Phil said. "You probably think all kinds of things after a breakup. Don't let your imagination mess with you."

Ed picked up a paper napkin and dropped it on the table. It puckered and sank as it soaked up the condensation.

"You know, Phil," he said. "One of the reasons Betsy left me was because I don't have any imagination."

"No?"

"Nope. None. I'm not an artist like you, or Betsy. When people screw me over, all I do is think of the worst thing that could happen to them. And it happens. No imagination involved. No 'summoning.' No candles. It just happens."

Phil licked his lips. He glanced across the room at the bar, where the waitress and the bartender stood watching him. Their expressions were blank.

"Ed, old buddy," he said. "That's kind of crazy. You know? The whole thing is pretty crazy." Phil rose to leave. He wiped his hands on his trousers.

"The numbers don't lie," Ed said. "Everybody lies, but numbers reveal the truth. That's what Betsy told me. And she was right! Thirteen people are fucked, all thanks to me and my lack of imagination."

"You said eleven. On the list Betsy came up with, you said there were eleven…"

"That wasn't including Betsy," Ed said. "Betsy, who by now is lying face-up on her kitchen floor in Brooklyn with a blade in her abdomen, one of those full-tang knives, the kind she took such good care of and handled so well."

Phil said nothing. His face was quite pale.

Beyond the window the street had gone pitch black. There was so little sound. Only the wet whoosh of traffic and the murmuring of strangers huddled under umbrellas in the darkness.

"So that's twelve, old buddy," Ed said with a smile. "Betsy makes twelve, and then, of course—you. All I can say is, I hope she was worth it. I really do."

LOST AND FOUND

Finally arrived. My heart's dancing. There's a slight chill to the air, a perfect greeting. Mist, too, but not like the constant drizzle back home. The streets are busy with people, buses, and taxis, nothing unusual. Yet it all feels different, and distant, the world I left behind going on without me.

I wish the people I work with could see me. They take vacations twice a year, usually to some awful place like Kauai or the Caribbean, where there's nothing to do. They lie around on the beach, and drink too much. Last year some of them took a cruise together. What a nightmare, sailing the Pacific coast with a boatload of your co-workers. Can you imagine?

This is my vacation and I'm doing exactly what I want, for a change. I tried explaining to my supervisor, who stared at me and said, "Oh well, have a good trip, try to get some sun." Stupid woman.

Here I am, at last, in the heart of Muriel Watson's hometown, in the hotel where she spent her childhood, where she honey-mooned, where she wrote her novels, and—I'm getting ahead of myself. I'm here. Hard to believe but all of it's real.

The train was full of tourists. I stood in line at the ticket booth while two of my fellow Americans harangued a young woman with blunt, jet streaks of eyeliner and meticulously drawn plum lipstick. She regarded them with the cruel patience of a child conducting an experiment on a pet hamster.

When my turn came I said as little as possible, hoping I might be mistaken for Canadian. The young woman studied the hotel name and address on my itinerary. She looked me over and asked if I knew the area. I said no. She took pity on me and wrote down my connections. She told me to be careful. I mumbled a brief apology for being stupid. I told her I didn't know which direction to go, to find the platform. She pointed and I mumbled thanks.

While I waited, standing directly under the sign for the train, feeling the cold rush of air from the tunnels swirl up around my legs, I heard my compatriots again, whining about the lack of customer service. Then they lapsed into what they probably thought to be a funny imitation of the ticket booth woman's accent. No wonder they hate us over here.

The Hyde Hotel is smaller than it appears in the photos online. Not as old as I'd assumed, refurbished many times, according to the front desk clerk.

"The cornices and balustrade are latter day embellishments," he said.

He was a young man who seemed middle-aged, rundown or broken somehow. Or am I being arrogant? I don't want to be one of those rotten tourists, accusing everyone of being dour. I have to remember why I'm here, and not become distracted with observations about how this is just like home, while *that* is so unlike what I'm used to. Always comparing things to other things.

The clerk didn't blink when he noted my reservation. He reminded me to exchange keys at the front desk each time I trade rooms. (They have actual keys here, not those key cards I despise.)

"Have you signed on for one of the local tours?" he asked.

"No, I'm on my own tour," I said. "Following the haunts of my favorite author."

"Oh?"

"Yes. Muriel Watson."

He frowned. "Sorry. I don't know the name."

"Her parents used to work in this hotel," I said. But he seemed to have lost interest.

I thanked him too many times. Should I have tipped? There was no bellboy, or porter, in sight. Only the clerk, a couple waiting to check in, and an old man dozing on a sofa in the corner. But it didn't matter. I only carry one small suitcase. "Don't pack what you can't hoist or drag by yourself," is my travel motto. Not that I've traveled much. Once to Vancouver. Once to Portland.

Upstairs, the corridors are so narrow I can't imagine two people walking side-by-side. Stepping out of the nausea-inducing "lift," which took off like a rocket and immediately slowed to a grinding halt on the third floor, I nearly fell over making the first turn toward my room. The hallway is curved, which seems odd in a building that looks square. Optical illusion, or an architectural compensation.

I found the room right away, 309. I stood staring at the number until I heard the elevator again. It's silly to be so excited. But I've come a long way on this adventure. I want to savor all of it. In fact, I wanted to take a picture, but I've lost my phone. (I used the lobby telephone to report it missing and cancel the service until I get home.)

The room is larger than I expected but also simpler, and less attractive. A narrow bed with pinstriped sheets and matching quilt. A nightstand with a lamp. One straight-backed chair and a small table next to the window. The view is a rooftop, with water stains and pigeon feathers, on the other side of an alley. I try to imagine Muriel Watson spending her honeymoon here and the thought makes me melancholy. Maybe the view was different in the early '60s. Maybe there was a garden next door. I don't know. The biography doesn't say.

I'm feeling very tired. Plane, train, bus. I was hungry earlier but now I only feel fatigue and a wave of something like sorrow. Chalking it up to too much distance covered in one day.

I've peeled the covers off the bed and I plan to rest for half an hour or so. Then I'll see what's available from room service.

***

SEPT. 25

Didn't know where I was when I woke up a little while ago. Thought I was still traveling. The rapid compression of places, names, faces I'll never see again. I replayed my journey while sleeping. Train stations beneath buildings marked with scaffolding and tarp. Above ground platforms, a distant whistle, vaulted canopies of rainclouds. A blank ticket in my hand. Trying to remember the name of my destination.

The sheets are damp with sweat. They don't smell like me, probably a composite of strange food and chemical and mineral differences in the water across regions. The bed felt fresh and crisp when I lay down. I'll have to remember to leave the housekeeping sign on the doorknob. Otherwise, my "privacy will be respected," according to the hotel greeting card.

Oddly enough, I'm not at all hungry, although I've missed the complimentary breakfast. I'll shower before I go out, and find a place for lunch while I'm exploring the neighborhood. On my first tour I'll track down Philips's, the bookstore where Muriel Watson gave the only reading of her all-too-brief career.

Can't help staring at the ceiling and wondering if the crumbling plaster was the same when she spent her honeymoon here. Or on countless occasions when she must have played games as a child, when her parents worked at the hotel. Did she hide in the rooms and stairwells, and jump out to startle the maids? Her biography doesn't say so, but it's a slender volume. One hundred and ten pages to convey a writer's life. If her books had been more popular, if her themes had been more universal, if she had nurtured the will to promote her work, or if she had won any of the prizes for which her books were nominated, the desk clerk might have known her name. But then she wouldn't be mine alone, all but forgotten by the writers' clubs and organizations to which she belonged. Her dark hair and pale gray eyes were luminous in the photo on the back of her books. Slim fingers arched elegantly around a cigarette. Lips drawn into a sort of smile, a resigned smirk.

I like to imagine young Muriel chasing shadows through a sun-dappled lobby. I like to think she was happy here, once. As a child, and maybe as a young woman. Despite the sad failure of her marriage to an aspiring poet named Timothy Davies, who shared this room with her so many years ago. Davies the Disappointed fled the marriage bed and returned to a bedsit in Islington.

Morbid today, probably the result of too much travel and, now, too much sleep. Shower, then lunch.

***

SEPT. 25

Before leaving the hotel, I stopped at the front desk. My intention was to check my directions to the bookshop on Merton Lane and make sure my room change is scheduled for tomorrow morning.

Everything looked a bit shabbier than I remembered. I must have been exhausted yesterday, not to notice the threadbare sofas and carpet. I expected the lobby to be busy. Or, I don't know what I expected. In any case, there were only two people, both elderly men wearing business suits, seated facing one another in armchairs, reading newspapers.

The same clerk who was at the desk yesterday nodded as I approached and listened politely to my questions.

"We have you booked into 219 for one day, following your stay in—"

He consulted a computer screen without typing anything and it occurred to me that the hotel was small enough to appear on a simple grid. "—309. Your key will be provided at check-in. Will you need assistance?"

"No," I said. "No, thank you. I wonder if you can tell me, which way should I start out to find Merton Lane?"

He studied my face for a split second, and turned toward the glass double doors at the north end of the lobby. He pointed but I couldn't tell in which direction.

"Is that to the left?" I asked.

"Left would be the longer route. Should you decide to take in the sights along the main road, you will end up at the market."

He didn't offer any further advice. I didn't want to waste his time. After all, I have a map.

I'm still a little confused, and embarrassed, about what happened next.

The way the desk clerk said "longer route" led me to think turning right would make the journey shorter but also less interesting. I hesitated just inside the glass doors, watching people on the other side hurrying toward myriad destinations. And then it was as though I reached out, pushed the doors open, turned right, and began to walk down the street. I say "as though" because I could see pedestrians on all sides of me, and I joined in the jostling crowd, happily making my way toward the corner where I planned to turn east, to venture through the midday chill.

Yet, in fact, I never moved. Never opened the doors at all. And when the desk clerk took hold of my elbow and asked, "Ma'am, would you like to sit down?" I let him guide me away from the lobby to an open area behind several enormous, velvet-leafed potted plants.

Tables had been set up for guests to enjoy meals from the hotel restaurant. I sat at one of these tables and the clerk placed a glass of water in front of me. Soon a waiter, slender and callow, flung open the metal French doors to the kitchen and conveyed to my table a meal I still don't recall ordering. A chicken sandwich with buttered bread, three sliced carrot sticks, and a pot of very hot, very strong black tea.

With every bite of the sandwich I felt more keenly how ravenous my appetite had become. Only when I had cleaned my plate and swallowed the last drop of tea did I notice three middle-aged women seated at the next table. They wore close-fitting hats which might have given them a vintage style if their dresses had not looked homemade and unfashionable, more like house dresses than outfits to wear while shopping for whatever was in the half dozen bags clustered around their feet. They were staring at me, one with her teacup poised midway to her lips.

A co-worker who had lived in London for a year offered me a list of social tips before I left home, to make my trip to the UK "more pleasant." Most of the rules were more offensive than helpful.

"Eat slowly, taking time to cut your meat into small bites. Tear bread into sections and butter each section, rather than slathering butter onto a whole slice and cramming it into your mouth. Don't say 'thank you' over and over. Say it once and then be quiet. Don't bring up politics under any circumstances but if you're confronted by questions about wars launched by your country, don't brag and do *not* claim any victory, moral or otherwise. Don't brush your teeth or floss in a public toilet. Never cut in line or demand special treatment.

"Above all, don't give the impression that you think you're important. They hate that. In fact, they hate us, but they're much too polite to say so. Not like the French, who live to show their contempt for our disgusting habits and ignorance. No. British people simply stand back and wait for us to fall on our faces."

You would think we were born in a barn, if you listened to this woman talk. And there I was, finishing off my first meal since I'd arrived, and I'd somehow made a spectacle of myself. The women at the next table went on staring at me while I signed for the meal. I made my way out of the dining area toward the elevator. (No use calling it a "lift," the word doesn't describe that lurching sensation any better than the American term.)

I intended to freshen up, splash cold water on my face, and start out again. But the elevator ride, the cramped quarters combined with that too swift, trundling motion, left me dispirited and sleepy. In the corridor I turned to the right and stopped. Somehow I'd lost my bearings. I must have taken a different route this time. The room numbers ascended toward the right, rather than descending. I turned left and soon found 309. In the privacy of my narrow room with its tousled sheets—I'd forgotten to leave the housekeeping sign on the door—I lay down and cried.

It occurs to me that I might be coming down with a cold. But the only symptoms are a weakened disposition and a craving for sleep.

***

SEPT. 26

I've been lying in bed staring out the window since 6 a.m. The sooty clouds threaten a malevolent downpour and I'd like to stay here re-reading Muriel Watson's biography. But I'll soon have to check into the next room I've reserved.

The ceiling over my bed is the one surface that doesn't appear to have been painted or repaired. I might be looking at the exact section of plaster Muriel saw, following her "attempted coupling" with her mediocre poet. This is the phrase her biographer used to describe the grappling that occurred, not in this bed, it's too new, but in a bed exactly like it. After which Muriel awoke in this corner, with the gray, dim light from the window breaking across skewed sheets and sprawled bodies. How long did they lie here, reassembling their thoughts, wishing to be rid of one another?

In a month Davies would be gone, last seen stepping into the path of an oncoming laundry truck, an absurd death Muriel would immortalize in her second novel, *Gin and Tonic*. By then she'd given up hope of earning enough money from writing, and had returned to teaching. How she hated that. She hated children. She hated not being able to smoke when she wanted. A woman of her day, with a two-pack-a-day habit she picked up as a girl of twelve in this hotel, imitating the maids who cleaned the rooms, traipsing along when they climbed the fire escape to the roof for a midday smoke.

***

SEPT. 26

If she had won any of the awards (including a Booker Prize) for which her novels were nominated in 1969, 1973, and 1975, she might have been successful. She would belong to the world, and everyone would know her name. Even her biography is out of print, a hastily written profile by a long-dead author for hire. Published by The Arts Council in the late 1970s.

I found Muriel several years ago, in the farthest back corner of a musty bookshop in Seattle, Washington. I'd lost my job, lost the apartment I shared with a younger, more successful technical editor named Giselle, who had informed me one day that she could "no longer live with the stench of failure everywhere." She was nice enough to refund my deposit and first month's rent.

I moved across the street to an older building, into a basement studio. It was brutally cold in the winter and I made a habit of taking the bus once a day, to warm up. One of the regular stops was in the U-District, near Burton's Books. It was a rundown place, the only entrance via cobbled alley, its façade bearing a plaque attributing construction to a WPA crew.

Inside the shop, the air was heavy with the musty odor of mold. Books, many of them yellowed with age, crowded every surface and cluttered the aisles. Little towers of them leaned against chairs and shelves. Each aisle led to a quiet haven containing an armchair where patrons were welcome to sit and read as long as they liked. This became my world for the winter, and on into the cold, rainy spring, until I finally landed a new work assignment downtown.

In my favorite spot at Burton's Books, a dilapidated crimson chair decorated with crocheted doilies faced a particularly dusty and neglected shelf. There a few Beryl Bainbridge novels met the tattered remnants of Bloomsbury Group essays and biographies. And someone had placed Muriel Watson's novels on the end, out of any order I could imagine and far from the highbrow classics occupying the front of the shop. All three of her books appeared to be untouched, unread, as if the set were opened on a long ago Christmas morning and immediately discarded.

In my depression and weariness, I accepted this meeting as something like destiny. I opened the first volume, *The Glass Houses*, and began to read.

The first page described a hotel lobby, and a room very much like the one I occupy now. The narrator moved on to the streets, pubs, houses, and factories beyond the hotel, creating an atmosphere of undeniable gloom made bearable by the author's wit.

Alice was terribly pleased with herself. Nine o'clock. On any typical day she would be seated at her desk by now, surrounded by the awful rumble of morning gossip...

I felt an intangible and, given the geographic and chronological distance between us, inexplicable connection to Alice, and to Muriel. She was young when she wrote this novel. She was engaged and fiercely determined to climb out of her own skin, and her hometown, using only words as a vehicle. Haven't we all had a dream like that?

I read that first novel in one sitting, at Burton's Books, and then bought all three. Online I tracked down a paperback of Muriel Watson's only biography. I traced her journey from the Hyde Hotel of her childhood, to the bedsit of her doomed poet in Islington, to a caravan on the beach where she spent a wild summer with friends who moved to Italy and never returned.

Muriel moved back here, to the street where she was born. After her parents died she lived on teaching wages and bravado, reading her work on the radio a few times, getting respectable reviews and award nominations, never quite able to escape the inertia of her time and place, never making crucial connections that could have led to festival readings and paid magazine writing. She joked in a radio interview that she was "shaking off the dust and going on holiday."

Holidays she spent here, at the Hyde Hotel, trying to write. In this room, 219. The one to which I relocated at check-in.

There is no view, not even a crack of sky above the rooftops. The ceiling is stained light amber from a past life, an era of evening cocktails and round-the-clock cigarettes. Hundreds of them smoked by Muriel as she sat staring at ominous white pages in her typewriter, her heart frozen to its purpose, fingers itching to do the only thing she knew how.

Did she realize she would only produce these three slender volumes of fiction? Her books were meant to be her escape. Yet who would read them? *An Unworthy Cause* would be her last novel. After a few decades, following her death, no one recalls her name. She isn't even listed in a recent *Guardian* roundup of the most obscure and forgotten British female authors.

Only I remember. Or seem to remember. Since she was dead by the time I learned of her life. Here are her books, on the hotel nightstand, come home. I reach out and touch the brittle covers as I begin to drift off, bone-tired after a day of disappointment.

***

SEPT. 27

Awakened in the middle of the night by the sound of someone trying to open my door. Pulling at the doorknob, rattling the key. I sat up in bed and turned on the light. But whoever was outside had moved on.

In the next moment I felt a wave of hunger that nearly knocked me over. Realizing I had eaten only a sandwich in the past 24 hours, I picked up the phone to see if room service was operating, and discovered there was no tone at all. The phone didn't seem to be connected. So I wrapped myself in my robe, pulled on slippers, and, clutching the room key in my hand, crept out into the hall.

Every door in the corridor was open, though dimly lit, and on each doorstep people stood talking, their words indecipherably soft and low. I took a step and one of these conversational groups broke apart, a man in a brown suit touching the brim of his fedora as I passed. From another room a girl of seven or eight jumped across the threshold and darted ahead of me. I felt another wave of hunger and decided to go downstairs to the kitchen. Surely someone would be there, if not cooking, then preparing for the breakfast hour.

My legs were unsteady but I forced myself toward the elevator. When I heard the bell indicating the door was open, I found the girl was already aboard. I followed. She didn't look at me, didn't speak, and I decided not to make conversation. There are parents who encourage their children to be sociable with adults, and many more who don't. I chose to err on the side of caution in case the girl's mother had a rule about not talking to strangers.

The elevator ride made me dizzy. I had to take a deep breath when we landed. The second the doors parted and the girl stepped out, the tantalizing aroma of bacon and eggs reached me. I let my hunger lead me down a passage with streaky black stains, apparent scars from years of food trolleys banging against the walls. The floor was slightly raked toward a set of metal doors, propped open, with bright light spilling out.

Among the steam tables, knives, pots and pans, a heavyset woman wearing a hairnet and white apron stood talking to the girl from the elevator. The woman held up one hand and seemed to be lecturing the child, who twitched and shrugged under her steady gaze. When I stepped into the doorway, both looked at me and froze. I heard a thousand voices, insect-like, murmuring. The hotel coming to life just before dawn, waking and stretching, putting a kettle on, dropping bread into a toaster, pulling on a clean shirt, lathering soap in a shaving cup, washing hands and face, sweeping the front doorstep, placing a sign on the pavement, opening curtains and blinds...

I woke up in my bed a few minutes ago. On the nightstand next to my books I found a small tray with toast and eggs, bacon, fried tomatoes, and a pot of tea. My head aches. I drink the tea in gulps, with generous helpings of sugar, and I eat with gusto, since no one can see me and take offence.

***

SEPT. 28

Nothing to report other than rest and reading. I fell asleep again yesterday, right after breakfast, and slept all day.

My itinerary is ruined. I no longer expect to visit Muriel's favorite bookshop, or the school where she taught grammar and composition to the children she called "an unworthy cause." It's all I can do to lie here, propped up by stiff, uncooperative pillows, re-reading her books.

There is an arc to her fiction. Beginning with the youthful jaunt, the green, lively attitude of *The Glass Houses*. The first chapter was written years before the rest, when the author was in school. It serves as a time capsule, then, an indication of her expectations.

"I will leave all of this, someday," the protagonist tells her mother. Yet by the final chapter the outcome is less certain, and we're left wondering if the bright, opinionated young woman will strike out on her own or spend her life working as a secretary at an insurance firm.

Gin and Tonic is more measured in tone. Its central characters make no pronouncements about the future. The only humor arises from the contrast between the protagonist's view of herself and the things others say about her. She rails against her fate as her mother's caretaker and part-time clerk at a company so boring she fails to identify its purpose. But she doesn't make plans to run away.

The old lady had taken a tumble. So said the pockmarked social worker from Hackney, who wore too much lipstick and badly scuffed high heels. The calmness of her voice assured everyone that a common accident had occurred, and there was no need for alarm.

Most of Muriel's third novel was written in this penultimate room. Afterward she struggled, and failed, to find a new story. Darker and more mature than her first two books, *An Unworthy Cause* alternates between an elementary school and a nursing home where the endless routine of meals, deadly entertainments, and bedpan collection add up to existential resignation. Life is sorrow and the sooner we accept it the better, the author seems to say. The few overtly comic moments are cruel in their depiction of elderly dementia and physical decay.

In a little while I'll be changing rooms again. This will require more energy than I have at the moment. So I'll rest now, and try to rally in time.

***

SEPT. 29

Room 206 is both more comfortable and more sterile than my previous accommodations. I wonder if Muriel chose it for these reasons. She knew the hotel better than anyone. She must have wanted a quiet corner in which to spend her last day. Or am I imagining? Nothing in her biography indicates that she planned, in advance, to end her life when she checked into the Hyde Hotel for a final visit. I've drawn my own conclusion from the fact that she stayed in this room and not her usual 219, the one in which she wrote her books, and later on tried to write, so painfully and unsuccessfully.

In these misted, green hills, are the premature buds wasting away, lured to their destiny by a brief, false spring?

The ending line to her last novel. Without words, Muriel had no life. She must have come to this room with a purpose. I believe that. After all, what is a writer without words?

I'm scheduled to begin the long journey back home tomorrow. To my basement studio. To rain and silence, to long hours downtown, surrounded by young people who find my sweaters too bulky, my hair too gray, my inability to discern their jokes amusing, my questions (as I work my way through their appalling documents) a sign of mental sluggishness. I don't watch the shows they watch, or listen to their music, or appreciate the nuances of their code.

Trying not to think of all that I've missed on this trip. If I think of it, I'll fall. Down that long, blinding chasm. My failure to trace Muriel's steps, to see what she saw, to know better than anyone alive what it must have been to create the world inside her books, this weighs on me and I can barely record the details. But one odd thing has occurred and I'm compelled to mention it.

I must have fallen asleep with one hand under my head. When I woke up I was groggy and sick. I fumbled my way to the bathroom, an obviously added feature so confining I bang my elbows on the sink and shower stall if I'm not careful. In the stark light I could see, clearly imprinted across my face, the bright pink ovals of three fingerprints.

I've been drinking water, glass after glass, but I'm still too tired to go outside in the corridor. The phone buzzes when I pick it up; when I dial, nothing happens.

If I just wait here, quietly, keeping my energy in reserve, I'm sure the desk clerk will send a porter eventually. When checkout time arrives and I fail to appear. When the maids lose patience and unlock the door, to get on with their rounds. When someone comes. When something happens.

***

HH Lost & Found Inventory Item, Ref No 12837, one handwritten journal, cover partially torn. No identification.

THIS
MANY

The costume appeared in a dream. In October the temperature was mild enough to keep the bedroom windows open at night. Maybe Lorrie's imagination was piqued by the mild vinegar scent of the blue jacarandas, slowly wilting in the Pacific breeze.

In her dream Lorrie stepped onto a dirt path at the bottom of a narrow ravine. She followed its twisted incline, walking through dry leaves all the way to her house, where the wooden gate stood open. Ahead of her, the trunks of the sycamore trees were etched white and gray against the lawn while high above a tiny fairy-like creature floated in midair. The creature seemed to be lit from within, her pink and ruby gown glowing, her diaphanous wings quivering.

Lorrie felt the color rise in her neck and cheeks. Warm light spread to her chest and arms. She felt that she, too, was glowing and euphoric.

When she awoke Lorrie reached for her journal and quickly

sketched the outfit she had seen. It was perfect, exactly what she wanted for Frances. The tricky bit would be the ruched velvet across the bodice. She knew she could match the pink and ruby satin, and build a sheer set of wings. She had conquered more ambitious projects, including the fully decorated playhouse that stood disused in a far corner of the yard, discarded after one summer of sleepovers and outdoor games.

The crafts store on Aliso Way would carry everything she needed. Lorrie could gather all of the supplies without leaving her neighborhood. She decided to make this a selling point during the unavoidable conversation with Kirk. He was a sweetheart. He just worried too much about the budget, which was natural for an accountant. And he didn't understand the difference between buying a pretty good, readymade outfit and making the extra effort to create a one-of-a-kind memory for their daughter.

Lorrie had given up trying to explain these matters. More and more often she fell back on her mother's example.

"She served macaroni and cheese for dinner, Kirk. Twice a week."

"So she was tired." Kirk said. "Single moms have a tough time."

"Macaroni?"

"I'm a little surprised you didn't demand sashimi." He grinned.

"Not the point."

"Honey," Kirk said, rubbing the back of his neck. "What is the point?"

"This won't cost as much as you think. It just takes time. I can get everything we need at Hobby Hut…"

"Okay, okay," he said, winding down, as he always did. "Do what you want."

Lorrie was glad to sidestep the question of when she might return to work. Their most heated debates centered on the subject. During the years since her generous maternity leave had become semi-permanent, Kirk had been promoted twice. They could live on his salary, even if they couldn't save or invest much.

Halfheartedly she'd begun to check a couple of job sites, but she didn't plan to call any of her contacts until after the holidays. Frances was in kindergarten this year, and there would be a million special moments to share. Where would the girl turn without her mom?

Lorrie thought back on all the school pageants and bake sales and kickball games her mother never attended. Sometimes she sent a proxy, usually a sullen twenty-something named Nancy who wore black T-shirts and sunglasses and had bad skin. Nancy was the daughter of another legal secretary and the sight of her could make Lorrie freeze. She had imagined when she was a child that this was how all daughters of professional women turned out: dark and silent and only tenuously connected to the people around them, applauding on cue but never giving a damn about anything. Nancy, with her greasy brunette hair parted on the side and her lips curled in a sneer, was no substitute for a mom. Only a real mom would sew an original gown and plan a perfect party.

***

During the second fitting, with a sheath of ruby fabric draped across her slender shoulders and the frame for fairy wings poised above her head, Frances announced her intention to be a witch for her birthday. Lorrie clenched the batch of straight pins between her teeth. She removed them and drew a clean breath before she spoke.

"Frances, remember how we talked about your wonderful dress?"

"Uh…"

"Mommy's been sewing all weekend to make you a fairy princess in time for the party."

"I want a black hat and boots!"

Frances did a bouncy dance step in place. Lorrie looked at

the wire and satin and velvet lying all around her on the living room carpet.

"Sweetie," she said. "I don't think a black hat will be pretty with a fairy princess gown."

"I want a black dress, like Annie's got."

They had run into Gloria Shepherd with her seven-year-old, Annie, at the mall. Frances blurted out an invitation before Lorrie could stop her. Annie was wearing a witch costume, which Gloria had personalized with a few Goth touches including mascara, lipstick, and a black choker decorated with miniature skulls.

One glance at Annie's tough-girl style and Frances started complaining. She reminded Lorrie that she had been Sleeping Beauty the previous year, and Strawberry Shortcake the year before that.

Lorrie could have killed Gloria Shepherd. All the way home she wondered about Gloria's shaky marriage to a much younger day trader. She also wondered who made the rules in the Shepherd family.

"But don't you want to be the star of your own party?" Lorrie asked, trying not to whine.

It was the kind of question her mother would have asked, playing on Lorrie's need to be the center of attention. Except Lorrie's mother, Caroline, would never have sewn a garment for her daughter. Anything she could afford pre-made, Caroline bought.

Her mother's scant free time had been sacred, reserved for facials, television, and naps. Lorrie only realized the macaroni and cheese dinners were not gourmet and her JC Penney clothes were not cool when she started first grade.

"I want a black hat with a pointy top," said Frances.

"Sweetie," Lorrie said.

She found herself fumbling for an answer a six-year-old would buy. Not griping about how much time she'd already spent on the dress. Not pointing out how adorable a honey-blonde girl with a cherubic smile would look with wings pinned to her shoulders and a petite, ruby-studded crown on her head. The "pretty factor" wouldn't work, thanks to Gloria Shepherd and her future heroin-addict daughter.

"Frances, it's bad luck."

The girl gazed at her mother with an expression of high seriousness. Her silence was difficult to read but Lorrie decided to press on while she had the advantage.

"Wearing black on your birthday is a no-no. I'm sure Annie won't wear black on her birthday."

"But," the girl thought hard. "It's almost Halloween."

"Oh, well, on Halloween, sure. You can be a witch to go trick-or-treating. I'm talking about your party, on Saturday. It's bad luck to wear black on your birthday."

"Oh."

Lorrie felt a blush begin to rise from her jaw to her cheeks. Nevertheless, she accepted the victory. Next year she could never get away with such a lie. But now, for at least one more set of birthday photos, her daughter would be dazzling.

***

On Saturday the air was still, and the cul-de-sac lay silent. The few neighbors who obsessed over their lawns had given up for the time being, even the old man next door, an octogenarian who loved to complain about the mess made by the jacarandas.

As of 1:15, no one had shown up. Lorrie poured a box of orange punch into a ceramic bowl and carried it out the patio door to a table on the lawn. The sycamores provided a light canopy and Lorrie had decided not to string the cheap plastic skeletons and pumpkins along the fence. If she couldn't afford the beautiful lanterns she really wanted, the trees would have to suffice as decoration.

Inside, in the foyer, she fussed with the ribbons on a bunch of helium-filled balloons. For a second she entertained the idea of curling the ends with scissors to make them more festive.

"Stop," she told herself. "Just stop it."

The balloons were printed with the faces of trolls, witches, werewolves, and vampires. Lorrie wondered if they were too intense for the younger children. It was the sort of concern Kirk would label "a first world problem."

"I saw *Nightmare on Elm Street* when I was five," he must have told her a dozen times. "Look at me. I'm fine. Kids need to be scared sometimes. It's healthy. How else can they learn to work through their fears?"

Kirk was also the champion of bike riding in the park without a helmet and rollerblading without kneepads. Whenever she threw a kids' party Lorrie sent Kirk to play golf and gave him an okay to smoke cigars with his buddies at the pro club afterward.

At 1:25 Karen arrived wearing surgical scrubs. Her twins were dressed as Hansel and Gretel. Hansel was in one of his moods.

"We had a disagreement about whether a Padres cap would be 'just as good' as this adorable, authentic-looking Tyrolean hat—"

"Monkey hat," Hansel grumbled.

"I found it at Kohl's. In the men's department."

"Retarded," the boy said.

Karen blushed. She lowered her voice and leaned close to Hansel.

"What did I tell you, my friend?"

Hansel studied his left hand.

Lorrie gave Frances a slight push forward.

"Welcome to my party," Frances said automatically, without smiling.

"Oh, look, kids!" Karen fussed. "Isn't the birthday girl beautiful?"

Frances stood, glum and wide-eyed, while they admired her

costume.

"How old are you today?" Karen asked.

"This many," said Frances, holding up five fingers.

Lorrie gave her a look, and she corrected herself by adding the index finger of her left hand. "I mean, this many."

"So sweet," Karen cooed. "And oh my god, this dress is unbelievable. Haute couture again! Frances, you're a lucky little girl."

As soon as his mother was distracted, Hansel sidestepped her and headed down the hall. He slowed long enough to navigate the cluster of balloons, punched one of the troll faces, and then wandered toward the sugary aroma of the kitchen.

Gretel was still fiddling with the beaded buttons on her peasant blouse. When Karen raised her eyebrows, Gretel went indoors. Frances followed. Karen waited until the girls were out of earshot.

"Sorry my kids are such clots."

"It's okay."

"No, honestly, if they weren't so stupid, I'd sell both of them. No offers yet."

"They're fine," Lorrie said. "Eight is a tough age."

"Don't be kind," Karen joked. "I'm thinking of having a maternity test."

"Sets of twins, switched at birth? What are the odds?"

"I'm clinging to this, Lorrie, don't shoot it down."

Both women punched the monster-faced balloons on their way down the hall. From outside came the first shrieks of children chasing one another.

A few minutes later the deluge began, and for the next half hour the hostess was busy non-stop. She greeted everyone at the door with an apology for the imperfect weather. There were thin clouds over Endless Vista Road extending north and east beyond Sunswept Mesa Drive and Glittering Sky Lane. Not enough clouds to ruin the day, but there could be sprinkles of rain later.

"I ordered a much better afternoon," Lorrie joked more than

once. With Frances in tow, she ushered all of the guests through her kitchen and on through the patio doors to the back lawn, where games and treats awaited.

"Why can't I just play?" her daughter asked between arrivals.

"Sweetie, this is how it's done. The birthday girl greets her guests," Lorrie said, eliciting only a sigh and a shrug.

By the time Gloria rang the doorbell most of the other neighborhood parents had shown up, bearing gifts and dutifully dressed in medical scrubs as Lorrie had instructed. Most of them stood sipping punch under the sycamores while their children played tag across the lawn.

Gloria handed over a cake on a tray with a makeshift foil cover, and then scratched at her maroon hair. Before entering the house with Annie the Goth witch, she asked if it was all right to smoke.

"Just one? Outdoors, of course."

"Afraid not," said Lorrie with what she hoped was a withering smile. "On top of everything else, we're coping with asthma. One of Karen's twins, Harris, that's Hansel. Or maybe it's Tina, that's Gretel. I've forgotten which. Anyway, sorry, no smoking."

"Annie had a touch of asthma when she was little, but we got her over that with swimming lessons."

Frances had crept up behind Lorrie to peek out at her idol on the doorstep. Annie shifted her weight but ignored the younger girl's adoring expression.

"Wow," said Gloria. "That's a hell of a dress, Franny."

Lorrie winced. She couldn't abide nicknames.

"Is that a prom dress?" Annie asked, wrinkling her nose prettily under the wide brim of her black hat, and giving Frances an insouciant once-over.

Lorrie could have strangled her.

"Mom made it so I have to wear it," Frances replied, and rolled her eyes.

Annie laughed. Frances laughed. Gloria laughed. And it

seemed to Lorrie that every minute she'd spent stitching and hemming, to say nothing of bandaging her needle-pricked fingers, had been dismissed as a waste of time. The way Kirk dismissed her bread baking and crocheting or the mommy-daughter ballet class.

"I like your costume too, Annie," Lorrie said. "Are you Hermione, or just any old witch?"

Even Gloria looked surprised.

Lorrie flushed red. Insulting a seven-year-old, she thought, what kind of mom does that?

To cover her embarrassment, she ushered everyone out to the back yard. She took the lid off Gloria's cake. It was pathetic. She felt better almost at once.

In the kitchen, Lorrie placed the cake on the marble countertop in front of Karen and sighed. They tried looking at it from different angles. No use. It was Gloria's standard-issue coconut vanilla, three tiers arranged on one level from small to large, the only dessert she knew how to prepare. And it was entirely inappropriate because Lorrie had baked a birthday cake.

"At least you know what to expect from her," said Karen.

For Christmas, Gloria stuck a hat on the smallest tier, added buttons and a frosted broom, and called it a snowman. For the Easter egg hunt she'd decorated it with floppy ears and jellybeans. Voilà! Bunny! Now the same recipe made a sad, third appearance adorned with a screaming O for a mouth and matching eyes, a mournful ghost for a children's party.

"Dismal," said Lorrie. "This is why I didn't want to invite her. She's a one-cake mommy. With maroon hair."

"At least she baked," said Karen. "I'll give her ten points for that. Rita's cookies are from Starbucks. I bet she raided the display case when she went out for a morning latte."

Lorrie laughed. Karen was the only mom on Endless Vista who could make her laugh. Both women had put their careers on hold to raise children. Together they planned group treks to

Disneyland several times a year, hosted holiday parties, and volunteered for Girl Scout bake sales.

The two women moved with their coffee cups to the sliding doors and gazed out at the wide expanse of lawn. On the other side of the glass were fifteen children, six women, and Gordon, whom Lorrie and Karen had dubbed the King of Dads. Gordon was a widower raising his daughter Kimmy under the watchful eyes and approving murmurs of the neighborhood mommies.

"I wish my dad had been like Gordon," Karen said.

"He's taking Kimmy to yoga class now," Lorrie murmured approvingly. "So sweet."

"So sweet."

They sipped coffee. One of the moms waved and Lorrie waved back. She noted the clouds were shifting again from sea blue to gray. There was enough space in the den to move the party indoors if it rained, but she preferred to keep the kids outdoors.

"Scrubs are such a good idea," said Karen.

"Am I a genius? I thought a theme would solve the Rita issue."

In a corner of the yard, near the deserted playhouse, Frances and Annie stood next to one another. Annie held her witch hat in one hand and inclined her head toward Frances, whispering in the younger child's ear.

"Thank you," Karen said. "I couldn't take another one of her forty-year-old cheerleader performances. That was so embarrassing last New Year's! Doesn't Gordon look adorable wearing a stethoscope?"

"I know," Lorrie said, waving through the glass at the King of Dads. "Granted, Rita's scrubs are a size too small, but at least the cleavage is under control."

"Progress has been made and duly noted. Although it does look a little like a doctor's office out there."

Both women laughed.

At 3:00 Lorrie presented the birthday cake. She was especially proud of the centerpiece, a pretty porcelain doll with huge eyes, wearing an exact replica of her daughter's dress.

"Oh, that's perfect!" Karen said, prompting a round of compliments from the other moms.

"Nice work, Lorrie!"

"You're amazing!"

"Look at that little doll! She looks just like you, Frances!"

"And you look just like your mom, you lucky girl!"

Only Frances seemed disappointed. She stared silently at the cake, until Annie whispered in her ear. At that, Frances grinned and the two girls linked arms.

The phrase "thick as thieves" ran through Lorrie's mind. She was ashamed to admit she was jealous of a child, so she smiled broadly and urged Frances to blow out the candles.

"Make a wish! Make a wish!" the kids chanted.

Frances took one last look at Annie in her Goth get-up. Then she closed her eyes and blew out the candles.

After cake and ice cream the grownups relaxed and the kids got jumpy. There was a minor scuffle when Hansel and Gretel told Rita's son Fred he was too fat to be Spider-Man. The boy picked up a Frisbee and hit Gretel in the face with it.

"Little jerk," Karen said under her breath. She went to break up the fight.

"You keep an eye on things, okay?" Lorrie said. "I'm going to wash my hands."

"Sure," said Karen.

A few minutes later Lorrie was studying her face in the bathroom mirror. She had never considered Botox before but the lines emerging across her forehead were more pronounced than the last time she'd paid attention. Maybe Kirk was right. Maybe it was time to go back to an office job. Her daughter would be fine. Wasn't that the whole point of all this effort? To raise a child who could face the world on her own?

The doorbell rang. Lorrie decided to let Karen see to it.

Anyone showing up this late didn't deserve a personal greeting from the hostess. A few seconds later she heard Frances call out.

"Welcome to my party!"

Lorrie had to give Karen credit. She knew how to follow rules. Even in Lorrie's absence her friend had made a point of including Frances in the greeting. And for once the child sounded like she was enjoying herself.

Lorrie dried her hands and wandered out to the kitchen. Her coffee cup stood on the counter, where she'd left it. She took a sip while she watched the party on the lawn. She smiled and held up the cup in salute when Karen caught her eye.

"Thanks!" she called out.

"For what?" Karen mouthed with exaggeration.

"The door," Lorrie said, pointing toward the front of the house.

Karen stared blankly at her. Then she shrugged.

Gordon had organized the children into a friendly game of freeze-tag, pulling in even the shy stragglers, all except Frances and Annie, who stood near the back fence watching and smirking. Lorrie noted with a rush of irritation that the girls had exchanged headgear. Frances wore the pointed black hat while Annie had topped off her Goth witch outfit with the ruby-studded silver crown tilted at a rakish angle.

Lorrie stood perfectly still behind the patio door, breathing. She counted from one to ten, and back, and then started again. She had to do this several times. It was all she could do not to dash outside and tear the crown from the girl's head. The numbers began to glide naturally into a head count.

Idly, all afternoon, Lorrie had been keeping track of the number of children and parents. It was a habit. Frances was popular enough to drag friends along on a lot of their excursions. Lorrie frequently found herself counting heads. Even when they were in the car or the living room, she was always running a quick tally.

Something was off. Including Karen there were eight moms,

fifteen kids, and Gordon. But that didn't seem right. Thinking she must have stupidly included herself twice, Lorrie started with Karen and counted the moms again: Eight. Plus Gordon.

Then she remembered the doorbell. Of course, another parent and child had arrived while she was in the bathroom.

"I wonder," said Karen as she returned to the kitchen and picked up her coffee cup, "is it better to make them behave politely, or teach them to be honest and break the news to Fred about his weight problem? Don't answer. I know I'm a monster. I shouldn't be allowed near children, right?"

As she started counting heads again, Lorrie made a discovery. She knew all of the fifteen children, no one had been added, but there was one adult she didn't recognize.

"Who is that woman?" Lorrie asked.

"Which?"

"Over there. The woman with dark hair."

A woman in scrubs was pulling one of the boys aside, asking him something. The boy, Charlie, was dressed as a pirate. After a second Charlie responded to the woman by holding up his right hand, fingers splayed.

"Oh," said Karen. "I don't know."

The woman's costume was the only one that looked authentic. In place of the pristine blue and green surgical scrubs the other parents wore, hers were sagging and threadbare and, most alarming, decorated with blood-red stains. Her greasy hair wasn't brushed properly. Above the green surgical mask her eyes were opaque, without expression.

"Didn't you let her in a little while ago?"

"No," said Karen. "I didn't let anyone in. Why? Don't you know her?"

"I've never seen her," said Lorrie.

The woman was crouching next to Frances and Annie. Frances turned at an angle and the woman ran her fingertips over the girl's translucent pink wings. Whatever the woman was saying, the girls appeared to be enraptured.

"What the hell," Lorrie said.

"I don't get it. Why is she dressed like that if she wasn't invited?"

Both women set aside their coffee and went outside. They made a show of not panicking as they strode across the lawn, greeting familiar kids and neighbors along the way. When Lorrie reached the woman, who was still talking to her daughter, she stopped. Frances was holding up six fingers. Lorrie gently moved her little girl aside and stepped in front of her.

Annie and Frances wandered away. The woman stood up. She was a bit taller than Lorrie and thinner, with a rangy look to her limbs, as though she hiked a good deal.

"How do you do?" Lorrie said. "I don't think we've met. Did, uh, did one of the other parents invite you?"

The woman nodded.

Karen caught up and introduced herself. Lorrie gave Karen a scorching glance.

"Who would that be?" Lorrie asked. "Who invited you?"

The woman pointed vaguely across the lawn where the children were starting to wind down from their game. She murmured something indecipherable behind her surgical mask, which Lorrie could now see was stained with crimson flecks to match the rest of her outfit.

"Excuse me," said Lorrie. "I didn't catch your name."

The woman murmured again. Lorrie noticed a rank odor. It reminded her of the time the garbage disposal had backed up the day after Kirk tried to run steak leftovers through it. She wondered if one of the kids had arrived with dog poop on their shoes, but she hadn't been aware of the smell when she was greeting guests at the front door. She scanned the lawn and saw nothing unusual.

"So, where is *your* brat?" Karen asked the woman with the mask.

The woman mumbled and looked away. The odor grew stronger. And now it didn't smell like a garbage disposal.

Lorrie had only encountered such an awful, rotten, yet embarrassingly human scent once, when she was nine or ten years old. She had been standing in line with her chaperone, Nancy, at a pizza joint in Santa Ana when she smelled something that killed her appetite. The source was a bald teenager with her arms covered in tattoos and a head wound that looked like someone had tried to kill her with an axe. Despite several dozen stitches, the wound in the back of the teenager's head had begun seeping, clearly infected.

"Where's your kid?" Karen asked again.

The masked woman turned toward the crowd of children. Searching. Her eyes clouded over and she shook her head.

"She," the woman said through the mask. "She. She!"

The woman looked around the yard and back toward the house.

"Listen," said Lorrie. "I'm not sure how you got in, but…"

Before she could finish, the woman stepped past her. She made a beeline for the sliding glass doors and slipped inside the house so quickly and smoothly, Lorrie was stunned. It took her a moment to come to her senses and follow the woman.

"What the hell just happened?" Karen asked, trailing along after Lorrie.

"I have no idea," Lorrie said over her shoulder, controlling her nerves so she wouldn't ruin the party. "Gordon! Sorry to bug you. Could you come here for a second?"

Gordon caught up with them inside. The hall extended from the front door to the back of the house. Along the hallway an arch gave way to the kitchen and another to the living room, a door led to a half bathroom, and two sets of stairs led up to the bedrooms and down to the den.

"What's up?" Gordon asked.

"There's a strange woman here," said Lorrie. She inched along, wondering which way to go next, for the woman had slipped out of sight. The last glimpse of her had been a shadow cast on the floor of the hall, followed by the thud of footsteps on stairs.

"Strange how?"

"As in we don't know her," Karen said. "Right, Lorrie? You don't know her? Maybe we should call the police."

"Oh, I think we can handle this," Gordon said. "The kids are outside and it looks like we've got her cornered. How did she get in?"

"I don't know," Lorrie told him. She had to control the growing irritation in her voice. "I thought Karen let her in."

"I didn't," said Karen. "I've never seen her before."

"She must be crazy," said Gordon. "Why would anyone give up a Saturday to hang around with kids who aren't theirs?"

"It really isn't funny," Lorrie told him.

"No, it isn't," said Gordon. "Of course not."

"She smells." This just popped out. Even as she said it, Lorrie felt silly.

"She smells?" Gordon asked. "Of what?"

This was a question Lorrie couldn't fully answer without describing the scene she remembered from the pizza place. The thought turned her stomach.

"Sick," she told them. "Didn't you notice it, Karen?"

"No, but I didn't get very close to her. What do you think it was?"

"Something rank. Like a person who sleeps in a dumpster. Gordon, will you go down to the den and look around? Check the closets down there, too. Karen and I can look upstairs."

"Sure," said Gordon. "Stay together."

"Is that a joke?" Lorrie asked.

"No," Gordon said with a solemn face. "Of course not."

"Maybe she's homeless," Karen suggested. "Or one of those women you read about, the kind who steal kids."

"Let's not get worked up," said Gordon. "I think we can

handle this. We can call the police later if you think it's necessary. Right now we need to find her."

Lorrie drew a sharp breath. She trotted up the stairs to the bedrooms with Karen in tow. The violet, floral opulence of the master bedroom prompted Karen to say, not for the first time, "Lorrie, I love your sense of style."

"Thanks," Lorrie replied. "Let's stay focused, okay?"

"Sorry," Karen said. "Okay. Where do we go first?"

Lorrie considered the drapes. She took up a position on one side and Karen stood opposite. Simultaneously they yanked back the curtains. Nothing.

Next they rifled through the closet. Then Lorrie got down on the carpeted floor and crept toward the bed. She reached carefully and pinched a corner of the bed skirt. She heard Karen gasp when she pulled the skirt aside. Nothing.

In the bathroom Lorrie was the one who checked the shower. Karen gasped again, and Lorrie asked, "Are you doing that on purpose?"

"No," said Karen. She held up her hands. "Of course not. I'm a little nervous, that's all."

When they were satisfied the woman wasn't hiding in the master bedroom or the bath, they moved on. They surveyed every inch of the upstairs but they found nothing. They even rummaged through the linen closet. That was when Lorrie heard the unmistakable sound of children in the hallway below: stamping feet and shrieks followed by an outburst of giggles. She hurried back downstairs.

Gordon stepped up from the den just as Lorrie and Karen returned to the main floor. He shook his head.

"I checked the den, the closets, everything," he reported.

"I don't understand," said Karen. "We were right behind her. I thought we had her cornered."

"Who let the kids into the house?" Lorrie asked.

She heard the front door slam shut. She moved fast, dodging

manic kids and stray balloons, to see if the woman was making her escape. Instead she found Frances with her back against the door, dressed from head to toe in Annie's witch costume. For a moment, in her anger and confusion, she forgot about the woman.

"What are you doing with Annie's dress?" Lorrie said.

"I can wear it now," Frances told her.

"Children!" Lorrie shouted. "Outside, right now."

Karen began to herd the kids toward the patio doors. Gordon lingered near Lorrie as though he didn't know what to do next. Out back the other moms were drinking punch and chatting, ignoring the excitement indoors until their kids came pouring out onto the lawn.

Once the children moved away, Lorrie opened the front door. There was no one on the doorstep or the walk.

"Frances," Lorrie said. "What did that strange woman say to you a little while ago?"

"Which...?"

"You know which one, the lady who was talking to you and Annie."

Frances giggled.

"What's so funny?"

"She asked how old I am."

"What did you say?"

"This many."

Frances held up her right hand, fingers splayed. With the left she was grasping something, and she had trouble freeing her index finger.

"Did she tell you anything else?"

"She said I had to be seven."

Lorrie and Gordon looked at one another. Then Lorrie's gaze drifted automatically to the back yard, through the glass. She could see Gloria wandering among the children, searching for her daughter. And without even trying, Lorrie began to count...

Ten...eleven...twelve...

"Annie!" Gloria called out.

"She had to go now but she'll be back when I get bigger," Frances said.

Thirteen...fourteen...

"Next year," Frances continued. She opened her left hand so that Lorrie could see what she was holding. In the center of her daughter's palm a small, human tooth glistened with ruby-red saliva and a bit of pink gristle.

Fourteen...

Lorrie opened her mouth to ask another question. She was interrupted by a sharp, shrill sound from outdoors. It might have been the children playing a new game, or it might have been a woman screaming.

SOMNAMBULE

"Spirits have driven me from hearth and home…"
—*The Cabinet of Dr. Caligari*

***

"Positively lobotomizing."

"I told you," I said.

"Makes me swoon!"

Tubby tilted her head back and reclined next to me on the floor of my room. The glossy strands of her chestnut hair cascaded down her back onto the rug. Beyond my window the neighborhood drowsed under a waning crescent moon.

We lay on the fake Persian rug surrounded by record albums—the Beatles, the Buckinghams, the Turtles—all scattered and discarded in favor of my portable TV, a little black-and-white set balanced on a chair before us. The music to a jittering silent film droned beneath our conversation, end of the late-late movie, last broadcast before dawn. Uneven shadows flickered across our faces.

"You don't think it's too heavy, too sweet?" I asked. "Like sticking your nose in a magnolia?" I lifted the perfume bottle with the graceful S painted on its side. At once the fragrance began to overwhelm me again. I put the cap back in place. The voluptuous floral notes left me dizzy.

"Oh," said Tubby. "I don't think so." Her drawl was more pronounced than mine. Her family moved from Pine Mountain when Tubby was twelve and she had to practice to lose the guttural r-sound of her childhood. "*Photoplay* says Audrey Hepburn wears it when she isn't wearing perfume by Givenchy. You know, she's European and *très chic!*"

"Very well," I agreed.

"My mom only wears Chanel No. 5," said Tubby. "I think it smells like hairspray. Who is this mystery woman again?"

"Tubby, you won't believe me," I told her.

"If she wears this perfume, she must be divine. What's it called?"

"Guess."

"I can't. How did you get the bottle?"

"I'll tell you," I said. "But no interruptions and don't say I didn't warn you."

"Come on, spill!"

"It's a pretty strange tale," I began.

***

In the summer of my junior year of high school my parents insisted I take a part-time job. My mother said it would teach me responsibility. My stepfather said I ought to help with the household expenses.

I'm a lazy sort of person. Anyone who knows me will confirm this, not only my stuck-up stepfather. I didn't even read the classifieds to see what was available. I just walked down the street a couple of blocks and asked Pauline Bingham if she needed an assistant.

Miss Bingham was a middle-aged lady who took care of children at her house. Two or three times a year she placed a sign in her window seeking part-time help. Summer was a busy season with kids out of school. Ordinarily her charges were toddler age or younger, but some were joined by older siblings when school let out. This time of year she was overrun with first and second graders, and I showed up at the right moment.

Changing diapers, warming baby bottles, and chasing children around a neighbor's back yard might sound like a nightmare to most teenagers. I didn't mind. I only had to show up and follow Miss B's instructions, and I took home two dollars an hour in cash.

If you've ever taken care of children for hours, surrounded by shouting and crying and demands for one thing after another, you know it's physically tiring and mentally boring at the same time. When you get a chance to talk to someone over the age of seven, you jump at it.

On Friday afternoon, once the last child had been picked up, Miss B and I would sit on the back porch on a glider swing. From there we liked to watch the late sky changing color, and we would chat about anything that came to mind. On my third week she offered me a tiny glass of sherry. I made a joke out of scanning the back yard and the trees for spies. Miss B laughed and poured two glasses. Then she lit a Marlboro, the only one she would smoke all week.

"How'd you get started keeping kids?" I asked. Her bookshelves were crowded with novels by Jane Austen, Thomas Hardy, and Charles Dickens. There wasn't a bestseller in sight, exactly the opposite of my house where the tattered paperbacks all came from the corner drugstore.

She exhaled a rolling cloud of smoke and gazed at the honeysuckle vines leaning against the side of the house. I guess she was looking back in time.

"For twelve years I was a school librarian," she said. "My job was all right but I didn't feel a particular calling the way a lot of people do. And I don't mind telling you the salary wasn't very good. Well, one day, I happened to be collecting my paycheck in the vice principal's office when I heard a lady complaining about having to take off work early. It was a holiday weekend and the kids were let out an hour before the usual time."

"Wish I could leave school early for a holiday," I said.

"Oh sure," said Miss B. "Children love to be set loose. Give them an extra hour and they go wild all day. I don't think the schools do that anymore but back then it was common throughout the county."

"This lady wasn't happy about having a little more time with her kids?"

"She was not. She had a job with a very important member of the state legislature, she said, and even though she was only a secretary it was vital that she attend all of her boss's meetings. She went on and on about her shorthand and how she never made mistakes and that was why her boss relied on her so much."

I had to laugh. Maybe the sherry was making me giddy.

"Well, I gave it some thought and I started asking around," said Miss B. "There were quite a few women, in various situations, who could never seem to find a babysitter they trusted, or couldn't get a sitter to stretch their hours a little bit. What they all needed was a mature person who lived right here in the area, walking distance from school, who could change her schedule at a moment's notice. They needed a woman with no family obligations of her own who was reliable and who got along with babies and children."

"That's you," I said. Thanks to the sherry my voice was developing a drawl.

"Exactly what I thought," said Miss B. "I believe I discovered my calling that year. I turned the dining room into a playroom, and fenced in the back yard. One child came to my house after school let out, and then another and another. Word traveled, you see, among the mothers who had jobs. Some were already acquainted. About half the kids I take care of now have mothers who work at the telephone company. Well, once I was established and started hiring young people like you to help out, the mothers wouldn't have anybody else look after their kids. Whenever one of the mothers found out she was expecting, I'd get another call. Do you know most places will only hold a position for a woman for six weeks, at the most? These gals were desperate, so I started offering a little discount on second and third babies from the same family."

"That was nice of you," I told her.

"Oh, sweetheart, it doesn't cost a thing to be decent to people. And you can see the result. I've got more business than I can handle. I had to turn down two families just last week. Broke my heart but I really don't have enough room for more."

By this time I'd finished off my thimble-sized glass of sherry.

"I could offer you another," said Miss B. "If you think you can handle it." She smiled and I accepted a second glass. I reasoned it was no more than my mom let me sip on Christmas and Easter.

"Did you ever have to turn anyone down because you didn't like them?" I don't know what prompted such a bold question, maybe the sherry.

"No," she said. "Although I did lose one client due to circumstance. It's a pretty bad story. I'm not sure you'd like to hear it."

She might as well have said the story involved running off to an island with a French movie star. I was all ears.

"Well, then," she said. "I'll tell this the way it happened. But don't say I didn't warn you."

And she began the strange tale of Roberta Granger, whose name sounded vaguely familiar to me. By the end I knew exactly where I'd seen the name.

Roberta was one of the moms who enlisted Miss B's child-care the first year she was in business. Roberta was a part-time operator at the phone company but she wasn't referred. In fact the other mothers were surprised when they learned she was dropping her boy off early in the morning and picking him up midday. It seems Roberta had a reputation of some kind and the other women didn't like her much. She said she'd overheard a co-worker bragging about Miss B and decided her boy should have the best care, too.

"You meet a person," said Miss B. "And you think she must be normal, to have a husband, and a child. Her boy, Alan, was very quiet but he seemed all right at first. Maybe a little tired. Maybe a little thin. He had dark circles under his eyes. The way Roberta ran her hand through his hair and said nothing was too good for her baby boy made me feel odd, but not uneasy. I couldn't put my finger on what it was. She paid me the first week in advance, like all the mothers, and I decided I was being silly. This was back when I was getting started. I may have overlooked a sign I should have noticed."

For six months Alan Granger, age four, was left with Miss B at seven in the morning. More often than not he was half asleep when his mother dropped him off. By nine o'clock he was awake, though sluggish, and he spent his time playing quietly, mostly alone, with painted blocks and stuffed animals. He ate a light lunch at noon. When Miss B heard the huff and grind of Roberta's Mustang in front of the house at one p.m., she washed the boy's face and hands and combed his hair.

"My, my!" Roberta said every time she greeted him in the afternoon. "Aren't you a handsome young man?"

She laughed and cupped his face in her hands. Alan shuffled his feet. He never spoke except to answer his mother or Miss B. He never really came out of his shell with the other children. He regarded them with mild interest, the way a more active child might watch an exotic animal at the zoo.

Nothing very unusual happened during those six months. Alan was sleepy but never sick and his schedule remained the same. Then one night Miss B got a call from Roberta.

All the children had gone home. The house was silent and still. You can never know how quiet rooms are until you've seen them full of kids laughing and fighting and playing, and then empty. Miss B used the after hours for cleaning. She could have waited for the weekend but she said putting off a task led to laziness and laziness progressed to shiftiness if you didn't watch out. She made a habit of running the vacuum or the mop over every surface five times a week. This way her home was always sparkling and inviting when her charges arrived.

"Pauline," a voice on the phone whispered. This told Miss B nothing since she encouraged all of the mothers to address her by her first name.

"Who is this?" she asked.

"Roberta," came the husky reply, and now Miss B could tell the caller had been drinking or crying, or both. "I need your help!"

"What's the matter, dear?"

"I didn't know who to call," said Roberta. "I just don't have anybody. I'm sorry. Can I—can I please drop Alan off with you?"

Miss B consulted the kitchen clock next to the wall-mounted telephone. It was eight p.m. "Well, I don't know," she said.

Sobbing and a thin, whining noise came as a reply.

"Can you tell me what's wrong?" she asked. "Is Alan sick? Do you need a doctor?"

"No, no," Roberta cried. "He's all right, for now, but I need somebody to keep him for a few hours, that's all. Please. For his own good."

There was an edge of such poignant desperation in the young woman's voice. In good conscience, Miss B couldn't turn her down. She agreed this one time, for a little while, and Roberta thanked her profusely. When Miss B assured her things would be all right, the line went dead.

71

Fifteen minutes later the doorbell rang. Roberta stood on the porch holding Alan in her arms. The boy was wrapped in a blanket, wearing his pajamas, barely awake. He mumbled and rubbed his eyes and rested his head on Roberta's shoulder, his mouth dropping open. In her distress, his mother possessed the troubled, almost comical appearance of a raccoon driven from an attic nest. Tears and mascara streaked her face. Her hair, usually pulled up into a French bun, was hanging over her shoulders in unruly strands. The car coat she had thrown over her nightgown hung lower on one side than the other.

"I'm sorry, I'm sorry," she kept saying.

"Come in and I'll make you some coffee," said Miss B.

"I can't," said Roberta. "I can't. He'll kill me if I don't come right back."

"Who?"

"Frank," said Roberta. "My husband." She hoisted Alan across the threshold to Miss B, who could now see beyond her client to the street where the Mustang waited, engine huffing away. From where she stood she couldn't tell if someone was in the car.

A split second passed between the two women. A hundred calculations and assumptions came to mind.

"Roberta, do you need for me to call the police?"

"God, no, please, no!" Roberta said. "I've got to go home now. I'll be back as soon as I can." She stepped away, off the porch, and headed for the Mustang.

It was only when she was left alone with the boy that Miss B examined his condition. He was drowsy but not like a child suddenly awakened in the middle of the night. He didn't speak clearly. He never opened his eyes when she placed him in a small cot she kept in the guest room for those times when one of the kids didn't feel well. Wrapped in a clean blanket, Alan slept with his lips parted, a thin trail of drool sliding down his neck, one hand clasping the blanket his mother brought with him.

"Alan," Miss B said softly. "Alan, are you all right, sweetheart?"

The child went on dozing, unaware.

Expecting Roberta to return soon, Miss B made a pot of tea and settled down to read one of the Jane Austen novels she cherished for practicality and optimism. She drifted off in her chair around midnight and only woke up when she heard the doorbell ring at six a.m.

There was no mistaking the black eye or the purple marks on the left side of Roberta's neck. Miss B stood with her back against the door, stunned, waiting.

"I can't thank you enough," Roberta sputtered. "This is—I don't know what to say..."

"Dear," said Miss B. "Why don't you rest here while I call the police?"

"No, no," said Roberta. She pulled her coat closer and straightened her shoulders. She seemed less afraid than angry. "It's the worst thing you could do. Here," she said and peeled off some five-dollar bills and shoved them into Miss B's hand. "I'm sorry for the inconvenience."

"It isn't a matter of inconvenience, or money. You ought to call your family for help."

"Family?" Roberta laughed. "I've got a brother in the Army who hates me. If I even hinted I might leave Frank, my brother would punch my lights out. No, you take this money for babysitting."

"Why would your brother make you stay with a man who acts the way your husband does?" For the first time Miss B noticed more than the bruises. She detected sweat and a musky animal odor, both masked by the heady, sweet perfume Roberta wore.

"Because he told me not to marry Frank, that's why. He told me it was a mistake and I'd regret it. I can't prove him right, Pauline. I can't!"

After the tears subsided Miss B led Roberta to the guest room. Alan slept on as if the world of these two women, one weeping and the other afraid for his safety, never existed. Roberta gathered him up and left, whispering a promise to explain more of the situation as soon as she could.

Miss B put the bills in her purse without counting them. She assumed Alan Granger wasn't coming back that day, and his mother would take time off work to recover.

Two days later Roberta dropped Alan off at the usual time. She wore her hair in a French bun. Makeup covered most of the fading marks on her face and neck. Again she promised an explanation she didn't have time to offer at the moment. On her way out she thrust a small box into Miss B's hand. The rumble of the Mustang faded down the street and Miss B opened the box to find a bottle of perfume, an expensive brand she would never buy. She wondered if it was the one she had detected on Roberta the night she came to collect her son.

The violet bottle and the S on the label were familiar. She had spotted them on TV ads while watching *Bewitched*, one of her regular shows. In the ad a lithe young beauty in a mink coat splashed her wrists with the perfume, winked at the camera, and said, "Intoxicating—with a wicked little kick!"

Miss B checked her bottle to be sure. It was the same. *Somnambule*. Manufactured in Paris, the perfume had a heavy base note. Not a kick, exactly, and not very pleasant. It conjured perfectly the moment she had seen Roberta with her hair undone and her mascara running in black rivulets down her pale skin.

The next time Roberta needed help it was after midnight in the middle of the week. There was no preliminary phone call. She simply showed up, disheveled, holding Alan in her arms. Miss B was inclined to refuse, inclined to insist the young woman seek help, but the sharpness of Roberta's voice, the way she kept shaking her head and pleading, changed her mind. If she turned Roberta away, the distraught woman might return home with the boy, and who knew what would happen?

Alan slept deeply, as he had before. He finally woke up when the other children began to arrive. Miss B fed him breakfast. At noon he ate a light lunch. When his mother didn't show up at one o'clock he ate an afternoon snack with the kids who stayed until six. Then he had dinner with Miss B, who finally gave him his bath and put him to bed.

Remembering all of this, she said she knew it seemed strange but at the time she just couldn't think what else to do. She tried calling Roberta but no one answered the phone. Her instinct to alert the authorities was quickly muted by apprehension. Roberta had warned her not to bring in the police. If she did, there was no telling what they might find. And if Frank Granger was the kind of man who resented people interfering in his domestic life, anything might happen.

The next evening, after all the other children had been picked up by parents Miss B was beginning to view as paragons of virtue, Roberta showed up on the doorstep with a new collection of bruises on her wrists and neck. This time Miss B insisted on more than a gift and a promise.

"Tell me one reason why I shouldn't contact the authorities," she said.

"No one can help," Roberta told her.

"I think the police might want to hear about what's going on." This was the first time Miss B had encountered such a problem, and she had no real sense of how it should be handled.

"No!" Roberta shouted. "No, please! You're the only one who can help me, by not saying anything. I can't call anyone. It's my fault! It's all my fault!"

"How can that be?"

"I'll tell you," said Roberta. "I'll tell you, if you promise to keep it secret. Promise. Please promise."

This is how Pauline Bingham allowed herself to be compromised by a client she barely knew. For the rest of the evening Roberta sat sipping tea and recounting her story.

Being a telephone operator wasn't glamorous but it was a

good job for a girl who lacked a college education and hated the servile nature of secretarial work. As Roberta put it, "I didn't want to spend my life typing letters and pouring coffee for some fat, bald man in a tacky suit."

Her parents had died the year she turned fourteen, leaving their meager savings and Roberta's care to her older brother Gary.

"I saw myself as a hick. My brother's a hick too but he's seen the world. He wanted to study medicine but there wasn't enough money for that. He's a career Army man. He took a transfer and moved back home to raise me. He calls me Bird Brain and he ought to know. Pauline, do you mind if I have a cigarette?"

Miss B ushered her guest outside to the glider swing. Both women settled in and lit cigarettes.

"My brother's not a bad man," said Roberta.

This surprised Miss B. She hadn't given a thought to the brother, only to Roberta's husband, Frank.

"I stayed home as long as I could stand it. I wasn't much of a student, so I dropped out of high school. These other two girls and me, we shared an apartment. I was just doing what I could— cashier, car wash, waitress at a truck stop, greeter at a shoe store, anything. I was barely paying the rent.

"I heard the phone company was about to open another branch, and I applied. They said it might be a year before they were hiring. Pauline, I lived on lettuce sandwiches and spaghetti noodles. I got so skinny my clothes didn't fit. I was like a ghost, a ghost in a mini-dress. Can you imagine?

"Now you'll think I'm the worst thing in the world. I used to wander the aisles of the grocery store and steal food when I could get away with it. I also made a habit of picking up eyeliner, lipstick, hairspray, and Marlboros. I'm not showing off. I'm embarrassed about it now but when I did it I had to. I couldn't stop myself. I just took what I needed. I'd see some lady fiddling with her change purse and I'd get mad. It's not right. But I'd get mad. Why did she have everything she wanted?

"This sounds awful. I'm sorry. But I was so broke, and my brother wouldn't help me unless I moved back home. I was only about twenty when I finally got a chance to apply for a real job, as a telephone operator. I can't tell you how happy I was, just to be chosen for the aptitude test and the interview. Somehow I got the idea only women worked at the phone company. But it was a man that hired me. I flirted with him. It's true. I stuck my boobs out and I smiled and flirted, and he gave me the job."

"We've all done things we wish we didn't have to do," Miss B said.

"I've done a lot of things," Roberta told her. "See, the guy who hired me, who gave me the job I wanted so much, was Frank."

"Your husband?" Miss B shook her head and lit a second cigarette.

"Yes, ma'am. Except when I met him he was somebody else's husband."

Now Miss B raised an eyebrow. She poured tea and smiled at her guest but she started to wonder what she'd got herself into.

The man of Roberta's dreams was stocky, middle-aged, and going bald. He was a shift supervisor and it was a boring job. No surprise he fell for a woman half his age. Maybe he didn't see how desperate Roberta was. Or maybe he did see.

"My brother found out I was dating a married man and I thought he was going to kill me. You know what he did?"

Roberta told two stories about her brother. In the first he tailed Frank home one night and filled his gas tank with sugar. The second was less destructive but more frightening.

The sugar prank left Roberta's suitor without a vehicle. Frank couldn't see her again until he had his car repaired. On their usual date night she was home alone.

She showered and put on her nightgown. She turned out the lights in the apartment she now enjoyed by herself since Frank paid part of the rent. She could hear a radio faintly humming outside, down the street. The tune caught her attention because it was one of her favorites, "We'll Sing in the Sunshine." Quietly she hummed along to the bittersweet refrain about laughing and singing and then leaving the one you love.

The song ended and the radio faded in the distance. Roberta was drifting off when she heard breathing. She opened her eyes, assuming she'd been startled awake by her own gentle snoring. She lay very still. In a few seconds she realized the sound she heard was not her own breathing. Someone else was in the room.

She had to struggle not to make a sudden movement, not to jump up or scream. She measured each intake of air and tried not to tremble as she exhaled. She kept her eyes open. As they adjusted to the dark she glanced up at the ceiling, and then across the room at the door. Nothing moved. The closet was shut and the window was locked. As she lay there perspiring, trying not to call out, her hearing finally located the steady breathing. It was coming from underneath the bed.

As smoothly and quietly as possible she slid the covers off her body and rolled to her right, facing the door. She prepared every muscle for flight. She lay coiled and ready until she heard the breathing lapse into a kind of snuffling noise, almost a snore, and then she sprang from the bed. She landed halfway to the bedroom door, reached out and yanked it open, tore across the living room and out the front door. Unable to stifle it anymore, she let out a scream all the way to the next-door neighbor's apartment. She was shivering and hysterical by the time police arrived. She led two officers through the apartment but no one was found and nothing was out of place.

Roberta broke down when she told this story to Frank, who wanted to track down her brother and beat him up. Instead he comforted Roberta. He comforted her all night, and fooled his wife with a lie about an old friend, a drinking buddy. Two months later Roberta broke the news that she was pregnant.

She had a good job, she told Frank, and she liked living the way she wanted. Every time the subject came up, she refused his money for an abortion and she told him to go back to his wife. As she told Miss B, her plan was to scare him off. She didn't know whether or not she wanted a baby but she knew she didn't want to marry this pot-bellied old man who treated her like a child. Unfortunately her plan backfired. Frank told his wife about the affair and she filed for divorce.

Next thing Roberta knew, Frank had moved in with her while he waited for his divorce to come through. At first they had fun. Staying in bed all day on Sunday, eating cold spaghetti for dinner, watching old musicals and cartoons on TV, they felt like children getting away with murder.

Eventually the pregnancy began to show. Roberta bought zip-up go-go boots and dangling earrings to offset the feeling that she was turning into an elephant. The other operators started gossiping. Frank insisted she cut back her hours and work part-time. He was gruff about it, insisting his salary would be plenty for both of them.

When the divorce was final, Frank had to pay his ex-wife alimony. The amount, based on charges of cruelty and adultery, was devastating.

The new couple lived in a kind of fog after that, pretending nothing had changed. They went on watching movies on TV and singing along to the radio. But there came a day when Frank complained about eating stale donuts for breakfast. Then he informed Roberta they were moving to a smaller apartment, in a part of town where she had formerly vowed she would never live. "Hick Town" is what she called it, where hillbillies and their cousins shacked up when they couldn't find work in Atlanta.

After Alan was born Roberta tried to get full-time work again but Frank refused. He said she should stay home and care for the baby. But he wasn't bringing home enough money for that. So they argued. They argued about their budget. They argued about the money she spent on clothes. Most of all they argued about her smoking. She had smoked cigarettes while carrying the baby, and twice as much after he was born. The less money the couple had the more they argued, and the more Roberta smoked.

"It was the only thing that felt like it was just mine and nobody else's. After Alan was born we couldn't do anything anymore. No takeout dinners. No shopping. All I did was take care of the baby.

"Then somebody finally told on us, I don't know who. The phone company let Frank go, and refused to put me back on full-time."

"I can imagine how he handled the news," Miss B said.

"He tried everything. Finally he got afternoons and weekends handling inventory at a grocery store. You should have seen his face, Pauline. He kept shaking his head and saying this was the kind of work he did in high school."

"We all have to do what we can," said Miss B. "It wasn't your fault he got fired."

"It's nice of you to say, but it was my fault in a way. And then, after all the things that happened, I couldn't leave him. I mean I have to think of Alan, too. Right? I don't know."

At this point Roberta Granger broke down. Miss B put a hand on her shoulder, and the woman let loose and just sobbed. Once she calmed down she lit another cigarette.

"This," she told Miss B, "is my lover, my real boyfriend, right here. I swear, under the right circumstances I think I'd do anything for a cigarette. God, Frank hates it. Nothing helps. I'm already taking—what is it called, a tranquilizer, or a sedative? I can't keep up with all these new medical terms. Seems like it's all bad news these days, don't you think? I try to tune it out. The doctor said these pills would help me drink less. But they're not enough to make me calm down. I smoke like a chimney.

"Frank says if I don't quit, he'll divorce me and take Alan. Maybe he should. Maybe he doesn't mean it. I can't tell any more. But I feel so bad about everything, Pauline. I had to do something."

"What did you do?"

"On my break one day, I was reading the paper and I saw this ad. Madame Vivian, a hypnotist who specializes in non-smoking therapy."

"Madame?"

"I know," said Roberta. "But I was at the end of my rope. I needed a miracle. I went to see her the next day. She has a place downtown. Not really an office, it's more of a studio. There was a sign out front with a picture of a woman with her eyes closed and she's floating in the clouds. Inside the studio's painted white and gold. I expected Madame Vivian would come out wearing a turban and a caftan, carrying a crystal ball. But she was this petite, elderly lady in Capri pants and a white blouse and ballet slippers. She asked me to talk about myself, and all I could say was that I'm a mom and I want to quit smoking. Isn't that pitiful?

"She guided me to another room, smaller and very quiet, and asked me to sit in this sort of recliner. When I was settled in she let the seat back so I was looking at the ceiling. There were tiny lights up there, twinkling just like the night sky!

"Madame Vivian removed my shoes and loosened my clothes. For the first time all day I could breathe. She was speaking to me the whole time, nothing special, just how good it feels to relax and think about nothing, to let all the little worries and fears drift away. I could feel my body letting go, sinking deeper into the recliner, and it was almost like falling asleep except I could hear her voice. And I noticed a fragrance in the room. As I fell under the spell of her words the fragrance grew stronger, and it surrounded me and seemed to embrace me. I began to imagine myself as a caterpillar inside a—what do you call it—"

"Chrysalis," said Miss B.

"Yes. Not sleeping exactly but asleep and aware at the same time. Moving through a series of rooms with painted panels. People wandered behind the panels, whispering. The air was heavy with this scent. It was deep and sweet like an exotic flower, all around me, inside my head and all over my skin. I crossed a court-yard and saw a woman standing beside an open door. She was beckoning to me, and I obeyed.

"There was no sense of time. But when I woke up and checked my watch, two hours had passed. My hands, the palms of my hands were scarlet, smeared bright red with something like finger-paint. Madame Vivian used a soft cloth to wash the color away.

"She asked how I felt and I told her the truth. I felt better than I had since I was a little girl, when my parents were alive and I would play outdoors all afternoon, finding beetles in the blades of grass and following their adventures. I took a deep breath and smelled nothing. The air was clean and bright. There wasn't a hint of the fragrance I'd smelled before."

"Well," said Miss B. "My goodness!"

"I know!" Roberta laughed. "When I walked out of Madame Vivian's studio I felt like a million bucks. I felt so good I went shopping. Not for anything in particular, just wandering around in a nice department store like a lady who could buy anything she wanted.

"I have no idea what drew me to the perfume counter. Every day, Frank was complaining about how I spent money. All I know is that I opened a bottle, right there in the middle of the counter, in the middle of the store, and when I inhaled the fragrance it carried me right back to the little room in Madame Vivian's studio. It was the very same scent!"

"How odd." This is when Miss B had her first inkling that Roberta might have problems beyond her marriage. "Did you buy a bottle?"

Roberta picked at the filter end of another cigarette. She resisted for a second and then lit up.

"Yes," she said. But she seemed uncertain. "I took three bottles. I hid them at home. If Frank knew he'd kill me."

"I'll give back the one you gave me," said Miss B.

"No! Oh no, no."

"I never wear perfume," Miss B insisted.

"I can't return it," said Roberta. "I didn't pay for it."

Miss B had to make a conscious effort to close her mouth at this point. She couldn't imagine a woman showing the audacity to shoplift three bottles of expensive perfume.

"See?" Roberta said. "I told you, Pauline. I knew you were going to hate me. I'm hopeless."

"Don't be silly," said Miss B. Before them the back yard glittered with lightning bugs. "I'm surprised, that's all. You must have had some lingering effect from the woman, the hypnotist, what was her name?"

"Madame Vivian…"

"What a ridiculous name," said Miss B. "She was a con artist. She took advantage of you. How much did you have to pay her?"

"Fifteen dollars."

"Well, that isn't too bad. But she cheated you. You're still smoking."

Roberta nodded. She crossed her legs and smoked in silence.

"I think I'm sleepwalking too," she said after a while.

"Sleepwalking?"

"I've been waking up in Alan's room. Don't know how. I wake up, and I'm standing next to his bed. One time I was holding a pillow in my hands." Roberta stopped. When she realized Miss B was staring at her, she laughed.

"What?" Miss B asked, amazed by her strange behavior.

"You know what I do? I wear the perfume whenever I smoke. Now, what do you say, do you think it's strong enough to cover half a pack of cigarettes?"

"No," said Miss B.

"No, I don't believe it either," said Roberta. "But you know what? Frank can't smell smoke on me when I'm wearing the perfume. He can't tell at all! Is that crazy?"

In fact Miss B had begun to wonder if the Grangers might

be unbalanced. Not merely troubled but somehow, in a deeper sense, unwell.

"What do you say, Pauline?" Roberta asked. "Am I going crazy?" She laughed again and this time her voice had a nasty undercurrent, a streak of real madness.

"Maybe all you need is some sleep," said Miss B. "Maybe you should leave Alan with me for a day or two and get a good rest. Might do you a lot of good."

The night was still except for the lightning bugs. The porch light was dim on purpose. Miss B didn't like neighbors to spy on her evening smoke. In the shadows her guest's face lit up suddenly, illuminated by the tip of her cigarette when she took a draw. Her eyes were dark and fierce like a nocturnal animal's. She exhaled and smirked.

"Pauline, you're a very nice lady," she said. "I've got to get home."

Briskly she gathered her things. Her last words to Miss B were spoken on the doorstep with her son Alan asleep in her arms.

"I'll mail you a check to settle up for the rest of the month," she said. "That's fair, right? You'll have to find someone to replace Alan." She turned away before Miss B could answer.

Miss B held the screen door open. She watched Roberta step nimbly from the walkway to the street where the Mustang was parked. Miss B moved forward, down the steps, and saw someone—a tall, broad-shouldered man—leaning against the car on the driver's side. Had he been there, waiting, the whole time?

Roberta hoisted Alan into the back and tucked him in with his blanket. Then she climbed into the passenger's seat. The man took the driver's seat, and started the engine.

"What happened after that?" I asked.

"Not a thing," said Miss B. "I never saw them again."

"Did you ever get a check in the mail?"

"No, I did not," she said. "But she left me that bottle of

perfume, and it's still here. You can have it, if you want. I don't have any use for it."

***

"So, she gave me this," I told Tubby. I pointed to the night-stand, to the bottle with an elegant S printed on its side.

Tubby was in bed beside me, eyes half closed, with her hair spread in chestnut waves across the pillow. She turned to me with a wrinkled brow.

"But what happened to the woman?" she asked. She reached up with one fist and rubbed the corner of her eye. The childlike gesture silenced me. We needed sleep, especially Tubby. She was singing a solo in the choir next day.

"Oh. Nobody knows," I lied.

In fact I knew, and Miss B surely must have known. Roberta Granger went to prison for murdering her husband and her little boy while they slept. Frank Granger's throat was slit with a butcher's knife and their son Alan was smothered with a pillow. Roberta claimed to be under the influence of tranquilizers, and made mysterious references to a hypnotist who was never located during the trial.

Tubby was such a good girl, in every respect. She didn't need to know how the story ended. She wouldn't know what to do with a story like that.

I rolled over with my back to my best friend. As dawn crept across the windowsill I began to drift into quiet slumber. With my hand beneath my head I could detect just a hint of the per-fume I'd dabbed on my wrist.

In my dreams I saw a woman dressed in white standing beside an open door in a courtyard, beckoning. I drifted toward her and heard her speak as I lost consciousness.

"Intoxicating—with a wicked little kick…"

FUR

Fleas were the part of her job she hated. But Mary accepted the fleas, as she accepted many things nowadays, with a shrug: A necessary evil, what could be done about it? Fleas occupied the fur on so many of the dogs she groomed, the fat, lazy dogs of clients who paid extra for bows, extra for bells and silk ribbons. Cheap trinkets.

Mary knew that the really wealthy pet owners took their dogs to the Kennel Spa down the street. At the spa, they paid hundreds of dollars so their canine children could sit in a sauna or get a massage.

"Stupid," Mary's mother said whenever the subject came up. "What dog needs a facial? I need a facial."

"They don't do facials, Mom," Mary told her a hundred times. "It's a mineral pack, makes the coat shiny." But her mother wouldn't listen.

"Kennel Spa," she said. "It's a stupid idea, but it makes money. You should work there. Nobody goes for just grooming anymore."

"Our clients do," Mary said. "Not everybody has a million dollars in the bank, Mom."

"We sure don't," her mother said. She always complained at the breakfast table. "Your dogs have got fleas. Why? I don't think Kennel Spa dogs have fleas." She poured Mary's coffee. "Dogs with fleas. It's a shame."

Over the past three years Mary's mother had become the background noise to her life, a steady cadence like the radio. Mary dressed by it, brushed her hair by it, said goodbye and caught the bus from Phoenix to Scottsdale.

Brenda was already there. She opened the shop every morning, because she owned it. She had worked here all her life, and she inherited the shop when her mother died.

No matter how early Mary arrived Brenda was there, wearing a frosted wig and several pieces of turquoise jewelry, blue jeans and a ratty T-shirt. Brenda always started the day wearing mules or sandals, and ended up working barefoot. Mary wondered how she could stand the feel of animal hair sticking to her feet, but Brenda never noticed.

Mary thought about the fleas while she combed the silky coat of a Pomeranian notorious for his sharp little teeth. She had his mouth strapped shut with a muzzle and she worked steadily until the dog dropped a turd on the white Formica table.

"Bad!"

Mary put her hands on either side of him and spoke firmly, and he snarled up at her through the muzzle.

"Yeah, I know," she told the Pomeranian. "You'll kill me as soon as you get the chance, right?"

She had never struck a dog, but she had seen Brenda lose her temper and give a little one-finger thump to the noses of dogs that gave her trouble. Brenda always had trouble with the Schnauzers. She said they reminded her too much of her ex-husband.

Mary finished brushing the Pomeranian and returned him to his cage. Then she prepared to shampoo and blow-dry a poodle whose name she could never pronounce, so she called him Foo-Foo. That's when she noticed the flea on her arm. It jumped and tumbled on her skin. She slapped it away. But she kept thinking about it: the thin line between the dogs and herself, and how the fleas seemed happy with both.

Fleas came with the job, although Mary and Brenda took pains to introduce their new clients to a reliable topical treatment. Some clients were grateful and some were not, like the over-exercised Barthe woman, the one who wore real furs and fake jewelry. Mary's husband had once given her a jacket made of rabbit fur, but she never wore it because people gave her dirty looks. She never wore jewelry either, but she could tell at a glance the big baubles on Mrs. Barthe were cheap imitations.

Mrs. Barthe's Chihuahua was named James but she called him Jimmy, and she strapped him into a custom-made car seat and took him wherever she went. In his brightly decorated seat, Jimmy sat quietly watching traffic, like an emaciated baby.

The smell was part of the job, too: a wet, beauty shop aroma. Soap couldn't touch it. Worse, it was a dog hair smell. Mary's mother complained about it, and they sprayed the house every day with a spring bouquet room freshener, but it came back. Not at once but gradually. It lingered between the couch cushions until someone sat down and—whoosh—the dog hair smell would come up and surround the surprised guest like an invisible cloud.

"If that Jimmy squirms around when I clip his claws today, I'm gonna chop his tail off and tell Mrs. Barthe one of the dogs bit it," Brenda said over coffee, stacking her feet one on top of the other on the rim of a wastebasket and leaning back in her chair. Then she laughed at herself.

"I need a vacation," she said.

It was the Christmas season. In Phoenix, that meant

Styrofoam Santas wearing sombreros perched merrily on the streetlights, and the temperature dropping to fifty-five degrees. The weather was perfect for shopping. Tourist season was in full swing. On the freeway people drove like demons looking for an exit from hell.

When the last client picked up the last dog at the end of the day, Brenda let out a sigh of hallelujah and flipped over the CLOSED sign on the front door.

Brenda and Mary sat in the cramped waiting area, watching traffic and sipping a final cup of coffee.

"I told you and told you, he's all right," Brenda said. "Why would I set you up on a date with a rapist or a psycho or something?"

"Why did you set me up at all?" Mary asked. "I don't need a date. I'm happy."

"In a five-room bungalow, with nobody except your mother?" Brenda made a face. "Is that all you want for yourself?"

Mary didn't like to talk about her future. Life was hard enough when all she did was go day by day. It wasn't always so. During the years of her marriage to Johnny, Mary thought about the future all the time. She had plans, but she couldn't explain them, especially to her husband. He was only interested in what Mary wore and how she looked in it.

"What do you want?" Brenda asked.

"I don't know," Mary said. "But I don't want another husband telling me what to do, and how to do this and that and everything."

"Then dumping you for a younger woman," Brenda reminded her. This was the real dividing line between the two women. Brenda never treated Mary like an employee, more like a partner. They split the clients and tips. But Mary's husband had left her in the middle of the night after he fell in love with a 21-year-old cashier at their neighborhood 7-Eleven, while Brenda had the good sense to throw her husband out of the house for gambling. It was a difference that gave Brenda free rein to offer unsolicited advice.

"You should've taken his .38 down to that motel and shot both of them in the butt," she told Mary at least once a week. "Then you'd feel better about it."

"Yeah, yeah," Mary said. "Good riddance, okay?"

"Fine, okay," said Brenda. She scratched her leg. "I hate the winter, man, I get this dry skin."

Brenda turned her attention back to the traffic beyond the shop window.

"Anyway, he thinks he's picking you up at eight o'clock. So just meet him at the door and say you've got the flu or you hate men or whatever," she said.

First thing when she got home, Mary took a warm bath. In the tub she ran through the scene in her mind, imagining what her mother might say to get rid of her blind date.

"No, my daughter isn't well. She grooms dogs and one of the dogs bit her so she can't go out with you. Sorry."

It was ridiculous, and guaranteed to make both her mother and the guy feel stupid. There was no way out. She had to go.

At eight o'clock Mary sat in the living room under the smiles of three saints framed in gold. She was bathed in light from the miniature Christmas tree and surrounded by the smell of dog hair. She wore the only dress she owned that could be called nondescript—a brown cotton shift with a tan Peter Pan collar and sleeves that were added on by her mother to turn a spring outfit into winter.

At eight-ten Mary turned off the Christmas lights and decided to go to bed. The doorbell rang.

She told herself she had not anticipated anything. She had, in fact, made a firm resolution not to expect one single thing. It was a habit that kept her fear low to the ground and manageable. But when she opened the door and saw her date she felt her jaw muscles tighten.

He wore a brown suit—the same shade of brown Mary was wearing. The carnation in his lapel was already wilting. She noticed it was an unnatural yellow, probably over-dyed.

Otherwise, he was the most handsome man she had ever seen. At least, he had the most handsome head she had ever seen. A romantic, poetic head with large, dark eyes and thick, black hair and a lower lip that made her own lips move involuntarily as if she had something on the tip of her tongue. A gorgeous, glamorous head—attached to a square solid frame with a beer belly. He looked to be about 5' 3", which was a good three inches shorter than Mary.

She tried to shake the idea, but there was no doubt in her mind: He had a body that wanted to be under someone else's head, a bald butcher's head.

"Hello. You must be Mary," he said, and his voice was so deep and artificial it seemed to be traveling through a giant megaphone to Mary's ears. She imagined him practicing his deep voice in front of a mirror.

"Hello," she said. "Do you have a car?"

She would go. She would go with him and call it a date. Fine. She could do that, but she would not invite him in and let him judge her and her mother because they lived in a house that reeked of dog hair. He was okay, but he wasn't perfect, and she wouldn't stand for any judgment. She made up her mind. She didn't want to know his opinion of her.

"My name is John, you can call me Johnny," he said as soon as they were seated in his weather-beaten Plymouth Fury.

"Thanks. Okay," Mary said. She stared out the window at the night full of palm trees and wondered if she would end the evening by screaming out loud. She knew Brenda wasn't malicious enough to set her up on purpose with a guy named Johnny, so she figured Brenda didn't know him as well as she pretended.

"My ex-husband was named Johnny," Mary said flatly.

"Do you have another nickname?"

"Oh," he said. "Not really. Sorry about that."

They cruised along in silence for a while. Then Johnny took another stab at conversation.

"Brenda tells me you two work together," he said, stopping at a light.

On the corner a grizzled old man was fighting with a bulldog for a scrap of what appeared to be carpet. The light changed before Mary answered.

"We groom dogs," she said.

"Hey, that must be interesting," Johnny replied. His eyes were fixed on the old man and bulldog in the rearview mirror.

"Why?" Mary asked.

"Oh, I don't know," he said. "I thought, you know, you probably learn a lot about people—uh, people with dogs."

Mary stared out the window.

"See, I work at the zoo," he explained. "You'd be surprised how much you can learn about an individual from the animal he spends the most time watching."

"At the zoo?" Mary pictured this dark-haired beer-bellied man shoveling scat out of wire cages.

"Yeah. Like—the people who are attracted to the big cats? Usually middle-aged men starting to put on weight. They like the tigers, the leopards."

"Chubby men like big cats?" Mary asked. She tried not to look at his belly.

"And the fat women, they always go for the exotic birds," Johnny said as they came to a stop at a Sonic Drive-In.

"Birds, huh?" Mary said. "How about that."

They studied the menu for a minute and then Johnny asked what she wanted.

"Oh, I don't know," said Mary. "A milkshake—no, wait, a diet soda. And French fries."

Johnny ordered for both of them and if he gave the

waitress the once-over, Mary didn't catch him at it. The skinny high school girl in a tight uniform had taken a good leisurely look at Johnny, though. Mary thought it was only natural. Judging by his head and shoulders, he was quite a catch. Then a mean thought crossed her mind.

"Do you eat at the drive-in a lot?" she asked.

"Not really," he said. "Why?"

"Just curious," Mary said. Now she was sorry she'd thought of him taking all his meals in his car, so he wouldn't have to stand up and reveal his body.

"So every person likes a different animal, huh?" She tried to sound interested.

"Yeah," he said. "It's pretty funny to watch. They don't even know it."

"I don't like dogs," Mary told him.

The night sky was etched with clouds.

"I brush their hair and give them a bath because somebody pays me to do it," she said.

"What kind of animals do you like?"

"None," Mary said honestly. "I don't like animals very much."

"So, how did you decide on a job like that?" Johnny asked.

"I knew Brenda for a long time. I needed a job, and she taught me." She didn't want to talk about dogs and she didn't want to talk about herself.

Across the street a man and woman were walking toward a gas station. The man followed the woman, reaching his hand out to try and touch her. The woman pushed his hand back, but she didn't run away.

"Brenda hates dogs," Johnny said. "She likes reptiles." He laughed. "They don't have to be groomed."

Mary had to laugh, thinking of Brenda trying to unsnarl the nappy curls on a terrier's back. First the dog would bare its teeth and growl. Then Brenda would bare her teeth and growl, then the dog, then Brenda.

"But most women don't like the snakes and lizards," Johnny said. "They like the animals with fur. Something about it."

"Yeah, they probably imagine themselves wearing it," Mary said.

Johnny seemed confused by this. He took the tray from the girl in the Sonic uniform, and handed Mary her soda and fries. He ate his cheeseburger and onion rings like a starving man, without stopping to talk.

Halfway through her fries, Mary noticed the familiar tingling sensation on her forearm. Anyone else might have mistaken it for a stray hair, or a grain of salt. Instantly, Mary recognized the minute crawling of a flea on her skin. She turned and brushed it off quickly before Johnny knew something was up.

They heard raised voices outside. The man and woman across the street were shouting at one another.

"Want to see something?" Johnny asked. The expectant smile made him seem naïve for a moment.

"What is it?" Mary didn't want to see anything. But Johnny was reaching around the seat, fumbling through paper and empty cans on the floor behind him. He found a hand-sized gold box and offered it to Mary.

"Open it," he said.

Mary accepted the box, unable to refuse with a mouthful of French fries. She nodded thanks and opened the gold box. Inside she found a piece of what seemed to be fur—only a scrap, but it was black and glossy like mink. She ran her hand over it several times until it lost its coolness and began to take on the warmth of her fingers.

When she looked up, Johnny was watching her. Their eyes met for a second, just a flicker, and her face flushed red. The car seemed to close in on her. The dark, the night, kept her there, trapped with him. She was excited, and infuriated by the knowledge that she couldn't leave. It was too far to walk home now. She was stuck with him.

"What is this?" Mary asked, holding up the scrap of dark fur.

"It's from one of the black bears. He died a few months ago. Beautiful, isn't it?" He was staring at her, making her blush more deeply.

"It's a pretty color," she said. "What's it for? Small piece like this, you couldn't even make a collar out of it."

As soon as she said it she felt sorry. Johnny looked at the fur, then at Mary.

"I'm really tired tonight for some reason," she said. She closed the box and handed it back to Johnny. Reluctantly, he returned it to the floor behind his seat.

"Hard day at work?" he asked, smiling.

"Just tired."

"Well, I wanted to show you one more thing on the way home," he said. He tossed their trash into the can beside the car, placed the tray on top, and started the car.

They drove in silence again. Mary didn't look at Johnny. She hoped he couldn't tell that she was grinding her teeth.

There was nothing, really, wrong with this man. And she kept reminding herself there was nothing wrong with her. But it was an unusual moment when her ex-husband's voice didn't play in the back of her head, telling her she was getting fat, she should never wear shorts at her age, she ought to think about having her nose fixed, maybe she should see other men to get some more experience, it might help their marriage, he wasn't going to stop flirting with other women as long as they found him attractive, and on and on.

It was a marriage her mother disapproved of, from the beginning. So it was all the more humiliating when Mary had to ask her mother if she could come home because she could only afford to pay a few hundred dollars a month for rent. The rest had gone to creditors and lawyers.

Mary's mother reminded her, every day, that she would never get another job and make more money unless she went back to school. She would have gone to school a few years earlier, but now the idea of sitting in a desk in a classroom with a bunch of people ten or fifteen years her junior made her feel like crying. She often told herself that she was in a transition, and she needed to let things rest for a while. She would figure out what she wanted to do next, but now she was tired and she needed to coast and not feel anything, for anybody, just for a while.

On the west side of Central Avenue Johnny turned south down an alley, then right into a large cul-de-sac and ended up in front of "the most decorated house in Phoenix." A sign proclaimed this triumph and the name of the newspaper running the annual contest, but it was barely visible in the glare.

There wasn't an inch of the dirt lawn that didn't pulse with Christmas lights. The roof was covered in bright white fake snow, with a giant plastic Santa riding his sleigh pulled by reindeer. A life-sized plaster Mary and Joseph and the Magi smiled from both sides of a wishing well in the yard, where pilgrims were encouraged to make a donation toward the electric bill.

On the roof a neon sign flashed: "Have." Then darkness. "A." Darkness. "Merry." Darkness. "One!"

"That's pretty," Johnny said as they huddled in the car and gazed out through the crowd of people who had come to see the house lit up at night.

"What do they come here for?" Mary asked, watching the crowd watch the house.

"To see something they can't see anywhere else, maybe."

Mary studied the scene. She tried to understand what the fuss was about.

"It's a waste of money," she said, finally. There was nothing else she could offer.

Johnny started the engine and slowly pulled away from the curb, watching the Christmas lights in his rearview mirror, all the way to the corner.

"Look!" he said when they turned down the next street. "You can still see the glow, over the rooftops!"

Mary pretended to look.

"Wow," she said and stifled a yawn.

They said nothing on the way home. Johnny drove a little over the speed limit, and Mary watched the street lamps flash by, dressed up in their sombrero-and-poncho-clad Santa Clauses.

At her house, Mary said thank you and good night in the car, explaining that Johnny didn't have to see her to the door, her mother was asleep, and the neighbors liked quiet. He said nothing about the piece of fur in its box, and she wondered if he had meant to offer it to her as a gift. Maybe she had misunderstood and embarrassed him.

Mary couldn't get over the feeling that she was crawling with fleas, that they were taking over her body and her mother's house. She wondered if Johnny would find any fleas in his car on the way home, and forever think of fleas when he thought of her, if he ever did.

She waved goodbye and unlocked her front door. She turned off the porch light before he drove away. She let out a ragged sigh now that she could go to bed and not have to talk to the stranger with the beautiful head stuck on the wrong body.

In the next room her mother was snoring lightly in the dark.

Mary opened the door to her own small room. She sat on the narrow bed but she wasn't sleepy anymore. Outside a tepid breeze ruffled the palm trees and a dog barked.

Mary opened the closet as quietly as she could. She found

the bundle of plastic wrapping by touch and pulled it out. Then she stripped the rabbit fur jacket of its plastic cover and put it on over her brown shift. The jacket lay heavily against her body. Feeling its weight and the stifling warmth enfolding her, she clung to it with both hands, lay down on her bed, and closed her eyes to shut out the night.

ANIMAL HOUSE

The first semester of 1997 proved to be more challenging than expected. Tuition hikes and a scarcity of affordable housing favored the resourceful students. When Dave, Abigail, and Marla found a comfortable place, and discovered it was remarkably cheap, they felt fortunate.

The house sat unevenly behind a weedy lawn on the corner of 12th Street and Derwood, eight blocks from the university. There was little traffic and no reverberation of music from parties. Most of the fraternities claimed larger, traditional housing on the opposite side of campus.

The three students met the day they answered the ad. Finding they were compatible in their personal taste and prone to an easy sarcasm, Abigail suggested they share the house. She joked about something fateful bringing them together at eight o'clock on a rainy Saturday morning. The house was their destiny, she said, for the school year, anyway. Dave and Marla agreed and so they signed a contract with the pale, nondescript man who managed the property. He seemed happy to settle the matter and end his workday. Before he drove away he pulled up the "open house" sign on the lawn and tossed it into the trunk of his car.

Thereafter, whenever the kitchen plumbing grumbled, the new housemates grinned at one another. "Destiny," one of them would say with a shrug, to make the others laugh. When a doorknob fell off, or a window frame popped loose, they hauled out a roll of duct tape and applied a quick fix.

All three were satisfied with the rundown condition of the house because it was temporary and they could afford it. The peeling plaster and cranky radiators were a colorful part of college life. No one questioned the stale odors wafting from the closets. A clutch of potpourri from a flower shop on The Ave was enough to take the edge off.

There was no reason to venture beyond the kitchen, bathrooms, and bedrooms. No one inspected the attic or the basement. The manager left them a note confirming mousetraps had been set above and below living quarters a week before they moved in. They were sleep deprived and distracted by school. If they imagined a swift, light scuffling from the darkest recesses of the house in the soft minutes before daybreak, they ignored it.

"Not my property, not my problem," was their motto.

***

One Saturday afternoon early in their residence Marla and Abigail sat on deck chairs on the lawn, chatting. They rambled, comparing opinions about the campus racquetball courts, library renewal policies, and the lack of feminine hygiene products in the Student Union bathrooms. Only when they reached a quiet pause did they notice two elderly women on the other side of the hedge. The women were pulling up weeds and tossing them into a bucket, carrying on their own conversation as they went along.

"...Better with young people," said one of the women, who wore a wide-brimmed hat despite the overcast day. "Since they're less attached."

"Well, I've said that for years," said the one dressed in overalls.

"But I can see the advantage of families, too."

"Do you remember the Maxwells?"

"Before my time."

"Oh, listen to you!"

Both women laughed. Then they seemed to lower their voices because all that Abigail and Marla could make out were the words "animal" and "house."

"*Animal House?*" asked Marla.

Abigail shrugged. "Do they mean this house?"

It had been years since either of them had seen the movie, a satire about the seedier aspects of fraternities. The gradually sinking, dowdy porch and the bowed plank steps of their rented home wouldn't have lasted one night under the wear and tear of frat life. Yet the name pleased both girls. Later that night they told Dave the story, and he laughed.

Afterward whenever the housemates mentioned where they lived, they called it Animal House. Most people laughed. The elderly man who delivered their daily newspaper did not find it funny. He ducked his head the day Marla greeted him with, "Welcome to Animal House!" From then on he left their newspaper in a plastic bag on the sidewalk.

***

Kirsten was a necessary addition at mid-term. After a late-night, tearful conversation about who was or wasn't pulling their weight, Marla was forced to admit she couldn't keep up with utilities, groceries, and school expenses without help from the father she despised. The group solution was to post an ad on a kiosk at the student center and split the rent four ways instead of three.

Although several people called to inquire about the ad, only Kirsten showed up for an interview. Quiet, plain-faced, wearing a wrinkled cotton dress and a kimono robe that bunched up around her waist, Kirsten struck both Marla and Abigail as trustworthy, dull, and a bit sad.

"Where have you been living up until now?" Dave asked.

"With friends," Kirsten said. "I need to move."

"Why?" Abigail asked.

"My friends had a problem with vermin."

"Why do you want to live here instead of a dorm?" Marla asked.

"The dorms are full. And. Um. This is a good place." Kirsten glanced at the ceiling and grinned. A caterwaul from her stomach caused her to blush and place one hand over her mouth. "Excuse me," she said, and burped.

The minute Kirsten gathered her backpack and traipsed out the door, the original three (as they had come to think of themselves) began their assessment.

"At least she didn't fart," Abigail said.

"Vermin?" Marla said with a smirk. "Who says 'vermin' outside of a Russian novel?"

"Are we judging her on digestion or vocabulary?" Dave asked.

"Do you want to judge her based on grooming habits?" Abigail asked.

"What do you mean?" Dave looked from one girl to the other, baffled.

"Our prime candidate is—sort of—hirsute," Marla told him. "She could use a good wax on her forearms."

"Or a comb," Abigail added. "And she's poor. I can tell. The kimono robe was probably right off a hanger at Value Village. And what was she doing with those lacquered sticks in her hair? It's like she picked up fashion tips from a magazine she found in her mom's closet."

"It doesn't matter," Dave said. "We only need her to pay one quarter of everything. How could anybody not afford this place?"

Marla gave him an injured frown.

"Not a dig at you, Marla," he said. "Why would you take it that way? I'm just—never mind. What do you think?"

"She's okay. A little dumpy."

"I guess beggars can't be choosers," said Abigail. "We need her to pay rent this month."

Marla frowned and said, "I think she's okay."

***

Kirsten moved in the next afternoon while the original three were in class. Later there was no sign of change except the locked door upstairs. Although Marla claimed to detect a slight scent of burned meat in the air, the others smelled nothing and they teased her about her olfactory sensitivity.

"It's probably the lingering aroma of a meatloaf from the 1960s," Abigail said. "A ghost loaf."

Marla rolled her eyes. "Forget I said anything."

Roughly the same size and dimensions as the other three, the bedroom occupied by the new housemate claimed its own small floor at the top of the stairs. Like Kirsten, the room was an add-on, constructed out of the attic space at least a decade after the house was built.

The original three had each considered and rejected the fourth bedroom. Equipped with the same amenities as the others—clanging radiator, partial view of the street below through a jungle of oak leaves and ivy, the skittering of branches and squirrels across the outer walls—something about it, a barely noticeable difference in one of the angles, an indefinable offense to their nascent sense of *Feng Shui,* sent them scuttling back, one by one, downstairs to the first or second landing, to settle behind slightly crooked doors with duct-taped knobs.

The add-on housemate settled in quickly and silently, to the relief of the original three. In only half a semester they had developed a comfortable routine they were loath to give up: morning coffee, toast, and amiable gossip; a dash to campus on foot or bicycle to their various lecture halls; days filled with classes, meetings, labs, a stop at the library; and then each made the short journey home to crash for the evening meal in front of a rickety TV rescued from a sorority trash dumpster. Most nights ended with a review of notes and assigned reading for the next day, followed by an incoherent stumble to bed.

They were vaguely aware of Kirsten's presence in the room above although they paid no attention to her comings and goings. They assumed her schedule was much like their own but they didn't ask. She never joined them on the slouchy sofa and dilapidated chairs in what they jokingly referred to as "the family room."

One night, during a meal of pizza and popcorn, the original three heard a massive groan from the plumbing overhead. Dave gazed up at the ceiling and said, "Must be Kirsten eating dinner." They laughed until they felt sick.

There was no mess in the upstairs or downstairs bathroom. Each month a day before it was due Kirsten's money order for rent and utilities appeared on the kitchen counter, and this was enough contact as far as they were concerned.

***

"I'd almost trade places with you, if your housemates were hot," Dave's friend Rob said over lunch at the Union one afternoon.

"Screw you," Dave told him.

"Bet they wouldn't, though," said Rob. "Bet they like each other. Am I right?" He grinned stupidly.

"Shut up."

"You should've signed up for Fall Rush, dude."

"I'm not frat material," Dave said.

"Well, watch out. Sooner or later girls get hormonal, and they go crazy."

Dave's answer was to hurl a handful of potato chips at Rob, who ducked and laughed louder. It wasn't the first or last time they had a version of this conversation. Rob teased Dave about his living arrangement every time they got together. Dave knew a lot of guys would envy the situation. He was glad none of his friends had seen Kirsten. If he had to be honest, she was kind of mousy, and pathetic in the way only plain girls who refuse to admit how plain they are can be. The way she'd dressed the day they met, it was obvious she was taking a stab at some glamorous image. Her inability to pull it off made him feel sad and a little queasy. He was glad she didn't try to hang out with him.

Marla and Abigail were okay. They weren't his friends. They were rental partners, a way to save money, and they were less messy than the guys he would have been paired with in a dorm.

At least Abigail tried. Apparently Marla had led a more sheltered life before college. She was still learning to pick up after herself. Abigail nagged her, and Marla made a halfhearted effort to keep her clothing, shoes, books, and backpack off the floor most of the time.

Dave couldn't understand Marla's reluctance to hit her dad up for cash. But he figured the reasons were personal and none of his business. He guessed at the degree of strain between them, based on Marla's whispered phone conversations with someone she never identified, someone who sent care packages of expensive sheets, extra blankets, homemade cookies, and checks in small amounts for special treats like dining out once a month.

Dave figured Marla's mom was on the other end of her lifeline. He didn't care, didn't pry, but he was the one who had suggested a fourth housemate. He was afraid Marla might ask him for a loan. He didn't want to explain how he had worked every summer during high school just to afford state college and a meager existence off campus. In a more vague sense he was afraid she might screw up the balance of his easygoing, temporary home, respite from parents who drank too much and forgot to pay the gas bill on time.

Being up-to-date on all the basics in life appealed to him very much. He needed to know this feeling could go on indefinitely. He was comfortable. So whenever he noticed a distant squeak in the rafters at night he remembered the manager's assurances and paid no attention to the noise.

***

Abigail's greatest fear in the century-old house was fire. Her worries were not entirely imaginary. One of her cousins had been trapped and disfigured beyond recognition in a fire on the east coast when Abigail was nine years old. An ill-advised hospital visit had sent her running down the hall, sobbing and terrified, into the arms of a nurse who scolded her parents for being thoughtless.

Afterward on the plane trip home, and for the rest of the time she lived with them, Abigail could no longer see her parents as responsible adults who carefully considered her well-being. Every new outing or event was fraught with potential disaster, from car crashes to rock slides. She came to think of her home as a minefield as she picked her way fretfully from one room to another. Even now during moments without the distraction of homework she might begin checking electrical cords and appliances, turning off lights when Marla or Dave stepped out of the room for a few minutes, locking and re-locking the front door.

Before she fell asleep each night she engaged in a mental review of escape routes. From her room on the second floor she could climb out a window onto a narrow deck surrounded by a painted railing. If the portico below were on fire, however, this would mean certain death.

She could run for the door she kept ajar all night (to avoid a backdraft in case the hall was engulfed in flames) and take the stairs. If the stairwell were impassable she had a third choice, to risk opening Marla's door to climb out her window, down a crumbling lattice on the far side of the house.

Running to the top floor wasn't an option. She couldn't identify the apprehension she associated with it. Only that something mean and feral frightened her, not exactly hiding in the shadows but a part of them, as in a dream. It reminded Abigail of her mother talking on the phone, years ago, about the fire and the way her cousin's skin had melded together with the curtains and bedspread.

She would run for Marla's room. In a real emergency, she would choose what she knew. She would choose what she could define.

Usually by the time she reached the end of her escape routes she was drifting off, murmuring about safety zones and backdrafts. In the dream forming, shifting, and taking the place of the objects around her, Abigail was unable to separate the noise of hinges from the gentle squeal of something distinctly alive overhead.

***

The frustrating thing about people who didn't grow up with money was the way they hesitated before every step. Marla's housemates were sweet, intelligent people but they were not exceptions to the rule. She could almost see the hairs rise on the back of Dave's neck when the rent was due. Abigail was worse, always guessing what things cost and how much people earned. She sometimes opened her change purse right in front of everybody at the grocery store to count the one-dollar bills wadded up like used tissues.

Gardner, the housekeeper to Marla's family, was nothing like that. No awkwardness, no fumbling over price tags. Gardner had grown up poor with ten siblings but she wasn't afraid of people of substance. The fearless little woman with watchful, deep blue eyes had been Marla's lifelong protective barrier, first against inappropriate conversation and cuddling by her father, later against bullies at the snobby school her mother insisted on.

When no one else had the nerve, Gardner stepped in to gently adjust the landscape. Without fuss and without being explicit she was able to influence every aspect of Marla's life, from family sleeping arrangements on holiday to which courses Marla was expected to take. Nothing was beyond Gardner's reach and however things turned out she was always standing by with good advice and comforting snacks. In all the ways that mattered, she was Marla's real mother.

The only thing Gardner couldn't control was how much money the girl received from the family estate. Once Marla turned twenty-one this would no longer be an issue. Her paternal grandmother established a trust fund the day she was born. Someday she would have her own home, with a private suite and sun deck for Gardner's retirement. Then she would forget all about this place.

A poor little state college, a major in art history, and rustic living quarters were Marla's revenge. While waiting for her trust fund she saw no reason to go along with her mother's plans for an ivy league school and marriage; her mother's life had been ruined by the very path she wanted Marla to take. Her escape, her sojourn among penniless students, was more fun.

As punishment for slumming instead of stalking a rich boy, Marla's parents stopped sending her the little extras that made life bearable for other girls of her social standing. She was forced to beg for scraps.

Temporary poverty proved to be interesting although not the lark she expected. Having to admit the limitations of her funds to Dave and Abigail was mortifying. Given time she could have worked something out with Gardner's help but Dave had stepped in before she could make arrangements, practically demanding a fourth housemate.

Who was this Kirsten? After a brief interview she became part of the household with the same rights and obligations as the original three. Yet they never saw the sad girl in the shabby robe. She never ate dinner with them, and never shared coffee in the morning. Marla had never run into her on campus or on the stairs. The only indication of her presence was the monthly money order on the kitchen counter, an occasional scent of hamburger lingering in the air, and a barely perceptible but persistent squeak like the movement of rusty bedsprings late at night.

***

Over the winter break the original three went separate ways. A few weeks later, after enduring the usual family rituals and discomforts, they returned to the ramshackle house at 12th and Derwood.

Though they arrived at different times on various days each was struck by the same sense that the place had undergone a fundamental change. The doors still fit crookedly and the odor of mildew continued to travel from corner to corner with every draft. But the housemates had a new and slightly invigorating feeling of self-consciousness, of being observed from afar. They couldn't name this sense, didn't admit it to one another. If asked, they would only have identified it as a sort of buzz, an internal white noise—and no one asked.

They didn't share these sensations with one another. They never mentioned the dreams they had upon returning to the house. All of the nightmares began the same way: awakening in darkness, confused and alone; being shifted from side to side; a nauseating suspension, the sensation of dangling in space; and a gray light stretching from a window far above. In certain variations the light spread across the floor to reveal the dreamer's torso crushed to a pulpy mass. In others the dreamer crawled on broken limbs through a winding tunnel, faster and faster, with a whirring noise catching up a few more inches at every turn. The worst dreams were the ones without form, in which nothing could be identified except the pulsing dark all around, blinding, paralyzing, burning away the skin.

Soon after being reunited they fell into their old routine but without the energy they had felt throughout the first semester. They associated their restless, unproductive mood with the laziness and rich diet of the winter holidays. They expected to grow more focused as time went on. But each day they were more inclined to sleep late, to move slowly, and to give in to listless channel surfing instead of studying.

It was several days before anyone thought to mention the fourth housemate, Kirsten, and wonder where she might be. When her monthly payment appeared as usual, speculation ended. So long as she paid her fair share on time, they didn't care where she was or what she was doing.

***

In early February a week of rain ended with a sudden drop in temperature. The sidewalks iced over. Streets became perilous to navigate. It just happened that all of the original three had one non-essential day when nothing was due, no meetings were scheduled, and no important chapters or subjects were being covered in lecture. They decided to stay home, to rest and avoid the nasty weather.

The novelty of their coincidence inspired them to remain in flannel pajamas, pop popcorn, cook frozen pizza, and hunker down in front of the TV for a marathon of old situation comedies. They soon discovered a common bond they had never known, childhood nostalgia for a maudlin comedy-drama called *Every One of Us*.

Each episode posed an unlikely moral dilemma for a member of the Conklin Family—a widowed father, his two divorced daughters, their three children, and wise, wheezy Aunt Lorraine—who shared a New England home that resembled a lighthouse. No matter how implausible or convoluted the story, all was resolved in the last five minutes and most episodes ended with two or more members of the family hugging and vowing never to misunderstand one another again—a moment that prompted the original three to utter a little "aw" of satisfaction. The second time it happened they laughed. By the third episode they were chortling and goading one another as the final "aw" moment approached.

Somewhere between the last slice of pizza and the fifth hour of the show they heard a noise issue from upstairs. All three looked up and waited. Dave muted the TV.

The sound was a loud, persistent squeak. Rusty and rhythmic, it seemed familiar to all three listeners. They didn't say so because they couldn't recall exactly where or when they'd noticed it. Before they could comment, the sound changed, deepening and widening into a metallic grinding of gears accompanied by a guttural emission like gas bursting through broken copper pipes. Following this crescendo it settled into a low, steady rumble.

"What the hell?" Abigail asked.

"Go see what's happening," Marla said to Dave.

They looked at one another. Dave realized he wasn't under any obligation to represent the group but Marla's command conveyed an edge, a reminder that he was the one who suggested a fourth housemate.

He stood and brushed crumbs from his pajamas. He hesitated for a split second, long enough to allow the girls to change their minds and let him stay. No one spoke, so he went to the bottom of the stairs and began his ascent.

He slowed on the first landing. He considered going back downstairs and saying everything was fine, Kirsten had a date and he was a noisy bastard, no big deal. But when he glanced behind him, Dave saw Marla and Abigail close together at the foot of the stairs, gazing up at him. He was the man, and they were the girls. There was no way out.

By the time he reached the second landing he was moving so slowly his muscles ached with the effort. He hoped the rumble would stop but it grew in intensity as he approached, softly grinding like a broken engine. The trouble was, it seemed to fill the space, as though the source were as big as the room above.

He turned the final corner and took the last short flight of steps in a state of near paralysis. He noticed his hands were drawn up to his ribs, clenched and useless. At this proximity the rumbling was deafening, its point of origin both mechanical and organic, its volume unbearable.

Dave's legs trembled beneath him. When he tried to call out—whether to Marla and Abigail below, or to Kirsten, he couldn't decide—his voice caught in his throat. There was a familiar layer to the vast sound starting to surround him, a chord he remembered but couldn't identify. He reached for

Kirsten's door but couldn't touch it. He put out both hands and instantly he couldn't see them, reached for his chest and face and felt them come apart, the molecules of his body separating and redistributing, becoming waves, becoming nothing.

In his panic he tried to scream but the roar of an unseen, enormous beast enveloped him. He was no longer standing outside Kirsten's room. He was inside, and the sound whirled about him like the wind. Swept up in its momentum were bits of clothing and tufts of hair. Rising up on powerful haunches before him, emerging from the shadows and confusion, there came a creature twice the size of a person, its claws twitching and its teeth sliding over one another, sharp as scissors.

At the bottom of the stairs the girls were holding hands, stunned, shivering in their pajamas. All noise had stopped. In the awful silence they waited until they couldn't stand it any longer. At last Abigail found her voice.

"Dave!" she shouted. "Dave! What is it?"

The panic in her voice triggered Marla, who began echoing her.

"Dave!"

"Dave!"

"Come back!"

"Come back!"

"Stop it, Marla!" Abigail shouted, and punched Marla in the arm when she repeated the command. "Shut up!"

"Shut up!" Marla yelled. "Oh, god, I can't stop, I can't stop! Where is he? What happened? Why did the noise stop?"

Above them something shifted weight, something as wide as the roof and as deep as the attic. There was a new sound like a great sigh, and the walls above began to move. They expanded, the wood beneath decades of paint groaning, stretching until the contortion split the surface and clouds of plaster came huffing out. Both girls watched the stairs, unable to speak, registering the exact moment when it—whatever it was—inhaled and began its descent.

Abigail heard her teeth chatter once, twice, and she clenched her jaw. Her thoughts raced through emergency phone numbers, escape routes, plans for tomorrow and the day after, the grocery list in the backpack in her bedroom, the dopey smiles on the faces of her parents the day she left for college, the busted zipper of her favorite jeans, the way the elderly neighbor leered at her as she walked past his yard, and the burned flesh of her cousin's face as she dreamed it so many times, melting in the fire, blood and skin sputtering like plastic.

Behind her Marla had silently retreated to the door, and now stood with her back braced against it. *Stupid girl*, Abigail thought, *she doesn't have a plan in the world.*

While Marla sank to the floor, Abigail took a step backward, then another, and another. She turned and made a run for the nearest window. Suddenly the stairs creaked and began to split into fragments.

With cold, stiff fingers, Abigail ripped loose the layers of duct tape holding the window frame in place. She caught a peripheral view of Marla crying, frozen, a pool of urine spreading on the floor around her, and something as big as a grizzly reaching down, tearing off Marla's head with one swift slap.

Abigail groaned and shoved the window open. She scrambled over the ledge, shredding her pajamas and cutting her legs. With one glance backward—at blood-red eyes, at matted fur on massive arms—she jumped. The hard landing hurt her ribs and her shins, left her breathless in the ice-cold air.

Feeling the heat of motion in her wake, she got to her feet. She slipped in the wet grass and fell on one knee. She wanted to scream but she couldn't breathe. She forced herself to stand and to move. All she could hear as she limped down the slick sidewalk away from the house was the triumphant roar of something tearing loose and standing to its full height, preparing to pounce.

STAG IN FLIGHT

Benny's session began at dusk every Thursday. He was scheduled after all of the regulars because he was a charity case referred by a meddling neighbor.

"I'm writing my dissertation and doing my internship at the same time," the neighbor had yammered at the back of Benny's head one afternoon while he checked his mailbox down the hall. "My committee decided to allow it. I'm a special case."

He could tell by the shadow before him, the woman's fists were clenched and resting on her hips. Her arms spread wide, wing-shaped, on the wall. He didn't dare turn around.

"If I were assigned to you, I know exactly what I'd do," she went on. "First of all, I'd get you out into the open air, on a day like this. You should take a walk in the park."

He had ducked his head, clasping to his chest the feeble stash of mail—a gas bill and two coupons to cheap restaurants that delivered—while heading back to his apartment. She had trailed him all the way through the umber carpeted, dim corridors, breathing hard to keep pace with him.

"Sunlight's full of vitamin D, you know," the neighbor said. "D fights depression better than Zoloft or Prozac or anything I've seen. It almost never fails."

He took the long route to avoid facing her—up the unlit stairwell he hated, down the hall, holding his breath and hoping no one would emerge from an apartment on the second floor, then back downstairs with his heart doing flips, to number 103. He nearly wet his pants with relief when he saw the number, his number, on the door. He jiggled the key and shoved his way inside, slamming the door shut with his back.

"I know it's hard, but you need to step outside of yourself. That's the key. Exercise and a change of scenery would do you so much good. You should be signed up for talk therapy, and maybe physical therapy. I notice you have a slight limp…"

She perched on his doorstep, her face inflated and distorted by the lens of the spyhole. She was still talking long after he barricaded himself inside with three locks and a kitchen chair.

Afterward he had tried to calm down. He avoided filling out his unemployment log; it might make him hyperventilate. He did some breathing exercises. He read an article about a 12,000-year-old skeleton found in the Yucatán Peninsula. He sat silently watching dust motes drift on a stalk of light between the velvet curtains of his living room. Nothing helped. He shivered through the night on sheets that smelled pleasantly of bleach. At 4 a.m. he fell asleep, and his usual nightmare began. Patches of water-stained wallpaper shifted until shadows emerged, hands reaching and opening drawers, windows, doors, lifting the roof at one corner…

The next day he debated whether to risk another trip to the mailbox. Once he was satisfied his neighbor wasn't hiding nearby and decided to try it, he discovered a business card taped to his door. His neighbor had scribbled her name, Kit, above the contact information for a therapist named Dot Dougherty.

Under ordinary circumstances Benny would never place a call to a stranger. He wouldn't call anyone, since he had no phone. But on the day when his neighbor left the business card he had been planning his suicide. No longer listing pros and cons but sketching out every step. His trip to the mailbox had served as a test. To be sure he was in sync with what the universe wanted he had devised a simple experiment.

"If I open the box and it's empty again, I'll do it," he had decided. "If the mailbox is empty, this is my last day."

He wanted to say this more poetically but he couldn't. Words flickered and fell silent in his head. Conversationally they served so little purpose. He ended up setting most of them aside. During the years he had worked in the archives department at the library, he had seldom spoken to anyone. He had eaten his lunch alone every day, and taken the same bus home every night, creating a protective barrier against other passengers by reading a book. His mind knew so many words he never spoke. Now they roamed through his consciousness, playing hide-and-seek like sullen children. At times he would find himself staring at a wall, repeating one word until it had no meaning. One day he said the word "platitude" seven hundred times, and found he couldn't lift his arms.

The fistful of coupons and the gas bill had thwarted his intentions. All the way back to the amber-tinted lamps and overstuffed furnishings, the stacks of reference books, the meditative quiet of his sanctuary, the neighbor had nagged him with advice and terminology—agoraphobia, bipolar disorder, Asperger syndrome—reeling off one diagnosis after another, even after he closed the door in her face.

At least she hadn't promised to say a prayer for him. The rotund lady who approved his eligibility for food stamps presided over a desk teeming with stuffed animals and toys. The wall behind her was decorated with gilt-framed Bible quotations instead of diplomas. She sent him away with a pat on the back and a vow to pray for his recovery. Of all the people Benny had to endure—on days when he was compelled to report to one agency or another, or when he had to venture down the block to the corner market past homeless beggars and the sly, contemptuous glances of prostitutes—the praying food stamp woman was the worst. What did she mean by "recovery," anyway? He didn't have an injury or a condition. His sickness, if anyone wanted to call it that, was himself. He couldn't feel joy. Anticipation was the same as anxiety. There was nothing pleasurable about it. From the second he decided to do something—anything—he began to perspire and the knot began tightening in his stomach.

He had a few guilty indulgences but these soothed him a little, rather than bringing joy. Marmalade. Ripe mangos. Immaculate sheets. And every morning he watched—with a shameful combination of envy and hatred—as a parade of troubled men and women took the stage with Dr. Bob, celebrity shrink, on his TV show. In less than an hour Dr. Bob would isolate the concerns of each guest, explain how they had started, and describe how they could be rooted out with a few altered habits and the will to be happy.

This was the name of the show and the title of Dr. Bob's bestselling book, *The Will to Be Happy*. At the end of each episode the audience cheered for Dr. Bob and the miraculous changes he had wrought.

After the show Benny turned off the portable TV and unplugged it. He longed to watch for hours. But the apartment's wiring was dodgy and the TV cord drew sparks from the outlet. He would sit staring at the blank screen, pondering the same questions every day.

Dr. Bob never followed his guests home, never interviewed them after they returned to their shadowy rooms or their houses crammed full of yellowing newspapers and stacks of unopened mail. Benny had to wonder if their problems were truly solved. Did they return to the habits they'd spent a lifetime learning, or were they altered forever thanks to Dr. Bob? And what if they were cured of depression and self-hatred? Would they be happy then? What did it mean to be happy? Was it an emotion or a state of mind? What did it feel like? And why was Benny, alone among all the people he had ever met or expected to meet, unable to achieve such a transformation? Why did the smiles and assurances of the happy guests on TV make his heart plummet? What was missing, and how could it ever be replaced?

No matter how he tried to summon the will to be happy, Benny only thought of these questions. They made his stomach hurt.

It seemed to him the people who laid claim to happiness had to keep reminding themselves—and other people—how happy they were. Why else would they say, to strangers on the street, "Cheer up!" Why did they bare their teeth like dogs in photos, their smiles undermined by the frantic light in their eyes? They wore brightly colored T-shirts stenciled with the command, BE HAPPY!

Wasn't happiness enough, if they possessed it? Why did it look so painful? Benny thought of the newly happy as a frayed wire, compressed by duct tape and sputtering with a current they couldn't handle.

When Benny placed the call to Dot Dougherty's office he wasn't planning to make an appointment. He could never afford to see her. But he wondered about the coincidence. Of all days, the card had been taped to his door on this one, the day the mailbox decided he would live.

Dot insisted on meeting with him as soon as he mentioned his neighbor, her friend, Kit. Dot told him she and Kit went "way back." They were "practically sisters." And "for old times' sake" Dot would waive her normal fee. He asked her to repeat this last part, and she did.

"Of course, I can only fit you in after my other patients," she said. "If that won't be a problem, I have an opening late on Thursday."

He didn't know what to tell her. He was on the verge of explaining how he planned to die and was only interrupted by the mailbox and his neighbor, when Dot said she would see him soon, and then disconnected.

Benny hung up the pay phone receiver and hunched inside his jacket for the walk home. At once the bile began to rise in his esophagus. Here was a new thing he had to face. Since the city cut the budget for libraries and Benny lost his job, the world had become a minefield of new things.

He flinched at the sight of two limber boys with long hair and knit hats riding skateboards on the sidewalk, heading straight for him. He would have to skitter to one side or they would pretend they were about to crash into him, whipping their skateboards off the pavement at the last second with a metallic shriek. It happened every time he walked more than a block from home. Anyone, skateboarder or pedestrian, who saw Benny approaching automatically included in their navigation a little extra time to fake him out. This occurred no matter what he wore and no matter how he carried himself, slouching or shoulders back.

These were the everyday fears. He was accustomed to them. His new worry, burning like acid on his tongue, came from sheer anticipation of his first visit to Dot Dougherty's office. For he would have to prepare and map every step, decide what he would wear and which bus he would take. He would write list after list, each designed for a different mistake he might make. The one certainty was this: he would make mistakes.

He would skip meals and lie awake, growing more exhausted and sick every night, knowing he could never account for all contingencies. And in the haze of his eventual slumber the hands would reach out from shadows to flick the bedspread, tug the curtains apart, toss his clothes from the bureau onto the floor...

A number 7 would take him within two blocks of his destination. But there was an express bus every thirty minutes, and if he got on the express by mistake he might end up miles away, lost on some nameless avenue in a desolate part of town among deserted warehouses, tagged security fences, and snarling watchdogs.

Number 43 was slower and had more stops. This was closer to Benny's pace. But the number 43 would be crowded. He might have to wait half an hour for a bus with vacant seats. He might have to sit in the back, with teenagers, who would study him like an animal they wanted to chase and kill. They would point to the sweat stains on his shirt, and nod to one another, and snicker. This had happened one time, years before, when he had missed his six o'clock bus home from the library and had to settle for the six-fifteen. He had never made the same mistake again.

By the fourth day of mapping his route, Benny was feverish and his stomach was swollen tight. He paced his apartment. He drew up list after list, enumerating items he might otherwise forget during the last-minute panic. A real person, he believed, would not forget such things, but he might. He would, if he didn't write them down.

Underwear

Shoes

Bus schedules

Bus fare

Mango ("in case the bus stalls and there is no food")

Socks

Clean shirt

Trousers ("hang up in the bathroom at night to un-wrinkle")

The day of his first appointment finally came. Dressed,

groomed, re-groomed, Benny urinated, staring into the yellow ring of the toilet bowl, imagining the pee turning crimson. He washed his hands, walked to the front door, decided to urinate again, and returned to the bathroom. He did this five times.

At last he yanked the door open and stepped outside, checked the lock behind him, checked it again, checked it a third time by twisting the handle, and headed out. He was brisk, moving quickly before he could change his mind. He could fool himself for a while. Soon the distance would become real and he would struggle to breathe. He counted on momentum to carry him past this point.

A quarter of a mile from home, every street might as well have been a different planet. He scanned for recognizable landmarks. The world was in motion and wouldn't stop for him to catch up.

At the bus stop he stood beside the empty bench and watched as it slowly filled with people. He had once brushed a bench with his hand and found it was coated with cold phlegm.

He waited for ten minutes. He concentrated so hard on the number of his bus, the digits came loose and switched places. He boarded the wrong bus and skidded to a stop in the aisle. Flapping his schedule at the driver and shouting, he was let off at the next corner and had to trudge back to his starting point taking long, deep breaths. He was close to tears when he finally spotted the bus he needed.

A few blocks from Benny's destination, a man in a shabby suit climbed aboard and collapsed into the seat behind the driver, across the aisle from Benny. At the next stop the man dragged himself from the seat, back down the steps, and onto the sidewalk. The bus pulled away from the curb.

The driver swore, slammed on the brakes, and got up to examine the vacant seat, where a puddle of liquid excrement shimmied on brown leather. The driver swore again. He wiped down the leather with a newspaper and turned to Benny.

"Did you see this going on?" he asked.

Benny shook his head.

"Guy took a shit *right here*," the driver said. "Three feet away, and you didn't know this was going on?"

Benny was craning his neck so hard he thought it might be frozen in place. If he gave the driver all of his attention, maybe he could see that Benny had no connection to the shitting man. He had never seen the shitting man before. He knew so little of the shitting man he couldn't even tell the man was taking a shit right in front of him. Surely the driver could see all of this.

"Fuck me!" the driver said. "I hate this goddamn job."

Benny hid behind a paperback. He'd brought the tattered book along to fight the tedium of the trip, but then he'd felt too disoriented to read. This time, his ploy didn't work. The book was no protection. A woman sat next to him and demanded to know what he was reading. He tilted the cover and listened to her say the title out loud.

"Oh, I like that one," the woman said. "But you know what I read around the same time and really loved, that you should read before you read this one…?"

Fifteen minutes later the woman stopped talking when Benny exited the bus.

The rest of the afternoon and evening would be a permanent blur—a warm greeting from Dot, a tour of her office and introduction to her pet birds and tropical fish, listening to the history of Dot's youth and college days, leafing through a batch of brochures about mental illness, examining the pills Dot gave him, hearing the tinkling chimes of the portico as he left arm-in-arm with Dot, who insisted on giving him "a lift home," the clean, well-tended scent of her car with its dashboard array of red and amber lights. This was the only time Dot gave him a ride but from that night on he felt something had changed ever so slightly. He was no longer entirely alone.

He was able to visit Dot Dougherty's office thirteen times. He couldn't tell whether or not he was improving. He didn't know what it would mean to improve. He wasn't sure what was expected. And in a way his lack of progress gave him confidence in Dot. He had not been fixed, repaired as Dr. Bob's guests were, slapped with happy faces.

He didn't know what happiness felt like, and didn't expect to. But one day, on his way to the bus stop, he noticed a bank of gladiolas in bloom, early evening heat shimmering across a pale green lawn, and briefly he sensed that he might, someday, believe in the possibility of happiness—not for himself, but for someone, somewhere, happiness might be possible.

Meanwhile he relied on the pills in the sample pack Dot gave him each month. White for mornings, orange for sleep, blue for panic, a plastic dispenser, and a promise not to tell anyone. ("In which case I'd have to charge you," Dot said. "And I'd hate to do that. You wouldn't believe how expensive these are.") He slept without dreaming. He began to feel less terrified by his weekly jaunt. He liked it when Dot asked him how he was feeling.

On his thirteenth visit, the session was bumped up an hour; another client was on vacation. Benny had never seen Dot's office in sunlight before. He marveled at the riot of pink and fuchsia throw pillows against a jungle of philodendrons. He revisited the birds and tropical fish, calmed by their placid presence.

The afternoon was close and warm. A window stood open to catch any passing breeze. Yet Dot sat before him swaddled in her favorite pink shawl. The garment left fuzzy trails wherever she went, reminding Benny of cotton candy and plush toy snails.

He began, as always, with his foster family. The Bishops, Ted and Amelia. Good people, everyone said. And they were good. At least, they weren't bad. They drank every night in the privacy of their two-story home in a quiet cul-de-sac in a neighborhood where the only outrage was the paperboy's habit of landing his deliveries under parked cars.

Mid-session Dot stirred and gently shook her head. It was a mild, tremulous motion, slighter than a sigh. She edged forward on her chair. She stared at him, her voluptuous mouth wrinkling involuntarily. Her lips were glowing with pink gloss.

Under too much scrutiny and despite the pills he had consumed that day, Benny started to sweat. His scalp tingled. In the world outside of therapy, this was a warning sign, the moment when he should excuse himself and rush home. A flutter in his chest told him it was too late.

But I don't have to, he thought. *I can choose not to panic.* Out loud he said, "I have a choice, don't I?"

"What...?" Dot asked, still staring, enraptured. Her eyes, often languid, were strangely quick and bright.

"I'm feeling a twinge," Benny told her. "But I'm not giving in, right?"

"What in the world *is* it?" she practically shouted.

"This is the sign," he tried again to explain. "You wanted me to tell you..."

"No," she said. "No, no. I mean, what the heck is *that?*"

He was unable to follow.

"Look, Benny!" she sputtered. "Right there! Crawling up your shoulder!" She pointed at him.

Benny turned his head to the left. His eyes focused and he gazed down at a large beetle poised upon his shoulder. The triangular labrum was thrust forward. Mandibles hoisted to a sharp angle, the creature ambled on six elegant, slender legs toward his neck. It proceeded with this daring march until it stood beneath his chin. There it stopped, frozen in a posture of primitive worship.

Sweat fell from Benny's scalp. He had a fleeting thought

that he might rain on the insect. Instead he reached up with his right hand. With thumb and middle finger he thwacked the insect across the room, to the windowsill. It landed with a slight crack, exoskeleton against wood.

For a sickening few seconds all six legs struggled for purchase. Then the beetle rolled, righted itself, and stumbled to the outer ledge. Despite the clumsy size of the mandibles it spread its stiff, translucent wings and vanished in a froth of sunlight.

Benny was stunned. His every flickering thought rebelled against what he had done; it was abominable, unthinkable, a bitter act of unkindness. He had done what any mean-spirited person might do. He was alarmed not only by his involuntary reaction but also by the speed with which it occurred. He turned to Dot, certain she would understand his predicament and offer words of comfort.

His therapist was bobbing up and down on the plump cushions of her chair. Her hands held tight to the velvet-upholstered arms. Her lips quivered. Sounds began to bubble out of her mouth.

"Oh! Oh! Ha-ho-ha-ah!"

There was a crazy pitch to her voice, a shrillness, an animal noise entirely too personal, drawn from crevices Benny could only ignore by pretending they didn't exist. Mortified, he tried but he couldn't look away. He couldn't move. He sat there stranded between surprise at discovering an insect on his shoulder and confusion at Dot's spasm of what seemed—no, not seemed, but was now unmistakably—wild amusement.

She had never laughed at anything he'd said or done during previous visits. Week after week, while Benny writhed and sweated beneath her gaze, Dot had smiled. She had nodded and raised an eyebrow and furrowed her forehead and grinned and paced and stretched her arms and arched her back and opened her mouth in surprise and squinted and coughed and folded her hands and tilted her head and adjusted her shawl. And she had talked. Endlessly, she had talked. But laughter was new. He had never witnessed Dot doing this before. With growing alarm he realized it was ugly, maybe the most ugly thing he'd ever seen. He thought of a mollusk stranded by the receding tide. The way her glossy lips kept spreading and opening, closing, and re-opening, revealing the inside of her mouth and its damp, pink walls.

The flutter in his chest grew more insistent. He ground his teeth until he could hear his jaw crunch. He wondered if Dot could hear this, too.

He watched her laughing and laughing. While he watched, he reconsidered the wisdom of this weekly habit. What was he doing? Sitting in front of a stranger, locating and labeling all the nuances of a shameful, private despair. After two months this had begun to seem to Benny a necessary and solemn act, a step in a long process.

Now the only person he'd ever allowed to hear the tedious details of his existence and advise him in her fussy, maternal fashion was doubled over, consumed by hysteria and gasping for air, because of a beetle on Benny's shoulder.

Maybe she was imagining something he couldn't see. She often implied (never stated, only hinted) that perhaps he lacked imagination. She had given him homework, sayings to repeat and visual exercises to practice, to help build his "capacity for wonder."

Dot herself had imagination to spare. At the age of six she had shown her first paintings in a gallery run by a friend of the family. She had won a prize and had been profiled in a local magazine. And this was the least of Dot's many childhood exploits.

Maybe she envisioned the bug as a crusty mountaineer scaling Benny like Kilimanjaro. He forced himself to picture this and as he did he thought, as hard as he could: *Surely I'm being imaginative right now. This demonstrates how colorful my thoughts can be...*

Whatever she imagined under all of those blond curls, Dot was in the throes of mirth bordering on insanity. When she rolled to one side in her chair, Benny caught a horrifying glimpse of her underpants. The object of such mania couldn't be a beetle, could it?

The insect was gone. It wasn't funny to begin with, and once it was gone Dot should have stopped laughing. The object of hilarity, Benny decided, had to be himself and his discomfort. He had been thrust into the role of an object, a mere lump beneath a scrambling, adventurous insect. He had been robbed and that was why he had lashed out—wrongly—at the creature. The beetle had robbed Benny of his role. It had taken over in that brief moment and become the central character in his life.

Tears poured down Dot's cherubic face. She couldn't speak.

"Oh, oh," she simpered. "Oh, ah, oh!"

Benny had more time to ruminate. He was starting to crave supper. His jaw ached for food, for the crunch of it, the breaking sound.

He wondered if Dot admired the beetle's daring. The creature was intrepid and Dot probably loved that. She worshipped the strong and the plucky. The opposite of everything Benny was.

She knew his history. Benny had been placed in a foster home when he was seven. The disinfected linoleum maze of an orphanage was replaced by the dank solitude of a basement bedroom with fake wood paneling and a private TV. His bed was a rollaway. He ate dinner every night from a TV tray. His favorite meal was fish sticks with macaroni and cheese, which he gratefully devoured four nights a week, to his harried foster mother's relief.

In every session Dot had found a reason to extol the virtues of her own upbringing. At first it seemed odd, since Benny was there to talk about himself. He reasoned these detours must be part of the therapy. Now, gazing into the open maw of his laughing therapist, he knew her digressions had been a respite from his mundane troubles.

He couldn't win. His purpose was to recount his life. Its ordinariness was dull. He was here, in part, because he knew this. He had tried every exercise Dot recommended. He had bought balloons on his way home but he lacked the nerve to inflate them. He had worn a suit and tie to a fast food diner and ordered a cheeseburger. He had intended to enjoy it with gusto, as Dot directed, alone at a table in full view of the other customers. But his stomach hurt and he had asked for his order to go, and he had eaten in the dark in his bedroom that night.

He hated his own memories, the ones he could talk about. But where could he find better ones?

In this overstuffed floral office tangled with plants, photos, mementos, and pets, Benny's discontent was stripped bare, reduced to a series of complicated, unimpressive issues. But the central question, Benny knew, was whether or not he had the guts to conquer himself, to take charge, to end his deadening point of view. His task was to be something other than what he was. He had fooled himself into thinking this might be possible.

Every week Dot had asked how he was feeling. But she was asking about his physical state, how he felt on the drugs she was giving him. Was he getting stronger? Was he becoming normal? For the first time it occurred to Benny that he might be part of an experiment, a study concocted by Kit and Dot.

Why else would she give him medication for free, without a prescription? Was she writing a paper about him? Was she testing him? Was this why she was constantly comparing her life to his? Pointing to a framed portrait of her beloved, golden, biological parents during a conversation about his myopic, fake ones. Mentioning the glorious weeks her extended clan used to spend together, in the Alps. Benny's parents had never taken him on vacation, certainly not to the Alps where Dot's family had lodged at a cousin's chalet. He imagined them flying by on their skis in winter and prancing across glistening meadows in springtime like manic von Trapps.

Dot's family had shared meals around a great wooden table inherited from her grandparents, hand-carved by Nordic craftsmen and laden with dishes miraculous to behold. Even the sauces and condiments she described were probably more nutritious than the stuff Benny called food. Dot's brothers had mischievously added her monogram to the table's carvings. Three generations had eaten there.

Her mother was a famous artist. Her father was a pediatrician who had longed for Dot to follow in his footsteps. Yet she had taken the route of New Age Therapy, as her Viking brothers called it, and no one was disappointed. Her father cherished his Dotty-doodle. She was his only daughter. She must have been so precious to him, reading by the time she was two and a half, quoting Emerson at the age of six. She graduated from college at seventeen, earned a master's degree at twenty. She could read three languages and stumble reasonably well through two more. She could fly a Cessna, she said, and she had vacationed in South America too many times to count. She had photos of herself smiling in the arms of lithe, sunburned college friends on the terraces of Machu Picchu. From the embrace it was obvious she had cavorted in the nude with these same friends, probably drunk on wine.

The universe meant for Dot to be happy. Thanks to her good start in life she was unfettered by self-doubt. It was astonishing what unconditional praise could do for the psyche.

Benny's parents could only relax with a combination of vodka, sedatives, and TV. They had encouraged Benny to watch science and nature programs to improve his education. He was so quiet in class, and so fragile, his teachers recommended home schooling. In fifth grade his parents agreed, and his limited social life ended forever.

From the heated rush of school, where he dodged elbows and hung his head while other boys stole his lunch and wrote obscenities on his notebook, Benny retreated to the basement at home. The gnawing hunger grew worse. The nightmares and the loneliness held him in their grip. There were times when the loneliness hurt so badly he held his stomach and lay on the floor, expecting to die. How could it hurt so much and not kill him? His only hint of contentment came with the fragrant rush of an evening breeze through an open window, in the dark solitude of his bed. Even then he knew happiness would never belong to him.

Setting aside the past three months, he had spent his life trying to hide from people like Dot, who was finally winding down from her fit of laughter and dabbing at the crinkled corners of her eyes with a balled-up linen handkerchief. She had no use for paper products. Anything common to this melancholy world, overpopulated by creeps and malcontents and people who didn't know how to select wine, was unthinkable.

She must hate him so much. How could she relate her family saga and not feel that he was pathetic by comparison? Of course she must know he wasn't getting better. How could a creature like Benny ever get better? How could Dot counsel him, and murmur halfhearted affirmations about his progress? What progress? He was what he had always been. Nothing could change inside him. He saw that clearly. He was not going to get better. He had sent a brave and magnificent creature sailing through the air to writhe on the window ledge. Out of spite, out of envy and spite.

A man on his belly in a sea of blankets, tugging his penis into bleach-scented sheets; a boy on a concrete basement floor scuttling under the cot where he used to sleep, sniffing for company among the ants and roaches. This was all that Benny would ever be. The story of his life wasn't worth telling. He was not the adventurous beetle. He was only the lump of flesh sitting under the black and glistening body of a far more dashing insect.

Dot was coming to her senses. It wouldn't be long before she resumed comparing her wine-and-cheese-toting, multilingual super-parents and abnormally devoted brothers to Benny's sofa-bound, sad suburban family unit of three. Both of his foster parents were long dead. They had never adopted him formally, never even suggested it. He would never be a family, alone. And who was his therapist? Who would she be, stripped of her nauseating memories?

"Oh," Dot whimpered. "I'm so sorry!"

Smiling broadly, she dabbed at her eyes again, cleared her throat, and straightened her posture like a child reprimanded at the dinner table. She could seem so good. She could smile so well. She said the words of caring and becoming. Benny knew better.

"All right then, Benjamin. Carry on!" she commanded.

She made a luxurious noise, the verbal equivalent of a stretch, a yawn apprehended too late. She settled amid her pink shawls and layers of chocolate-infused flesh. (Her favorite saying was: "Take anything, but leave the chocolate!")

Her opulent mouth puckered. Then it relaxed. She seemed to be testing herself, making signs of bursting into laughter again and then stopping. Yes. She was demonstrating self-discipline, for his benefit. She often said he could wear brighter clothing, and he could exercise, and he could practice small talk. He could do so much for himself, she said. Just look at all she had accomplished without using her father's famous moniker.

How did Benny know so much about her, in so little time? How did she not know the depth of his hungry sorrow?

He was the suffering one and Dot was the goddess to whom creatures like Benny crawled for help, only to be silenced. Only to be smacked aside. Only to feel smaller than when they arrived.

Before she could prod him again, he stood. And before she could stop him, he walked out of her office. The night was warm. The sound of Dot calling his name faded as he headed for the bus stop.

He wasn't feeling anything by the time he shambled onto the number 43 and took a seat. His mind was numb. He stared out the window at mottled lights of one street after another. If anyone spoke to him, he didn't answer.

He wasn't aware of the movement along his arm until the beetle reached his elbow, propped against the window frame. When he recognized the creature he was certain their eyes met. The beetle was even larger than he remembered. It held its enormous mandibles, which were black, above a glossy brown thorax and abdomen, and waited for a response.

Benny reached up with his right hand but this time he didn't flick the insect away. With patience learned in abject boredom, he pointed his index finger and held it before the beetle. He was surprised to find he could touch its sleek body without provoking any sign of distress.

Walking in the night air away from the bus stop, Benny kept his arm crooked and the beetle remained on his elbow all the way home. In his apartment he sat immediately in a chair with broad arms, and the beetle climbed down. The creature spent the next hour ambling on rugs and furnishings, stopping to examine shoes and lampstands and books. With preternatural grace it flew from the floor to a comfortable plateau on a stack of volumes, touched down for a moment, and flew back to the floor.

Benny shuffled through the stack and found a guide to North American insects. By flipping pages and studying the intricate diagrams, he soon determined that his new companion was a male stag beetle. The remarkable claw-like mandibles were used to attract females and to frighten other males. In a conflict they might serve a more violent purpose but this was unusual.

He pondered the beauty of this quiet warrior. Without raising its most powerful weapon it could command the respect of all other insects. Best of all its attributes, the stag beetle liked to eat ripe or rotten fruit. The mango slices Benny piled on a plate and lowered to the floor served as their final bond. The beetle staggered from one slice to another, devouring and rejoicing.

Benny had never had a pet. His foster mother had been allergic to everything. They had considered a hairless cat but one look at an exemplary photo had sent Benny into a spiral of despair. How could humans be such assholes, to breed these sad, shivering animals in order to have a cat without the physical characteristics of a cat? It crossed Benny's mind at the age of eleven that people would stop at nothing in their selfish cravings.

Within a few days the stag beetle and Benny were living comfortably together. They lived on the fruit Benny purchased at the corner market and occasional meals delivered by cheap restaurants. The stag beetle stood watch while Benny flushed his medication down the toilet.

He searched his field manuals and smirked at the small, bulbous abdomen on the female. Of course she was less impressive than the male!

He held his cock in his sleep. He woke with a hard-on every day. His thorax thrummed. He felt alive for the first time.

This wasn't joy or happiness but a crimson darkness flourishing inside him, an awakening of the senses in the absence of anything human. His passion allowed him to see the leaves beyond his window in stark relief. Their viridian skins absorbed the light. His companion watched for signs of rain, loving the stickiness of the damp wood chips Benny fetched for him.

During this gorgeous interlude, Benny recovered memories he had long forgotten. He was thrown back thirty years, to the cement floor and macramé owl and rooster decorations of his childhood in the basement. Lying prone on his bed as a boy he took flight every evening, surveying the roof, the road, the cul-de-sac where his caretakers lived.

After Benny stopped taking medication these dreams returned and carried him high above the apartment building. Every night he took flight, his mighty crepuscular armor gliding through the air, his whole body shimmering with a confusion of desires. He traversed the lawns of his neighborhood. He knew the trees and patios, the open windows, the steady snores. He stole in and let himself run wild, traipsing down the length of a thigh, rolling off a lampshade onto a breast. Surveying the nipple with antennae until it stiffened into arousal.

And he dreamed of Dot. Luscious, pink-lined bitch Dot. Night after night in dreams he returned to their final session. With her fit of mirth finally subsiding, he burned to tell her the one achingly beautiful thing he knew. If only to show her! If only to shut her up! If only to feel what he felt, alone in the dark, with his companion waiting patiently beneath his bed! And then the sound, pouring out of Dot, rising from those unfathomable regions of her body, orifices he wasn't supposed to notice.

"Ghjh...nh...ng..."

Was that the actual sound? In his dreams, Benny cocked his head. Again he heard the sound.

"Ghjh...nh...ng..."

Dot wasn't laughing any more.

There was no mistake in the dream. Everything was sharpening. The air was clearing quickly. A warm, humid evening would follow the dappled light of day. He wanted so much to see it. He wanted to reach down and masturbate in front of Dot. Make her witness his transformation, and label it if she could.

He leaned back and back and back. He shook his head side to side. His labrum gleamed in the light.

Blood dribbled beneath Dot's chair. Benny opened his sleek mandibles just enough to confirm that Dot's broken mouth parts had, indeed, said:

"Ghjh...nh...ng..."

He clenched once more and went on pressing until Dot's head stopped talking with a final crunch. Blood oozed out of her mouth and ran down the sides of her neck. After that the only sounds were a low-pitched buzz in his glistening thorax and a click of camaraderie from the windowsill.

"Benny!"

Dot's voice was muffled.

He wasn't dreaming any more. He wasn't asleep.

"Benny! Open up right now!"

He shook his head and brushed the hair from his face. The sheets lay in all directions and his clothes covered every inch of the floor.

"Please open this door right now!"

Through tunnels and sewers, night clouds and falling leaves, he had a dim awareness. The voice was familiar but it couldn't be Dot. Each thud of a fist against wood brought him closer to being sick. He inhaled and his stomach turned from the scent of rotten food permeating the apartment.

Stumbling through clothes and shoes, Styrofoam containers and cardboard boxes, Benny made his way to the front door.

Behind him, on the windowsill, his companion stood guard with mandibles poised. And behind the stag beetle morning light flooded the window.

The thudding started again, causing the wood and metal frame to vibrate. The creature Benny spotted through the spyhole was two-headed and female. Dot and Kit were taking turns shouting.

"Benny! For your own good, we have to talk!"

"Open the door! We want to help you!"

A smirk twisted Benny's lips. Over his shoulder he took in the beauty of his wasteland, and his heart began to sing. He saw his companion on the windowsill, and the shadow of its antennae and claws spread across the wall, enveloping him.

MS. X
REGRETS
EVERYTHING

2015

Gray-haired, your face both plump and lined with age, you wait with your hands demurely folded in your lap. (A state-appointed somebody recommended this trick years ago, for calmness and the illusion of calmness; once learned, you've never forgotten.) Your smile is faint. The skin of your arms, flaking with eczema, itches beneath regulation overalls. A sparrow traces a pale, diagonal course across the sky, its pattern framed by barred windows reflected in your new bifocals.

Pine-Sol permeates the corridors, the cafeteria, and a labyrinth of concrete cubicles. Even the skimpy mattress on your bunk bed reeks of disinfectant.

No rock albums or heavy metal is permitted, only white gospel tunes and psalms on Sunday. There is no rattle of handcuffs; they're made of plastic like trash bag ties. And plastic benches have replaced chairs, for safety. You miss the legs of wooden chairs scraping linoleum floors gruffly, the sound akin to terriers barking in a courtyard.

In this facility every recollection is handled and cherished until it wears away, its contours ruined, stained, its origin thrown into question. After decades a youthful memory becomes paper-thin, almost too fragile to unwrap.

You have trouble separating yourself from recorded events. You lived. You dreamed. You hallucinated.

At your trial forty years ago, a mob of pregnant women burst into the courtroom, shouting your name. In the alley between the van and the courthouse they spat on you and tried to shove guards aside to tear out locks of your golden hair. They wished you Hell in prison at the hands of an imagined battery of avengers. The pregnant women cursed you with a nightly beating that never occurred.

They didn't know. Hell is nothing. Hell is boredom. Hell is absence. You have no friends, no allies, and no enemies.

Nothing prepared you for all of this maddening cleanliness and civility. Daily and for decades you were bound and broken by the order of it all, swaddled and smothered by decency, prescribed drugs for docility.

Everything here is reduced to routine. Even death has its protocol, and nothing is unexpected. No wonder you want out, even at your age. You know you'll die ever so quietly, unclaimed, and your bed will be cleared for another inmate, and another.

Today the news reports seldom mention your name. When they do they include your entire biography. Otherwise no one would know who you are. No one remembers. You're no longer a wayward girl in love, committing unspeakable crimes. You're a menopausal woman who will never have children. Your narrative is dead.

On your behalf an attorney delivers aloud a list of your accomplishments in prison. Included are the reading and dancing lessons you give freely, for the benefit of all:

"Ms. X regrets everything. Ms. X recants her youthful rants. Ms. X would like the story to stop so she can go home and sit in a warm bath like normal people with the heady scent of lilacs in the air. Ms. X recounts her troubles and asks for reason to prevail. For the record…"

1962

The teacher told everyone to take home souvenirs of the day. You watched your classmates proudly stuffing book bags with greeting cards, flowers, and chocolate bars. No one noticed you. Alone out of twenty-two children you received nothing, and offered nothing. You were invisible.

Shambling from school with your coat pockets full of Valentines you cut from grocery bags and newspapers all week, with added flourishes in crayon. Nothing was certain. Nothing was limited. In a magical random cloud Valentines could flutter through the white sky to an unknown destination. All was still possible.

Shivering with cold and shameful desire, at the footbridge you dug inside your pockets and cast forty-three handmade Valentines to the wind. You watched them scatter down to be swallowed by the river and imagined a mouth protruding from the water, sucking in air, sinking, swallowing, surrounded by paper hearts.

"…Ms. X says a prayer before bedtime…"

1965

Daffodils drooped and wilted in your sweaty hands, stems crushed by clumsy affection. Anything tiny or helpless would die at your touch. Birds avoided the seeds you left on the ground. Wonder curdled to resentment and then disgust for daffodils and birds, and women with painted smiles in magazines.

Your mother said you missed your calling. "With your face you should have been a mortician." She laughed and the man she called your father laughed. Then he placed a calloused hand on your thigh and raised a can of beer.

"One day," he said. "You'll be just right." But he left after three months.

"You ought to be ashamed," said your mother. "You scared your own father away."

"…Ms. X wishes to remind the board she has grown in heart and mind and conscience and now has some regard for those she formerly referred to as farm animals…"

1968

Nubile and filthy in shabby jeans, halter top spilling your nipples for strangers to stare at, both hands out, begging for anything—a nickel for a spill, a quarter for a feel—you sat in the shade, in a parking lot, trading flesh for a cheeseburger.

"Please mister, please man, please…"

"Don't touch me."

"Pig!"

"Stay away…"

"PIG!"

You craved a man to fit you with a leash and put you to bed at night. You would gladly eat from a clean bowl, and sleep in a warm crate, and bark at the pigs that threatened your master.

"…Ms. X is in her dotage and poses no threat to society…"

1969

Eyes open wide, teeth bared, thighs slippery with blood, you gripped the knife handle. You braced against the floor on your knees straddling the redheaded girl, cutting her skin loose in rubbery slices. The knife struck home so many times the redheaded girl's white dress ran scarlet and black, clotting at the hem.

Nowadays you teach others to read. In your twenties you were famous for writing the words of a century. Who doesn't know "DEATH TO PIGS" autographed in gore?

Asked why and why and why again, your hands offered no reply. After smearing their message on defiled bodies and bloodied walls, they fell silent in the interrogation room. Your lips and voice replied, "Nothing. It was there, and it was right."

A thousand journalists have interpreted those words.

It was right for the moment.

It was right for the occasion.

It felt right to you.

It was right for him.

It was right for the night.

It was right for the cause. Because there was a cause, right? It was so much more than the bruised ego of a filthy, angry middle-aged man. Right?

"...Ms. X has gained insight into her history and psychology..."

1990

Aided by Klonopin and encouraged by a writing teacher, you began to list reasons why you did what you did:

1. Charlie was controlling your mind.

2. Who wouldn't turn crazy when the chemicals took hold?

3. Daddy left and Momma died.

4. Sanctuary was the home of a heroin-rattled sister.

5. The world. Read history, man. It's all there.

6. Human nature. Read psychology. Or don't read it; just watch what people do.

7. A hollow space inside the chest cavity and cranium, where every step echoed and every face reverberated. Did

other people feel the way you felt? Were they alive? Did they dig in dirt and scream at night and crawl inside the flesh of strangers and tear them apart with dirty fingernails? Why, or why not?

8. A normal need for love, or the normal desire for love, or a normal yearning for love, or the normal allure of love. In short, love. Normal love like everyone wants and is entitled to seek.

Nine. The number nine, so sacred it must be spelled out every time.

10. Charlie was controlling your mind.

"...Ms. X practices self-discipline and seeks peace of mind..."

1995

A volunteer therapist recommended relaxation techniques to facilitate sleep. You fell in love with sleep, when you could slip all the way. You wished you could hypnotize yourself, and hypnotize Charlie when his torso crawled from under the cot, or when he slithered into your cell clasping the back of a centipede.

"Termination...Elimination...Assassination...Execution...Liquidation...Butchery...Murder...No!" Wide-awake again, you would shiver and turn onto your belly and begin again.

"Termination...Elimination...Assassination...Execution..."

"...Ms. X has successfully engaged in mutually satisfying relationships with numerous individuals..."

2005

You were allowed to receive fan mail. You kept your favorite letter in a tattered cigar box.

"Dear Ms. X,

In 1970 I was ten years old. I remember seeing your story in the newspapers and on TV. My parents were terrified. They feared Satan with a crusty beard and wild eyes. Good suburbanites, they locked all the doors and barred all the windows against intruders at night.

I wasn't afraid of Satan. He was 5' 2" and he dressed like a cartoon caveman. He reminded me of a boy at school who stank of masturbation and baloney. I knew I would smell Satan's approach from a mile away. He memorized passages from *How to Win Friends* and he stole the techniques of a knife-wielding pimp in prison. He was no one, a figment of our fantasy lives, a crummy little hustler and worse—an old man. Not my generation. No.

My nightmares were about Satan's wives, Jane or Suzy or Mary with an insipid smile, wearing a black cross on her forehead. *She looked like me*, broad-faced, ordinary, and not very bright. *She was like me*, bad at conversation, wide at the hips, unlovable. She grew up in the suburbs, like me. She whined for scraps of attention at the dinner table.

Jane Suzy Mary Anybody was a vacuum, a void. She was a girl stripping new leaves from trees and pulling the wings from dragonflies. Her touch was poison, envy, anger, and anonymity. A thousand strangers met her and saw her hunger, saw the scars on her arms, read the panic in her eyes. All of them turned and walked on without a word. A thousand times she fell to her knees and begged for tenderness, not money, not sex, just a split second of acknowledgment. *I am here! I am alive!*"

You removed this letter from the cigar box twice a day and caressed it with both hands. You felt the longing behind the words. You imagined this woman as she used to be, as a girl. This was a girl like you. This was a girl like you who spread her legs and gave herself to animals before she was allowed to sleep.

This girl, your fan, would sit on the lap of the high school music teacher and let him fondle all of her openings, if only he would say her name. She would lie down in dirt and ask Satan to walk across her, to keep his feet clean. She would think, proudly, *I am the one who bears his footprints on my back.*

No one wanted her except to piss on. She was no one's favorite. Eventually she stank of everyone who had ever touched her. She dressed badly, never brushed her teeth, and never knew how to style her hair. She was awful and ugly and overweight and irritating and unwanted.

In every way on any given day, she was you; her rotten breath, her skin erupting in acne, the rolls of fat beneath out-of-fashion sweaters, and more than all of this, the humiliation of longing, the embarrassment of being a girl whose name no one could remember.

You wanted to find this woman and follow her back to her childhood. You wanted to chase her as a girl through the park, into the woods, and hurl stones at the back of her legs. You dreamed of knocking her to the ground, pinning her down, and smashing her face with a sharpened stick again and again until her dress turned scarlet and her lips stopped begging for mercy, mercy, mercy...

"...Ms. X regrets the pain she has caused. She did not recognize pain until she relived it in dreams of her former life. The sorrow written by her hands on another woman's body did not convince her the pain was real. Now she knows it was real. Now she knows other people are real, their blood is real, their names belong to them, their unborn infants are not dolls to fondle and taste, their mothers are not shadows, their fathers are not rapists, their homes are not stolen, their desires are more than a trail of garbage, their pleading voices deserve to be heard, their screaming is not the howling of animals…"

1955

Your first lesson, as a child, is empathy. The place and time and circumstances were forgotten until today. While your attorney drones on your memory drifts, and suddenly you remember every detail.

Your mother is on her knees. She doesn't pray. Only the weak pray. In her grip you are sodden with tears and piss and fear.

"Do you know how it feels when you bite your sister?" your mother shouts, and shakes you until you feel your head snap forward. "Do you know how this feels?"

You throw back your head and wail when your mother's teeth make contact and pierce your skin. You feel it pop like the casing on a sausage.

On your left arm, even now you can see the uneven imprint, a pale arc to remind you what is right and what is wrong, what is good and what is bad.

"…Ms. X politely requests a glass of water during this parole board hearing. She is prone to hot flashes and water helps to soothe her nerves…"

2015

A guard retreats to the corridor to fetch water for you—in a paper cup, of course. With one hand he offers you the water, with the other he taps the holster at his hip. You smile shyly, surprised to find you can yet frighten a middle-aged man carrying a deadly weapon. In days gone by you might have offered him sex and stolen his gun and killed a family with it. You could do anything.

1969

Charlie found you sleeping on a piece of cardboard behind a trashcan. He washed your face and fed you from a jar of baby food. He named you Roses because he said, "One rose ain't enough for you."

Charlie's women sat in the weeds and yellow grass near a freeway exit. Dust flew with each passing car. The women waved. They sent up a loud cheer of contempt when a camper barreled past, its driver barely concealing a sneer.

In a shopping center parking lot Charlie stole a car and took you joyriding with his women. They patted your face and hands tenderly.

"Let me braid your hair," you said to another girl in the backseat, another Jane Suzy Mary Anybody like you, the first person you were allowed to touch in this way, tenderly. Winding fingers through the oily strands, separating and weaving, tying the ends with blades of grass, you were as close as you would ever come to joy.

"Sunshine is joy," Charlie reminded you and the others every morning, and wiped your face with a damp towel. "Breathing is joy. A baby suckling your breast is joy. Forgiveness and smiling and bringing pleasure to your master will bring joy."

Your armpits felt raw and your teeth started coming loose. The blue pills weren't as good as the yellow pills and the white pills reminded you of your parents in Sunday clothes. The black pills made your heart race. Your heart was racing the day Charlie gathered the family to bury one of the babies. The other women marked the spot with crosses made from broken twigs. Some crying boy, a stranger wandering past, scattered daffodils on the grave and you followed him home. Charlie and the family followed you at a careful distance.

The boy lived in a trailer park a mile away. The campers were city dwellers. They didn't know better than to leave their garbage cans out overnight. You feasted on the food they discarded, scrambling through trash under the moonlight, like raccoons. Charlie sang an ode to the beauty of chicken wings and macaroni salad. Then you picked the crying boy's eyes out with a knitting needle you found in his mother's living room.

"...Ms. X would like to make it clear that she was not laughing when each of her victims died. She was in shock. She was on acid. She was young. She was wet and excited with her first love, and being called by her special name, and being someone to someone. She did not stab and stab and stab for joy. She did it *because* of joy, because she was afraid of losing joy, because she could no longer live and breathe without joy..."

2015

In your next decade your hands will lie useless on the tabletop. Your list of reasons will serve as Exhibit #97, a photocopy passed around the room. Some will hand it on without reading. Some will glance at the list and stifle a smile. The guard will stifle a yawn. The nature of your days will be determined by people who leave the nauseating scent of institutional cleaning products and walk into the light and the air, who drive home in a haze of dust and inexplicable sorrow, who kiss and hold their children when they arrive at home, who imagine the small bones of their children's hands crushed, their faces slashed into gaping screams, their cries for mercy met with derision and madness—and more than all of this, worse than all of their nightmares, their children calling out for Mommy, Daddy, expecting to be rescued right up until the fading of the dark, resilient pinpoint of life in their eyes.

Parole is denied at this time.

A CONDITION FOR MARRIAGE

"How's the weather up there?" I asked.

"Oh, you know," said Sandy. "Rain and more rain. October in Seattle."

The maple leaves would be scarlet, I imagined, the frosted cap of Mount Rainier gleaming behind a bank of clouds on cold, black, sparkling nights.

"Is it raining now?"

"Today? No," she said. "Drizzle. Yesterday we had rain, and for three days before that. Bet you don't miss it."

She was wrong. The previous year I'd accepted a new job and relocated to Southern California, land of dusty ravines, department stores, and six-lane streets. I missed plenty of things about Puget Sound, where Sandy and I grew up.

What I didn't miss (and felt guilty about not missing) was playing handmaiden, always lingering nearby to check up on my sister, and battling the vague sense of a long overdue catastrophe. It was a lot like having children without the benefit of watching them grow up and find their own way. Forget about vacations or anything resembling a normal life. So, when it came along, the job in California had offered a new start for me.

My primary role in Sandy's life ended when she met and married Jim. Good old Jim with his boring quirks and silly collection of beer bottle labels. He was the balm my sister needed, a methodical man, a guy who turned in his taxes early and never cheated.

"Come on, this season is your favorite, right?" I asked.

"Your favorite," Sandy replied. "It's yours."

"But you love autumn, too," I insisted. "How did you describe it, when we were teenagers?"

I heard a sigh. "Okay, sure," she said. "*I can smell the leaves, dying in their glory!*"

Sandy was the unofficial poet in our family, the sensitive one with all of the unrealized potential. She did temp work part-time for years, typing mostly, usually at law firms. Whenever the pressure got to her she would take a leave of absence, later returning to the temp agency for a new assignment.

I ended up a corporate accountant, like Dad. Not much more to say. The very mention of my profession has the power to put dinner guests to sleep. From an early age I earned good money, enough for Sandy to move in with me after our parents passed away. We were both in our thirties when that happened, and close to forty when my sister married.

The job offer was excellent, the house I rented was pleasant enough, and I'd settled into a comfortable routine. California wasn't home but this was the first time I'd lived far away from my sister. The distance was supposed to bring relief and new prospects.

Jim was an accountant as well, though his private clients were so wealthy and well known, he wasn't allowed to mention most of them by name. Jim was frugal, the kind of guy who saves every other penny. At forty-six he had been semi-retired and mortgage free. Then his first wife died and his world collapsed. Showing up for a lunch date with a paralegal, he spotted Sandy typing away in her cubicle and fell in love. As he told one guest after another at the wedding, my sister's resemblance to his dead wife was uncanny.

"Wish you could visit," said Sandy.

"Me too," I said, trying to force real enthusiasm into the words. "You've got the perfect weather for Halloween. I envy you guys. Hang on a minute…"

I put down the phone and chased Angus, my cat, off the counter. It was Saturday and I was baking cookies while Sandy and I talked. I'd made up my mind; there would be no tortoiseshell fur in this batch. Angus gave me a glance of contempt over one shoulder and sauntered from the room as though nothing had happened. I ignored him and returned to the phone.

"All right," I said. "I'm back. So, what are you up to this afternoon?"

The pause was long enough to make me wonder if she'd hung up.

"Sandy? You there?"

"Sorry, Natalie," she said. "Didn't I tell you before? I'm digging a hole."

"Okay…" I waited for the punch line but it didn't come. "Why are you doing that?"

"I decided the minute I woke up this morning," she told me. "Big project underway."

"Is Jim there? Is he helping you?"

There was silence. Then I heard a crunch of metal in dirt.

"Sandy, you're not doing this by yourself, are you?" I asked. Stress and physical exertion were two of the things she was supposed to manage carefully. She often forgot, so the responsibility for monitoring her activities, and her meds, fell to Jim.

He and I had gone over her schedule carefully. I had jokingly called it "a condition for marriage," to impress upon him the importance of a stable routine.

"It's a surprise. I've got Jim's gloves and shovel out of the tool shed, and I'm finally going to do what I always wanted." The next sound on the line was a snuffle or maybe a chortle, a gruff intake of air followed by silence.

"Sandy?" I watched Angus sashay across the living room and hop onto the coffee table like he owned it. "You're not over-exerting yourself, are you?"

"I need the exercise," she said.

Jim, when he wasn't crunching numbers, was often outdoors rearranging and planting. There was nothing he loved as much as digging in the dirt in the fresh air. Which would have been fine with most wives. But Sandy and Jim disagreed about the type of garden they wanted, so every time he headed out back with his spade and hoe she would whip out her basket of housekeeping products and start to clean the inside of their house within an inch of its life. That was Sandy's therapy, her way of working off mild frustration. This was the first time she'd ever attacked the garden itself.

"Oh boy," she said. "Tearing this place right up."

I speed dialed Jim's phone but he didn't answer. I knew he liked to spend Saturdays at the local arboretum, if he wasn't shopping at a greenhouse.

"Okay. So, what are you planting?" Knowing this wasn't going to end well and wondering what I could do to talk my sister out of it.

Jim was proud of his green thumb, and more than a little compulsive. The guy knew the exact time of year to start every bulb, every cutting. He studied soil composition, researched how many hours of light were needed, the whole caboodle. There were times when he could be kind of a pain about it. One time I made the mistake of casually asking what chemicals were in a certain fertilizer he used, and damned if he didn't stop what he was doing and list every ingredient in every product he'd tried over the past five years. He was like that.

"Sandy?" I said. "Isn't Jim still doing the cottage garden thing, the wisteria, the honeysuckle he likes?" I thought a mild reminder might jolt her out of any further damage until I could get Jim on the phone.

"Hang on a minute," she said. She must have set her phone aside; for a while all I could hear was the crunch of a shovel and the grunt of effort behind it.

Angus stared at me from the coffee table while I waited. I stared back. I thought maybe it was time Sandy adopted a pet. They say caring for an animal helps people to concentrate. Besides, Jim could be a tiny bit annoying with his attention to detail and his house rules. Without my company to mitigate the situation Sandy might be experiencing a little too much stress.

When they married a few years back, Jim seemed like the perfect mate for my sister. But it takes patience to accommodate a man who keeps a bathroom chart of his every meal and bowel movement, and who saves his used-up deodorant cans until he has four, before throwing them away as a set.

Sometimes I marveled at their relationship. They actually had little in common. Sandy loved to spend quiet afternoons on the sofa, reading poetry, working crosswords, or simply relaxing in front of a crackling fire. Jim had to be busy every second of the day or he would start to nag. The housekeeping, the way Sandy dressed, how much spoiled food was piling up in the fridge, how many minutes of talking or texting Sandy had used on their antiquated phone plan. It was always something but these gripes were acceptable, I thought, given what he had taken on.

I was startled when she came back on the line. "Jim's going to blow his top over this," she said, and laughed. It was a wonderful sound, when my sister really laughed, like bubbles spewing over the rim of a champagne bottle. I had to laugh, too.

Jim had lived with his first wife for seventeen years in the house on Queen Anne Hill. It had been a fairly posh neighborhood when he moved there, not so much anymore. Microsoft millionaires are scattered all over Seattle these days, knocking down landmarks to build their McMansions behind security fences. Compared to the homes of the nouveau riche, Jim's place—a 1920s Craftsman—was a quaint reminder of another time. I remember my sister's delight the first time she saw the place.

"Listen, Sandy, exactly what are you up to?" I asked. "Are you digging up Jim's rose bushes? Because I don't think it's a good time of year to plant anything new. You might want to wait until he gets home, and talk it over." Another speed dial to Jim's number went straight to voicemail.

"No. Listen to me," she said distinctly. "He can only blame himself. Damn it."

"Okay. What did he do?"

"He threw away my Tiki, the little wooden idol you sent me for my birthday. Threw him right into the garbage! I found him this morning, on top of the daily paper, with coffee grounds all over his face."

"Oh no," I said. "Well, that was a mean thing to do."

I'd wrapped the gift carefully, even though it was just a small wooden statue I'd found in a vintage store in Laguna Niguel, and mailed it special delivery. I knew how Sandy loved these out-of-place Polynesian ornaments. She'd fallen in love with the movie *Hawaii* when we were teenagers, watched it on TV late one night following her stay in the hospital. She always vowed to sail away to "the magical islands" someday. She was enchanted by this faraway place she'd never seen. The warmth and the promise of romance calmed her nerves.

Careful as he tried to be, mindful of my sister's need for balance and clarity, Jim sometimes let slip a stray detail about his former marriage. For example, he and his first wife had honeymooned on Kauai and vacationed there a few times. After he became a widower he swore he would never visit a tropical island again. This tiny difference between them had seemed insignificant when Jim and Sandy exchanged vows.

"Isn't it cold outside?" I asked. "Don't make yourself sick. Are you wearing a sweater?" With my sister there was a fine line between suggesting and demanding, and I had to be careful not to cross it.

"No," she said. "I'm fine. In fact, I feel great."

"Yeah?"

"Yep! I'm digging a hole in the back yard and Jim's going to shit a brick when he wakes up." So he was napping, presumably with his phone turned off.

The pause was infinitesimal. Then I busted out laughing. Sandy laughed. We laughed together for a long time.

"You're so funny, Sandy. I love you. You know that, right?"

"I love you, too, Natalie," she said. She always managed to put more heart, more tenderness, into these rare moments. It made me choke up, every time.

Outside my living room window I could see a bunch of people in neon spandex trotting past my house, doing a fun run. Southern California's nothing but idiots. Nobody reads. Honestly, if I ever saw someone reading a book in Orange County, I'd die of shock.

"Oh!" Sandy said. "I hear Jim. Gotta go!"

And she hung up.

I stood there watching the fun runners zip by my window. Some were fit and some jiggled like bright blocks of Jell-O.

***

When we were kids my sister used to make puppets and then stage little shows with them. Our parents praised her imagination and talent. She was about ten when these invented scenarios took a violent turn. However innocuous the original premise, after a couple of twists in the action one character would take issue with another and lash out. Sometimes the result was a swift, manic Punch and Judy performance. At other times she would leave the room in disarray, her strangely controlled acts of mayhem having broken all the puppets and scenery.

Dad learned to interrupt these displays before Sandy worked up to a full tantrum. A middle school counselor recommended medication. Before this method could take full effect Sandy pushed a boy down the stairs, breaking his collarbone. Our parents only avoided a lawsuit by committing my sister to a couple of months at a hospital specializing in young adult behavioral issues.

Upon her release, although Sandy seemed greatly improved, she had occasional lapses into a fugue state. She completed high school by correspondence, and we were relieved when she was able to earn a moderate income typing. To each temp assignment she showed up with a short list of instructions for the office manager. The only other oddity to her professional life was her need to take time off whenever the atmosphere became too hectic.

***

A couple of days before our phone chat Sandy and Jim had a disagreement about the décor of their home. This was what she told me on Saturday morning before I steered the conversation back to the weather. Sandy had been excited about the Polynesian idol I sent her. Without consulting her husband, she'd gone out and bought a couple of Tiki torches and a painting of the Na Pali Coast.

"Why do you want a picture of a place where you've never been?" Jim wanted to know.

"Don't you understand? I want it *because* I've never been there. From this point, at the tip of Kauai, you can see the world as it really is, thousands of miles of ocean compared to this tiny speck of civilization. The Pacific Ocean ahead of you on all sides, and these huge, green pinnacles of volcanic rock towering behind you. Oh my god, we're so small! Jim, we're just these little people trying to get by, we're like the Menehune when the first Tahitians arrived. Did you know, from Hanalei you can actually see the curve of the Earth out there on the ocean? Can't you sense these gigantic creatures coiling and uncoiling and swimming deep down in the sea? The sky and the water go on forever. And we're nothing at all..."

This was how she described their conversation. Before I could interrupt, she relayed the rest of her speech in a rush of words.

"Oh, Jim, let's go! I want to dig my toes into warm sand and let the waves carry me away! I want to learn to snorkel. I want to hang glide over the sea!"

"What did he say?" I asked. Measuring my words, trying to slow her down.

"He doesn't get it," Sandy said. "He went to Hawaii with his stupid dead wife and now we can never go there."

"Well," I said in my most soothing tone. "At least you have the Tiki idol I sent you, and you can always stream movies..."

"No." She sounded indignant. "Movies are not the same. I told Jim I want him to plant something tropical so I can enjoy the fragrance of Hawaii in summer."

"That's a nice idea."

"He said no. He said the plants I like would die in this climate and next year he's loading up on more of his English garden junk, more climbing roses, more poppies, more lavender. I hate lavender."

"Well," I said. "He did plant the garden."

The silence that followed was uncomfortable.

"He needs a new hobby," Sandy said. "Retirement is making him picky."

"Maybe he should have friends over more often," I suggested.

"Nobody likes him."

That made me laugh. This is when I decided to change the subject.

"How's the weather up there?"

***

The last of the fun runners jiggled down the street. I controlled my urge to make faces at them.

Angus meowed for his third meal of the day. I shook my head "no" while opening a fresh can of chicken and herring. Mixed signals were an element of our relationship from the start, along with a dash of laziness. At first I'd passed Angus over at PAWS while making the rounds. I was hoping to adopt a kitten, not an adult male with irreversible habits. A couple of violet-eyed, gray and white sisters caught my attention with their antics. They seemed very bright and lively. Then I noticed Angus, lying on his back spread-eagled, dead to the world, honestly not giving a damn if he was adopted or not. My kind of cat. A year later we were still a mutually indifferent item.

Once I had all the details about their argument, I thought it really was a cheap move on Jim's part, throwing that Tiki idol in the trash. Did he imagine Sandy would stop thinking about tropical islands, or a garden corner of her own, just because he threw away the gift I'd given her? I wished a little misery on him for that, while I slathered vanilla frosting on the cookies I'd baked.

***

The preceding month had been crazy at work. Approaching the end of the year, aside from tax concerns, we were factoring in bonuses and PTO. I had enough extra work to last all weekend. Yet for some crazy reason I'd promised my next-door neighbor I would help out with her daughter's Halloween party. Hence the revolting cookies with frosted vanilla skeleton faces.

Aside from baking, I liked Halloween but I didn't expect much. According to everyone I met, a dozen trick-or-treaters would have been a record breaker in our neighborhood. Another thing about Southern California, where the Pacific Ocean tantalizes, casting a magical light askance at even the lowliest inland suburb, is the way people join in games with their kids. You see parents in lame superhero costumes tagging along, checking their cells and pretending to have fun while the tykes beg for candy. It's pretty much killed the fun of the holiday, and it's no wonder most kids prefer to go to a party with their friends.

This is why I was parked in a lawn chair in my neighbor's back yard on Saturday night, wondering how much more cuteness I could stand before I had to run home for a glass of merlot. I knew my neighbor had a wine cellar but it was off limits during family hours. Five, six, seven kids ran past wearing costumes from the latest Pixar blockbuster, shrieking a song so familiar it made me want to shriek too.

My phone rang. In Seattle, even after she married, I'd been accustomed to calls from my sister at all hours. I wasn't accustomed to video chats. Sandy maintained she was more verbal than visual, and she hated having to check her hair before making a phone call. I figured she'd hit the FaceTime app by mistake.

"Hey," I said, leaning away from the noise of the kids.

"What's up?"

Something gelatinous and vaguely circular filled the screen of my phone. It might have been an eye or a squid or a drop of water or a tadpole.

"Sandy?" I said.

The sun had set. At the edge of the patio the squat, devilish jack-o-lanterns were glowing with candlelight. Screaming children were fighting over cookies. One boy started whining to his mom that his cookie had hair on it. I waved goodbye and made my way to the gate, motioning toward my phone as though I had an emergency call. I didn't want to be around if the hair turned out to be feline.

"Sandy?"

I made it to my own kitchen before the glob on my screen focused. Sandy's face came into view. She was disheveled, her hair uncombed and sticking to her face in spots where the perspiration had run down from her scalp.

"Jesus, Sandy, are you all right?"

"Yo!" she shouted. She gave a brusque little laugh but her eyes were wide and bloodshot.

"What are you doing?" I asked.

"Oh," she said. She took a breath and blew it out dramatically, casting a thin cloud of condensation. "This and that."

Ordinarily the phrase meant she'd been cleaning house and streaming her favorite TV shows. But she didn't look like she'd been watching television.

"What are you up to, *tonight*?" I asked.

"Tonight," she said. "Tonight is special, very special. Nat, I know you're busy. But things are going so well, I want to show you how much progress I've made."

The background framing her was in motion all the time she was talking. She appeared to be walking from her softly lit dining room, down the steps, out to the deck. The light failed until she reached the garden, where several Tiki torches were set up in a semi-circle. Sandy waved the phone in a swift arc to take in the complete arrangement.

"I was right about the garden," Sandy said. "I started by going back to the store for more torches. When the weather is better I'll add bamboo, hibiscus, maybe a couple of rubber plants…"

"Sandy," I said. "Honey, aren't you cold?"

"Nope," she said. "I'm warm as can be. Ever since I started my garden. Oh! I almost forgot." She swept to her left and the picture blurred. "The reason I called is my new Tiki man. Wait until you see this."

The picture went out of focus again. When the camera settled on one spot, the image was nothing but a swirl of light and dark brown. It took a moment but then it was just possible to pick out the gnarled contours of roots and an uneven surface of dirt. The brown soil was punctuated with smooth black stones and twigs. Holding the screen close and squinting, I could barely tell that something was moving or pulsing at the center of the shot.

Sandy zoomed in and then zoomed again. I stared at the screen until I could just make out a stained and bleeding face all but buried there, his body, neck, and head consumed beneath the surface. Jim's mouth was still moving but at strange angles and without uttering a sound.

***

Of course I considered calling the police in Seattle. I guess that would have been the thing to do, the thing most people would have done, if they had not spent their lives watching out for an unstable sibling.

There was my sister to consider. Sandy hadn't hurt anyone in a long time. She was a bit scattered, absentminded, but otherwise sensitive, even thoughtful. She was the kind of kid who gave away her overcoat to another girl who couldn't afford one. She was the kind of woman who walks twenty blocks to locate the owner of a lost puppy. Not the kind of person who bonks her husband on the back of the neck with a shovel and buries him up to his face in the back yard.

There was also a family sense of honor at stake. Our parents left Sandy to me, and I had taken care of her until a stranger came along and took her off my hands. Then I'd let her go, willingly.

Given all of the circumstances, there was only one thing to do.

***

The winters in Seattle are bitter cold these days, much colder than I remember. On most days I need three layers of clothing, minimum. These old houses are quaint but drafty as hell.

You should have seen the look on my supervisor's face when I announced I was leaving without two weeks' notice and flying back to the Northwest. I pleaded homesickness. I couldn't claim a death in the family. You never know how far a rumor might spread, or how many questions it might prompt. Above all, we needed to avoid questions, which, so far, we've managed to do.

Sandy's Tiki garden is wrecked every year by the elements. The torches stand sentry while icicles hang from the eaves over the deck. The ginkgo trees begin to shrivel. The hibiscus dies.

With each thaw, Sandy begins anew. Despite what Jim told her, some of the plants she loves have been able to thrive. I think it's sheer luck. She says it's the quality of the soil that makes a difference. Maybe it does.

All winter we sit indoors, sipping tea, reading, watching TV. We don't reminisce as much as we used to. We spread maps of the South Pacific across the dining room table and pick out fantasy destinations. Sandy comes up with elaborate scenarios for each one. We've even looked online at properties for sale on Oahu and Kauai.

Sometimes she asks when we can take a vacation. I always offer the same answer. "Soon." Lately she's begun to look at me with an expression I don't recognize.

What else can I say? We could never take a trip. We could never sell or lease the house and let someone landscape it properly. No. We read books on Polynesian history, sailing, and navigation, while Angus keeps watch over the garden from his favorite perch at the back window. Cats are lovely, fastidious creatures. Fortunately they don't like to dig, not the way a dog would.

Next year the bamboo will be coming in. We've got plumeria along with jade. Soon we'll add Tropicana lilies and red bananas.

The torches surrounding the ginkgo are perennial, so to speak. By night they illuminate a three-foot-tall hand-carved Tiki idol glowing at the center of their circle. We commissioned it from a local artist, brought it home and installed it ourselves, and we're very happy with it.

In the daylight the torches stand silently beside a burial mound overflowing with orchids. We have to order these from another state, of course. The local nurseries don't sell the species Sandy loves. As every landscape designer in town has patiently explained to her a dozen times, in this climate, nothing so delicate could survive without special care and constant attention.

THE SECOND FLOOR

From the back seat Jane's view of the house was divided but not entirely obscured, the left side glimpsed through a windshield cloudy with dirt, the right side framed by the window the Uber driver insisted on keeping open. The bed and breakfast was a remodeled Carpenter Gothic with a scruffy front garden and a flagstone walkway. The moss-covered birdbath had flecks of ice floating on its surface. A calico cat slept inside the ground floor window against a backdrop of lace curtains.

All along, on the staccato ride from the train station, Jane had expected the driver to light up a cigarette. But he never did. She had twice asked him to close the front window against the early November chill. Each time he had complied and then gradually lowered the glass again, so that she was continually buttoning and unbuttoning her coat to match the draft and the temperature.

She had chosen the route and mode of transportation

hoping to get a better look at the city. But a combination of drizzle and cloud cover neutralized the streets. There was a quiet sameness to the offices, shops, and condos Jane found both surprising and disappointing. Adding to the gloom, every block had its own collection of homeless squatters. Not the eccentrically attired poets and swashbucklers who once decorated, even dominated, these neighborhoods, but a shocking number of people simply huddled together on the pavement, their faces and clothing washed out, exhausted by the relentless search for food and shelter.

"2109 East Keller," the driver mumbled, prompting payment. He didn't offer to hoist out the suitcase wedged behind his seat. Jane handled the suitcase, tipped him despite the poor service, and headed up to the portico in descending twilight. The tires squealed when the car took off and she turned to watch it lurch up the hill and around a corner before she rang the doorbell.

A nest of white hair preceded its owner. The man who opened the door was slouching. Jane took him to be elderly but when he drew up to full height she could see he was a foot taller and perhaps only a decade older than she was.

"Yes?"

"Jane Morgan." She stuck out her hand, which became the object of the man's fascination. At last he wrapped both of his own hands around it. They were dry and cool as butcher paper.

"Poor thing," he said. "You must be so cold. Come in. I have a kettle on the stove. I'll pour you a cup of tea."

"Thank you."

The sick sweet odor of mildew seeping through numerous coats of paint greeted her when the man closed the door. She followed him into a small foyer with cherry wood baseboards and stairs. The gloom was lifted a bit by an area rug decorated with garish red and green apples. Both doors on the right-hand wall were shut. Between them an olive-green, velvet sofa looked as if its springs had collapsed years ago.

"My name is Leon, by the way. Come on back. Leave your suitcase there, it's fine."

Reluctantly, Jane drew her gaze away from the stairs. To the right, a passage led to the kitchen. All of it was so much like she remembered.

"You know," said Leon. "My parents used to run a theatre company in Everett."

"Oh?"

"Yes, indeed. My mother will be so jealous when I tell her Jane Morgan stayed here. Of course, I won't say anything until you're gone. Discretion is the soul of the bed and breakfast industry, you know."

"Thanks. I appreciate it." She wanted to be polite although she couldn't imagine being stalked by a theatre fan, not in a town where most people prided themselves on being unimpressed.

They had reached the kitchen at the back of the house. The arched window offered a broad view of the neighborhood down the hill, drenched in chill twilight.

Leon took a kettle from the Bakelite stove and prepared a steaming cup of tea for each of them. Jane noticed he had gradually resumed what must have been a natural slouch, so that they seemed almost the same height again. His Tommy Bahama shirt flared when he moved. His loose silk pants gathered in folds of at least a couple of inches over feet encased in wooly socks and Birkenstock sandals.

He made a motion, indicating that she should sit and make herself comfortable. She sat. She tried to remember if the tomato-red Formica table had been there years ago, and decided it was too nice to have survived the years of unkind wear and tear. Leon sat facing her and crossed his legs.

"Are you hungry?" He asked. "We have leftover blueberry muffins. I could heat those up."

"No," she said. "Tea is fine. I just need to warm up and get some rest."

They sat silently for a moment. Then Leon seemed to rally, to provide her with entertainment.

"Yes, yes, yes," he said. "My family is old Seattle and Everett show biz royalty. If ever there was such a thing. I don't remember a time when we didn't run a theatre. My mother acted and my father directed. My sister and I helped paint the sets, build the costumes. You name it. We handed out flyers on the street almost every performance night."

"What a wonderful childhood you must have had."

"Oh, yes, I suppose. I spent as much time in rehearsal as I spent in school. Endless musicals, dramas, puppet shows. You name it. We also rented space to all the touring companies. I even wrote a few plays we produced."

Jane nodded, knowing from experience never to ask a playwright for more details about his work. He might go on all night.

"Goodness, I must've adapted half the Jacobeans when I was a teenager. Then came the comedies, some fairly amusing Noel Coward pastiches. Wrote an original verse play about Marlowe…"

Leon did go on and on, for a few minutes, the wit and precocity of his youthful writing washing over Jane while she sipped the surprisingly delicious Jasmine tea. His story meant nothing to her. In this city, she estimated, every tenth resident had a similar tale to offer about their years "treading the boards."

"Enough about me," Leon said abruptly, and Jane wondered if she had betrayed her lack of interest by staring at the tabletop. She was awfully tired after the flight from California, the train from the airport, and the car ride, which she'd hoped would be more scenic.

"That's a fascinating life," she said.

"Not really," Leon replied. "Just your typical local theatre family. But you, you're a real, living legend, aren't you?"

Jane wondered if he was taking a dig at her.

"No," she said, playing it safe. "I'm a teacher, primarily a teacher, these days. I mentor and I do a bit of dramaturgical work. I haven't written a play in a while."

"But you have this amazing reputation," said Leon. "Aren't you accepting an award for lifetime achievement?"

"Nothing like that," she explained. "There's a city retrospective, not just for me. It's a festival. Excerpts from some of my plays will be performed, and short plays by other people, and there will be a dinner party."

"Sponsored by the mayor's office," he said. With a dip of his chin and a slight flourish he gathered a well-thumbed copy of a weekly arts journal—one Jane and her friends used to hate for its brutal reviews of fringe productions—and flipped to the calendar page. "A gala! My stars. A gala hosted by the biggest theatre in town. Oh, I wish I could go."

"Well the big event is tomorrow night but they probably still have tickets," she said, picturing Leon's bird nest of snow-and-bark-colored hair bobbing above the crowd wherever he went. She decided not to offer him a guest pass.

"I would love it," he said. "Truly. But Friday night is my crochet class."

Jane believed Seattle must be the national capital of this particular kind of insult. If she fell for the bait and took note of the insult, its perpetrator would become apoplectic with apology, scuttling backward into a sublime sort of moral shell, sputtering about over-sensitivity and not taking things too personally—assuring her that one more absence from crochet class would mean expulsion, given all the previous ones—although they had been unavoidable, since he (undoubtedly) had an ancient Aunty requiring frequent assistance. The unstated bonus insult being that Aunty was far more deserving than this ego-bloated, self-involved artiste before him.

Jane felt a new wave of exhaustion wash over her. She had spent so many recent years in a land of sunlight and mild enjoyment she had forgotten how tiring it was to cope with passive aggression from strangers. She placed her empty cup in the saucer and forced a weary smile.

"Well," she said. "Long day tomorrow. I should probably turn in."

Leon led Jane back down the hall toward the room with the olive sofa. She signed the guest journal and Leon carried her suitcase up to the second floor. After opening the door onto a cozy square room with a view of the hill below, and after pointing out where to find bath towels, Leon handed over the key.

"Only the owners and I have duplicates, so take good care of it. You wouldn't believe what they charge for a new set."

"Thanks," Jane said.

"Are you sure you don't want the room next to this one? We had a last-minute cancelation. The view is better. If we ever have a clear day, you can almost see the Arboretum."

"No," she said. "I'm satisfied."

"I could offer a larger downstairs room. But you'd have to wait while I clean up after the last guests."

"No," she said. "It's all right. Am I the only guest, then?"

"I'm expecting an arrival first thing in the morning. A couple. They haven't chosen upstairs or downstairs yet. And of course, there's our Miss Amy."

Jane hadn't realized the B&B had long-term residents but it made sense. The place was too rundown to be competitive in the hotel market.

"I'm happy with my choice," she told Leon.

"Suit yourself," he said. "As we say. I mean, make yourself at home. That's our motto."

At last he left her in peace. She considered the hardwood

floor, high ceiling, brass bed, and the sheer white curtains drawn to one side. She stepped on a slat in the middle of the floor and felt it give with a resounding squeak.

So she was home. She wasn't yet sure if the moment called for celebration. The worst years of her life were lived under this roof; drunk, delirious years. The time she spent with Sabina, Thaddeus, and Kurt.

Tearful secrets talked over with Sabina on the stairs after a botched audition or a frightening report from the gynecologist. Sabina's vow to marry a millionaire. Jane hurling a ceramic dish at Kurt in the kitchen during some disagreement about Strindberg's women, knocking him breathless, flat on his back, arms and legs splayed. Thaddeus enfolding Jane in his long, beautiful limbs when she cried over a script rejected by the same theatre now honoring her work. Jane's gratitude, mingled with a desperate yearning for recognition. The night she peeled off her wet slip and climbed on top of Thaddeus, on impulse, in the bath. Both of them surprised by a quick, sharp desire—and then shamefaced afterward, Thaddeus unable to face his boyfriend for a week. The way Jane and her embarrassed housemate huddled together on the steps outside and whispered, pondering the possibilities. Wandering through a landscape of brief mutual obsession, miraculous one day and absurd the next. Sabina calling them "self-tormenting twins," followed by Thaddeus crying and smoking cigarettes in the rain. The brute reality of the solace she later found with Kurt.

In California she had heard no rumors about the lives of these people who once defined the boundaries of her world. They had never been in the same state, let alone the same room, in all the years since Jane moved away. Always, however, they existed in her unconscious mind, in a dream state, their bodies more familiar and infused with kinetic energy than the man she had divorced the previous year. Martin. She had to think hard for a split second but she remembered Martin's habits without rancor, his fondness for Impressionist art, his insistence on buying every scrap of their produce at a farmer's market.

"Martin goes to market," she used to say under her breath, though not to Martin. Who was Martin? She still didn't know him beyond his CV. He was a scholar and a fellow teacher. An author with several volumes published on the subject of non-illusory performance. They were friends and colleagues who drifted into, and then out of, a marriage based on compatible schedules and a quiet, intellectual interest in theatre. Martin had moved into the mission style house where Jane kept an herb garden, a wine collection, and a hot tub. After the divorce he moved out and they went on meeting for lunch once a week.

Every semester Jane faced a fresh onslaught of smart, lazy eighteen-year-olds. In the early years students had been impressed by her credentials. As time went on, her authority became a thing in itself, taken for granted by all. No one cared that she didn't write plays any more. They, her students, were the ones who were expected to do great things. Their indifference toward her professional life was only challenged once, the day she mentioned the festival in Seattle and the gala celebrating several decades of local theatre, honoring Jane's work and the work of her peers. In fact, her announcement drew a round of applause. Today, especially after her conversation with Leon, she was embarrassed to admit how much that little shudder of approval had fueled her acceptance of the invitation.

Year after year, Jane's students were a grating combination of those fully committed to the stage and nothing else, and those who simply didn't know what they wanted out of life. Some were only majoring in performance arts in defiance of absent or disinterested parents. Most had money, at least enough to fall back on. They were nothing like Jane at their age. She had fought her way through undergraduate and graduate programs on scholarships and grants, recommendations and emergency student aid. Every semester brought a new form of desperation. Her drive had impressed people back then but it also earned her a reputation for being dour and difficult. Meeting Kurt after graduation, over an impoverished production of *The Seagull*, had opened a vein of passion she'd never examined before or since.

Kurt was the high-minded director and Jane the reluctant dramaturg who answered an ad stuck to a campus bulletin board. Their arguments about Nina and Konstantin had echoed into the night. Their collaborations attracted the best young actors and designers in town. Altogether they teamed up on six shows, most of them classics by Ibsen and Chekhov, all of them rough, wild, and magnetic.

Their arguments escalated over the years, fueled by wine, by Jane's writing ambition, and by an unspoken attraction. Unspoken for years, running just beneath the surface of every conversation. Until it was spoken, one terrible night on the roof of this house.

For a long time they had shared rent with Thaddeus and Sabina. All four lived in a flurry of activity, waiting tables, pulling espresso, leading tours of the Space Needle and Underground Seattle, anything to get by, anything to support their unpaid artistry.

Jane had turned to Kurt quite suddenly, without explanation, following her doomed flirtation with Thaddeus. After that, they spent every night together for weeks. It might have lasted longer if Kurt hadn't broken the animal spell with his declaration.

Jane's memory of the night was keen, as if no time had passed. She had craned her neck, leaning painfully, precariously, from her windowsill, shouting for sanity. Kurt had skittered this way and that on the rooftop, proclaiming a kind of love. Merciless. Undying. Vast. Beyond the cosmos. Between dimensions.

"Stop it!" she had yelled. "This has to stop!"

Kurt had opened his arms wide, smiled down at Jane, and plummeted to the ground. The cold thump when he hit the grass made her stomach lurch. More alarming still was the way he kept struggling to raise himself, to lift his head, to look up at her.

He was alive. Not entirely unharmed, suffering from a mild concussion, but alive and able to walk, talk, and recognize the paramedics who had revived him on two other occasions. Both were cases of alcohol poisoning. This time, one of the medics told Jane to get Kurt some help.

"But he's okay," she said. "He wasn't hurt."

"Do you know how drunk a man has to be to fall that far and not sustain an injury? Get him into a program or he'll be dead in five years."

The subsequent shouting matches between Jane and Kurt centered on this exchange. They never argued about life, art, or theatre again, only Kurt's drinking. He would rage and pace, draw his hands repeatedly through his black, slick hair. He called her names for interfering. She drank less as these rows went on. He begged to sleep with her again, and then denounced her when she refused. She led him on. Then she withdrew and tried to set terms. She said she wouldn't work with him again until he sobered up. He never did.

Jane knew Thaddeus and Sabina as well as she knew the contours and odors of her own body. Kurt had been her downfall, though. Jane could isolate in memory the exact night she sat drinking pinot noir on the back steps, eaves dripping icy rain, watching the lights of the neighborhood below the hill. She had said out loud, to no one, that she would never feel this way about anyone again. And she'd been right, thankfully, terribly right.

For six years Jane had lived in this room. The house had been a cheap rental but it had taken all four residents, and occasional drop-ins, to keep it going. The current cost of the B&B for two nights was more than she'd paid each month, as a starving artist.

In this room she had written her plays, all but one of them. On a PowerBook that Kurt fished out of a dumpster behind student housing in the U-District, she had spent endless nights meticulously crafting her two-character psychological dramas. They required no set, no music, nothing to distract from what she believed to be the essence of her work, the conflict within and between two souls. Most of these dramas played to houses of ten or twelve people at a small theatre located a few blocks away.

The one exception was a collaborative project funded by the city, a sprawling work combining musicians, acrobats, and found text. She had accepted the offer soon after Kurt's declaration of love.

For the first time, Jane had been well paid for her contribution. She provided bits of dialogue and phrases projected onto a wall, all of these clipped and rearranged from personal ads in a newspaper. The narrative unfolded non-chronologically over a series of performances in a converted brewery, the audience supplied with flashlights with gobos attached to create spontaneous, supplemental lighting effects.

The work was acclaimed by the local and then the regional press. Word spread. Jane was interviewed long distance by the *New York Times* and several theatre arts journals. The notoriety brought her to the attention of a college in Southern California. The project, called *Push/Shove*, was the crowning achievement of Jane's career and she didn't write a word of it.

As a result, she was offered a teaching position. The letter arrived on a morning of bleak hangovers throughout the house. Her mind was still spinning backward and forward through the previous night's arguments.

Kurt had called Jane a whore, but lightly and smugly, as if he didn't care. He'd vowed never to direct her "shitty little two-handers" again, blaming her because he wasn't hired to work on her only successful show. Sabina had announced a five-year plan to marry a doctor—any doctor—and buy a fat mansion on 10th Avenue, "the best part of Capitol Hill, you bitches. And I'm having four angelic children who sing in the moonlight every night." Thaddeus, meanwhile, sat on a cushion in the living room, in the exact spot where the olive sofa now sagged. He had sipped wine all night and shed sparkling tears while the only people he cared about in the world made plans to leave him.

When the offer came, Jane didn't give it a second thought. While her housemates slept off the bad burn of cheap wine, she glanced around, noted the mouse droppings lining the baseboards, wood slivers on the window frames, pale outlines of beer and vomit stains on the antique area rugs. Then she packed her belongings and moved away to so-called SoCal, where she had lived quietly and warmly for the past eighteen years.

Jane watched from her bedroom window at the B&B as the last gray and violet shadows crossed the hill and sank into darkness. She checked her phone one last time. No messages. She loosened the sheer white curtain and let it fall shut.

Early as it was, she barely managed to change into her pajamas before she felt too drowsy to sit up in bed. Her last thought was that the tingling, persistent draft creeping in through the floorboards and layers of wallpaper felt oddly natural.

Many hours later, and only in the most muffled and distracted way, Jane became aware of sounds on the landing, voices in conversation, followed by footsteps. She had sunk hard into sleep and had to struggle to raise her face from the pillow. Her phone read "3 a.m."

Her arms could barely lift her weight off the bed. She sat for a minute, her head bowed low, listening, gathering strength.

Although the footsteps ceased, she had an odd sense that someone was just outside the door. Hovering, hesitating. It was this lack of movement, the silence, she found troubling. And so she acted as she often did when she was uncertain. With unnecessary energy she sprang to her feet, crossed the room, and flung open the door to disprove the source of her fear.

"Oh, I'm sorry!"

This heartfelt whisper came from the woman whose marvelous eyes, the color of rain, met hers. Jane was so startled she couldn't speak.

"So very sorry," the tall, slender woman whispered. It was impossible to determine her age. With finely manicured hands she clutched a silk robe at her throat and waist. Her fine gray eyes fixed upon Jane, taking in every detail as though she had been alone for a long time and couldn't get over the novelty of company. She offered an almost imperceptible flutter of dense lashes. Her long face was in full makeup despite the late hour.

"Forgive me! I understood it would be all right…"

"What are you doing?" Jane asked, clearheaded at last.

"Excusez-moi, really, truly," the woman begged in that understated, husky tone. "The toilet on the first floor is backed up. There were three women visiting from Portland yesterday. Well, you know how girls sort of get in sync, especially traveling together. I think they clogged the pipes!" She gave an easy shrug and a grin. "Damn girls."

"Oh," Jane said. "Are you here for the bathroom?"

The woman shrugged again.

"It's right across the hall, there," she told the woman, and pointed.

"Merci."

"Sure," said Jane. "Sure. Good night." She closed the door firmly, the better to cover the slight rattle when she checked the lock. It felt secure enough. She went back to bed, shivering for a minute in the pre-dawn chill. She drifted off again and never heard the woman walk away.

In the morning the house hummed with the aroma of coffee and cinnamon buns. Jane showered quickly, noting both the blessed absence of any mess from the night visitor and the true measure of Northwestern cold, that moment after stepping out of a steamy shower stall with beads of water clinging to goose flesh.

Leon was waiting in the kitchen, legs crossed, wearing what Jane took to be a friendly expression, a lopsided smile. "Coffee?" he asked.

"Is that French Roast?"

"Oh, yes, and these buns are hot from the oven, my dear. Have a seat."

She let him fuss over her, pouring and plating, surrounding her with comforts she had seldom been able to afford when she lived here. She didn't ask about the guest who woke her the night before. Locals were touchy about so many things. Even a mention could be taken as a complaint, and she didn't want to get anyone in trouble. She just wallowed in the joy of being clean and fed and full of delicious brew. After Leon wandered off to "tidy and whatnot," she checked her phone.

At last she had a voice message. A reply to her pre-trip query: Would Sabina like to join her at the gala on Friday? The possibility, now that Jane was here, in town, filled her with images of Sabina: her rosebud breasts and hourglass silhouette glistening naked the day she shed her dress at a lake party and walked to the end of the dock to go skinny dipping; sobbing over a missing cat; shouting down a frat boy in the middle of the street on Broadway, chastising him for frightening Thaddeus with his taunts; teaching herself to play violin by wretchedly hammering away at "If I Were a Rich Man" thirty times a day until she mastered it.

Like girlfriends, they would catch up over a glass of wine. They would reminisce after seeing a play and discussing its merits, as they used to do. She might find out more about Thaddeus and Kurt, who had slipped from her life as though they were never there, only dreamed and abandoned. Jane's cheeks flushed as she hit the voicemail playback.

"Hi, Jane, it's Sabina. Wow. I just read your email again. I'm sitting here in my kitchen, baking zucchini bread, and I'm looking at the rainclouds and marveling at the whole karmic thing, the way we think we're traveling to some far-off place when we're really just walking in a big circle. You know? Sure you do, of course. You're the writer. Speaking of which. Congrats on the big thing, your, what is it, the gala! That sounds amazing, and you deserve it. Only the timing kind of sucks and kind of blows. Kipling, my youngest, is doing this project at her school on Monday, and—hey, did you ever get the birthday card she sent you last year? The handmade card? Sorry if it came out of the blue. I mentioned you one day and she wanted your mailing address at the university, so she could make you a card. That kid. So talented and smart. You'd love her. The others are on a field trip, hiking, building character, some bullshit. They're in this experience-based program at school, and it's a requirement every semester. I have to pick them up at the bus station tonight. And, look, no tears, but I've got surgery coming up soon. Jane, they're taking my ovaries out and I know that probably sounds like no big deal to you but I'm coming to terms with some real shit, you know? Kipling's eight, and, I know I'm greedy, but I really wanted to do it all again because—it was great! All of it, all four kids. Every goddamn minute of it. You know me, always wanting more! Anyway, we're good here. Family's good. Yeah. So, have a great night, and drink a glass of wine for me. I don't think

I've been to a show in fifteen years. Except school plays. Bless your heart. You should be so proud of yourself. Look at all of your accomplishments! Oh, by the way, that story you mentioned, about me taking off my clothes and jumping in the lake? That wasn't me, kiddo. And I never played the violin. I don't know who it was but you've got me mixed up with somebody else, I guess. Anyway. Yeah. Yay, you! Good luck. If you're ever in town again, give me a call."

She wasn't sure how long the silence lasted after Sabina's voice faded away. Then, all at once, Jane was on her feet and moving, hoping to avoid Leon and explanations. She retrieved her coat from the rack by the front door, made sure she had her key. Her need for light and air was acute by now; she fairly stumbled out the front door. She took the steps in one stride as she had more than a thousand times.

The cold breeze stung her face. She buttoned up and pressed on, up the hill one block, then two. Not meeting the gaze of several homeless men on the opposite side of the street.

She began to scan the houses, trying to remember where the theatre was, or where it used to be. She didn't know if the place still existed. She was afraid to check maps on her phone. If she found the exact spot onscreen, if it had been turned into a condo or if it was nothing at all, a blank, an empty lot, she didn't know what she might do. Better to ramble, to try and find it and probably fail, than to have her fear confirmed without trying.

As she walked, feet scuffing through brown leaves, she noticed a few impeccably dressed people in the neighborhood. Everyone was younger than she'd been when she lived here. All carried laptop bags and stared through the homeless as though they didn't exist. Some of the young residents wore headsets and nodded and talked to the air. They were clean in a way she just couldn't recall. Shining and, somehow, ready.

If there were remodeled houses she might have recognized

among the condos and duplexes, she couldn't tell. Everywhere she looked were private gates, security fences, signs warning of dire consequences for anyone who dared to linger too long. Some fences were marked with bits of graffiti. Others gleamed with new paint. One new building after another lined the streets.

Jane found she was accelerating, walking with a more and more urgent desire to locate the old theatre. She searched in every direction for at least one plain, old, lived-in home. Every surface seemed fresh. She sped up and rounded another corner.

Coming suddenly into full autumn light, she drew a sharp breath. For this was it, the ungentrified neighborhood she was seeking. A tumbling-down gray Victorian spread its weed-clotted lawn salaciously to the sidewalk. No fence, no KEEP OUT signs. A fat, lived-in Craftsman sported two armchairs and a ceramic bong on the porch. A shiver ran through the wind chimes as Jane passed. The next place was three stories high, with filthy, arched windows. The paint was peeling off in great scabs onto the yellow grass.

It was all so familiar; Jane felt she must be close to the theatre. This had to be the street, a lone survivor among newly scrubbed and over-managed, younger beauties. A compelling sense that she was just about to arrive grew stronger with every step. Even the maples lining this block retained some of their color, ruby and saffron burning away beneath the brightened sky.

With her face lifted toward the maple and alder canopy, Jane didn't see the man lying facedown on the ground until she drew alongside him. When he caught her eye she stopped abruptly. From the sidewalk she studied the man's back, wondering what to do, waiting for signs of life. His damp black and gray hair, his jeans and ruined corduroy jacket, suggested youth and old age at the same time.

Jane stood there for an agonizing moment. Then she saw the man stir. She could hear him. Breathing. Trying to breathe. A deep rattle reverberated down in his chest. His arms and legs were bony, brittle, and delicate. He began, with infinite slowness, to edge forward. Struggling, coughing, trying to raise himself on shaky, arthritic arms, both hands pressed flat against the icy dirt, he started to crane his neck, turning his head in her direction, as if to speak directly to her, as if to speak her name.

Before the man could lift his face, before she would be forced to look into his eyes, to see him as he was, a pitiful animal on hands and knees, Jane turned and walked away. Back the way she had come. Out of the only neighborhood she knew. Heart thumping in her ribcage. Chin set against the rising cold. Following an instinct she barely understood. Running away, quickly and silently, with all of her might.

DEATH AND DISBURSEMENT

Isn't it strange, the number of trivial things we can't help remembering, useless phone numbers of dead relatives, songs we listened to in high school? Compare this to the multitude of cherished memories our brains will jettison before we die. I often wonder what purpose memory serves. Are we only collecting, and sorting, bits of information to help us get through another day? Then why is it, at this time of year, when children dress up as ghouls and monsters and their parents worry about the dangerous people they might run into while trick-or-treating, my mind always wanders back to Garrison Reynolds?

I worked at Northwestern Residential Life for six years in a stuffy, file- and paper-strewn office in downtown Seattle. During the first two years I handled Disbursement payments. I have no idea how many accounts I processed during my tenure. Most of the clients must be dead by now.

"No Rest," as we called it, started out as an insurance firm in the 1950s, building a modest reputation during the post-war

189

housing boom. By the '80s, when they decided to branch out, regulations restricting stock investment to brokers had loosened up. Like a lot of corporations with only a sideways connection to portfolio management, No Rest seized the opportunity. Management created a sales team to specialize in retirement plans for K-12 schoolteachers, and the company made a fortune.

By the time I worked there in the late '90s the heat wave of ridiculous prosperity was winding down. Sales incentives had dwindled from first class vacations in Bangkok to a weekend of whale watching in Port Townsend. Other signs of trouble were emerging, rumors of financial impropriety coiling upward to the executive level. Most of us didn't care. We were making a living. The rumors only mattered to people who could recall the company's original mission statement, something lofty about hard work paying off.

Many of our clients had difficulty remembering my name. They grappled with health concerns and family issues that had festered over the years. They struggled to communicate through a haze of medication and dementia. In my mind, most of these people are now indistinguishable from one another. Yet I remember Garrison Reynolds and what happened to him with absolute clarity.

That year the Midwest was hit by a freak snowstorm a few days before Halloween. For once I didn't mind living in Seattle where the rainy season ran from October until early July. Cable news channels covered the escalating storm with on-the-scene reporters bundled in parkas, their eyes squinting in the blistering cold, voices intoning the latest weather statistics with an underscoring shiver. One reporter was killed when a van overturned and skidded onto the shoulder of the road where he stood waiting for his camera crew to set up. At least a thousand times the network repeated video coverage of the reporter turning and catching only a shadow of the massive white wall sliding toward him. He seemed to be drawing breath, presumably to scream, before he was obliterated by snow.

A few weeks earlier I had chosen Death over Disbursement, and for good reasons. First and foremost, I disliked talking to retirees on the phone all day. It was a job I'd survived for two years with plenty of coffee and too many snacks, and by using a characteristic I'm not proud to admit. Actually it was a skill, one I'd developed while my mother was in the last phase of her illness. When necessary I could withdraw from another person, swiftly and silently gliding backward into the shadows. From there I could peer out at the world and feel nothing. I became a ghost, a presence with no connection to the situation. This made me a prime candidate to deal with the tough cases: the crying octogenarian who insisted her dead sister was stealing her monthly checks; the schizophrenic man who inherited his father's account and called every other month to register a change of address.

People told me I was good at customer service, a real "people person," and I accepted the compliment. But it wasn't true. I was patient and helpful with each client because they didn't matter to me. My aim was to do my job well, not save the world.

At the beginning of my third year, Disbursement hired a new gal, Bonnie, to answer the phones. Bonnie was given the early shift, seven a.m. to three p.m., to cover calls from back east. Another associate handled the nine-to-five shift.

Bonnie was needed because I'd been promoted to fill a gap on the Death team. I tried to conceal my relief. After you've spent a couple of years listening to elderly people gripe about their rotten health and hateful children, it's a luxury to sit quietly in a private cubicle filling out paperwork to make their postmortem retirement funds the property of those same hateful children. Best of all, no one wanted Death. Older employees found it distasteful. New associates found it boring. I could pace myself because there was no competition for the job.

High on the list of reasons I was happy to leave Disbursement and take up the surprising backlog of Death was Garrison Reynolds. In many ways a typical client, Reynolds called Disbursement at least four times a month and every call lasted half an hour. No matter how often I reminded him of the due date for his retirement check—the 30th—he would begin dialing on the 20th or 25th. All because his payment had arrived a week early one time and he wanted to know why it wasn't early every month.

His impatience wasn't unusual. Quite a few of our clients led a frugal existence. Some lived desperately, the ones who had failed to invest enough cash before time ran out and they were pushed away by the employers they'd counted on for a living and a purpose.

Reynolds wasn't desperate. His mortgage was paid. He and his wife had no children. He didn't call Disbursement out of need. He called because he had no friends. No one wanted to talk to him. He had no hobbies aside from harassing the people who handled what was left of his money.

"Yes, I understand. I get it, I do." Bonnie's voice carried through the wall to my cubicle. I could hear the strain when she stammered, "We mailed the end-of-month checks two days ago, but we have no control over the weather. Sir? Sir? We're dealing with a very unusual, natural event. Sir? If we replace the payment now, it will just be delayed like the first one. Your best bet is to wait for the original check to arrive."

She paused and I imagined I heard the faint buzz of Garrison Reynolds on the line. In his gruff intonations he was, no doubt, telling Bonnie what she could do with her opinion.

In Seattle the season was in full swing. We'd had four consecutive days of rain. Not refreshing or cleansing but drizzling, a perpetual cosmic leak over the industrial-gray city. On storefront windows the scarecrows and black cats stood out in the glaucous wash. Doorsteps were cluttered with jack-o-lanterns.

At night the streets, ordinarily etched blue-black, were softened by the dull glow of orange lights and candles in windows. The Midwest snow and ice seemed far away, telescoped, a vague human-interest story flickering on TV screens.

"Sir," Bonnie said. Her voice cracked. "Sir, if you're going to speak to me like that, I have no choice. Mr. Reynolds? Mr. Reynolds? I have to hang up now. Sir? I have to hang up."

The next sound was the receiver snapping into place. Cutting off the tirade but not soon enough to prevent a crying jag. I rolled my eyes when I heard Bonnie whip a couple of tissues out of the Kleenex box on her desk and trudge around the corner to my cubicle.

"Katie," she said. Her lips were quivering from the struggle to stay calm. "I'm sorry to interrupt you."

I looked up from the files and forms on my desk, and refrained from laughing. Bonnie was still new. Maybe she would toughen up. Otherwise she would surely have to find another job. Talking to depressed or angry seniors and hearing the stray facts of their ever-diminishing lives would kill her if she didn't put some distance between herself and their misery.

"Bonnie, you can't take it personally," I said.

She drew a halting breath. She dabbed the corners of her eyes with the tissues crumpled in her hand.

"He asked me if I'm retarded," she said. "And. Well, we don't even use that word in my family. Or any of the other words he used."

"That's what I mean by personal," I explained. "It doesn't matter how you feel or what you do in your family. The person on the phone is a client. Nothing he says to you should be taken to heart. Just listen to his complaint and reassure him. If you decide his case warrants a replacement check, forward the details to one of the clerks in Accounting."

"His check isn't due until Thursday," she said, fighting a second wave of tears.

"Great," I told her. "Don't worry about it."

"He's called twice this morning. He said he's going to call every day because he already knows his check is going to be late."

"Because of the storm."

"He doesn't even watch the news. He says his check is late every month and it's my fault."

"All he has to do is look out the window," I said. "The storm's knocked out mail delivery. As of last night, even the FedEx office had to shut down."

"Oh God," Bonnie said. "What am I going to do? Kirk is out sick with the flu. He might not be back all week. Every time Reynolds calls, he'll get me!"

I was still young enough back then to feel a sliver of contempt for Bonnie in her sprawling Eddie Bauer sweater, her olive drab skirt and leggings. When she'd dressed that morning she must have believed herself to be fortified against a world she feared at every turn.

"Fine. Forward his calls to me," I said. "Only Garrison Reynolds and only this week." And because I'd written her off in that instant, deciding she would never succeed in Disbursement, I returned to my paperwork and ignored her blubbery thanks.

On the bus ride home that night, bone-tired from all the tedious facets of my job, I stared out the window at wet, black streets. House after house went gliding by, glowing with amber light, decked with festive pumpkins and cartoon witches. The homes looked warm and snug, but who knows what went on inside them.

The smooth hiss of electric cable overhead and the gentle rocking of the bus lulled me. In the dim alleys neighborhood cats traced a path from doors and gates to trash dumpsters and back. In my nearly dreaming state I imagined the shadows growing long and narrow, then separating into a multitude of dark figures scuttling between muted streetlights.

I almost expected Bonnie to call in sick the next day. But she sat straight-backed and smiling at her desk when I arrived. Apparently my taking over her least favorite client gave her a lift. I said good morning and she waved one hand toward a plate of muffins.

"These are home-baked pumpkin spice," she said. "Have one. Have two."

I'd barely sat down and arranged my desk for the day when the first call came through, a transfer from Bonnie. As I picked up the receiver I heard her voice on the other side of the cubicle wall.

"Sorry, Katie!"

"Northwestern Residential Life, Death Claims, how can I help you?" I said automatically.

There was a distinct pause on the line. Then came the sputter of an old man clearing his throat.

"What?" he asked. "What did you say?"

"Sorry, Mr. Reynolds," I replied. "This is Katie. I've been promoted to another team. How can I help you today?"

"What kind of a team?" he asked, his voice full of phlegm.

"I'm on a different team now. I've switched from Disbursement to another team."

"Why don't you call it a department?" he said.

"A team is a department," I said. "It's the same thing. What can I do for you today?"

"Well, if it's the same goddamn thing, why the hell don't you call it the same thing?"

This was his typical strategy. Bait and attack, lure and argue.

"Mr. Reynolds," I said gently and firmly. "How can I help you?"

"What happened to that other girl? She got sick of me, didn't she?"

I was holding the receiver in my left hand. This made it possible to continue filling out forms with my right.

"Mr. Reynolds, you're a valued client. We never get sick of you," I said.

"You're a goddamn liar." He cleared his throat again, a hacking, viscous wave ending in a cough. I waited until he stopped.

"Aren't we all?" I asked.

The hacking noise rose again, and expanded. It could have been wheezing but once it developed a rhythm I realized he was wheeze-laughing like a despicable cartoon character. I waited until he calmed down.

"A liar is lavish of oaths," he said at last. "Where's my check?"

"I've seen the weekly report," I said. "And your payment was mailed on time. I confirmed the date with Accounting."

"So, where is it?" he asked.

"Tomorrow is the 30th," I reminded him. "And the 30th is your due date."

"Don't give me that bunk!"

"Remember when you signed the contract to begin your pay-out?" I said. "The date you chose was the 30th. Since today is the 29th, your check isn't due. If it doesn't arrive tomorrow, please let us know."

A rustle on the line followed by a loud click let me know that Garrison Reynolds was gone. I sat staring at the small ceramic tableau on my desk: a Cadillac containing three manic skeletons dressed in dark clothing, holding down a figure with flailing arms and legs. Meanwhile a crimson Satan with silver horns sat laughing at the wheel. The tableau had been a Day of the Dead gift from an artist my mother used to know in Austin. It was the only office decoration I ever displayed on Halloween; its bright colors gave me a lift. Something in the devil's expression was strangely amusing.

"Go to hell, Mr. Reynolds," I said under my breath.

The rest of the day was quiet. I was able to hit my average in processing claims, so I treated myself to a Donut Day cruller at afternoon break. The sugar made me dopey. I almost fell asleep on the bus ride home.

On Thursday when I arrived at the office, Bonnie was absent from her desk. I imagined she had spent the first two hours of her day apologizing to Midwest clients for the delay in their payments. Two lines blinked on her phone. The Kleenex box lay on its side near a scattering of M&Ms. I took off my raincoat and hit one of the blinking buttons.

"Northwestern Residential Life, Disbursement," I said. "Would you hold, please?" I put the client on hold before he could speak. I hit the second button and repeated the greeting then placed the second client on hold. Finally I answered the first call.

"Residential Life, Disbursement. How can I help you?"

A damp wheeze identified the caller. He seemed to gather his words from a distance.

"What happened?" Garrison Reynolds asked. "Did you get demoted?"

He recognized my voice. I squared my shoulders. I forced a smile. Clients, my training had taught me, can hear a smile in the tone of your voice. The facial muscles contract even if the expression is false.

"Good morning, Mr. Reynolds," I said.

"It's lunch time where I live," he said. "And there's no check in the mailbox."

"Right," I said, visualizing the address in our database. "Illinois. Wow. You're in the thick of it. How are you doing?"

"I'd be doing a lot better with a check in my hand. You said to wait. You wasted my time."

Something caught my eye and I turned to see Bonnie striding back from the women's bathroom. She was clutching tissues in both hands and her face was a patchwork of pink splotches. She must have been crying for a while. She nodded but avoided making eye contact when she took her seat.

"Mr. Reynolds," I said. "Hold for a moment while I transfer you to my phone, all right?"

I took my time putting away my raincoat and settling at my desk. I saw the button light up when Bonnie forwarded the call. I heard her placating the next client in line. I paused for another couple of seconds, hoping in vain that he might give up and go away.

"All right, then," I said when I picked up the line.

"What's going on there?" Reynolds asked. "A goddamn party? I don't want to hear any more music. Stop putting me on hold."

"Sorry for the delay," I said.

"You can keep your apology. You and that Asian girl you hired to answer the phone."

Among his many charms Garrison Reynolds could count racism. After a knee-jerk impulse to thwart his assumptions by pointing out that Bonnie's family was Norwegian, I decided to ignore the comment.

"I'm sure I can answer any questions you have."

"Good luck!" he said. "Where's my fucking check?"

Somewhere in his original file I'd noticed that he had been a History teacher at a middle school for twenty-five years. I wondered if he'd spoken to students the way he spoke to us. How much was his wretched personality and how much of the salty sailor routine was put on for my benefit? Probably only his wife knew the answer. I pitied her.

"How's the weather in your neighborhood?" I asked.

"What?"

"Is it snowing in your part of Illinois?" I said.

"Hell, yes," he said. "The whole neighborhood's covered in it. What do you think?"

"Well, Mr. Reynolds," I said. "What you can see from your living room window is pretty much the same all over the Midwest at the moment. Even the FedEx office had to shut down for a day. Planes are grounded. Buses have stopped running. And the mail is delayed."

"The mail is never delayed," he said. "What about their motto, about rain and sleet?"

"I'm afraid the postal service has met its match this year."

"What are you telling me?" he said.

"This is a regional, possibly national crisis. It affects everyone."

"So?"

I had to marvel at the self-involvement of the old man. The little tableau of skeletons, holding their captive for the benefit of Satan in the driver's seat, made me smile, a genuine smile this time.

"No one is getting their mail," I said. "If we issued a new payment you wouldn't receive it."

He was silent for a moment. I could hear him murmuring in the background, as if he held his hand over the mouthpiece while he spoke to someone.

"Mr. Reynolds?"

"I'll call you back," he said. And he hung up.

I barely had time to feel fortunate before the light began to blink again. From the other cubicle I heard Bonnie's apology.

"Sorry, Katie, I'm so sorry. He's back," she warned as I answered the phone.

"Mr. Reynolds?" I said by way of greeting.

"Listen," he said, his voice reduced to a deep rasp. "I have to have that money."

"But I just explained…"

"I need it!" he said. "It's mine and I want it right now. Right now!"

"I would help you if I could," I said. "Didn't I replace a check that was lost in the mail last year? So you know, I only want to do what's right."

"Shut up!" he snarled.

"Excuse me?"

"Stop talking and talking," he said. His voice broke. "I don't have time. I need, I need my money right now. It belongs to me and you owe it to me."

"Mr. Reynolds, if there were any possible way..."

"No!" He was shouting again. "I need it this afternoon. Before it gets dark. They're coming back!"

I stopped staring at the little crimson devil with his silver horns and his grin of cruel delight.

"Mr. Reynolds," I said. "Could I speak to your wife for a moment?"

"Why?"

"Oh," I said, mind racing through a series of flimsy excuses. "I was reading your file yesterday and I realized we don't have her social security number listed."

"What difference does that make?"

If his nasty idiosyncrasies had all been a precursor to Alzheimer's maybe his wife should know about these multiple calls and complaints. I decided to lie to him.

"Before I can issue a new check, I'll need to fill in the information gap."

"Why?" he asked. "You've been paying me all this time without it."

"Yes," I said. "But now I know it's missing from the account."

"That's goddamn ridiculous! I want my money!"

"No," I said. Might as well make the lie as big as it needed to be, I decided. "If I can't speak to your wife I'm afraid I'll have to cancel your payment."

"What? What?" He was sputtering. "You can't keep my

money. I earned all of it. I spent years and years with those little monsters..."

The line went dead. Bonnie stepped into my cubicle. She had a strange expression, now that her tears had dried.

"What was all that about?" she asked.

"I'm not sure he's lucid," I told her.

"Oh my God." Bonnie shook her head. "Has he had a stroke?"

"Look," I said. "Later on, maybe I'll call his house and try to get hold of his wife. She should know how irrational he's become."

"That's so sad," she said. "Do you think she'll have him hospitalized?"

What a term. The same one I'd used when people asked how my mother was doing, in her final weeks.

"Poor Mr. Reynolds," Bonnie said.

It was irritating to make small talk like this about a client Bonnie couldn't handle. While we gossiped I was losing time I could have spent processing death claims. I started shuffling papers. Bonnie didn't take the hint. She stepped closer, and reached down to touch the Day of the Dead tableau with one index finger.

"You know," she said. "I actually took his first call this morning. About twenty minutes before you got here."

"Why didn't you say so? It would've helped to know he was already wound up."

"That's just it," she said. "I think he was wound up before he talked to me. He screamed at me. So I told him we wouldn't take his call until he calmed down."

"Well, Christ, Bonnie," I said. "Thanks for the head's up."

Her eyes welled with tears. I snatched a tissue from a box on the file cabinet and handed it to her. She sniffled and caught her breath.

"Katie," she said. "He sounded kind of crazy. He said

something was after him."

"Who?"

"Not who, I think, not a person. He said it was something hiding in the vacant lot next to his house. It freaked me out and I hung up on him. I'm so sorry!"

For the rest of the day I tried to push those words out of my thoughts. I reviewed notarized proof of identity and powers of attorney from two middle-aged brothers who were having their 80-year-old mother declared incompetent and placed in a nursing home. Placed. That was another one of those polite words.

Reynolds didn't call again all day. I didn't try to reach his wife. I decided to let sleeping dogs lie.

Every time Bonnie passed my cubicle she glanced at me with a ghastly expression I think she mistook for some kind of camaraderie, a sort of "we're all in this mess together" look. She frowned and shrugged at the same time. I don't know what she hoped to elicit with this ugly pantomime. It didn't matter because we didn't hear from Reynolds again that afternoon.

This time I fell asleep on the bus. October in Seattle is a dark night, pitch black under a slate cover of clouds. Condensation collected in the heated bus and ran in snaky streams down the windows. The throb of the electric cables, the too warm interior of the bus once it filled with bodies, the dark blur of Capitol Hill streets flashing by, acted like a narcotic on my frayed nerves. I only knew we reached my stop, and my head jerked forward into consciousness, because the driver knew my schedule. His shout had caught my ear in the middle of a dream.

The screech of brakes woke me. The driver sat at the front of the bus looking back over his shoulder at me.

"You're here," he said. His voice carried all the way to the back where I sat sprawled between my purse and my canvas grocery bag.

"What are you doing?" he asked.

I sat up straight and for the first time it occurred to me. If all of the passengers were gone, we must be at the end of the line, not at my stop. We must have passed my house an hour ago. I was going to point this out but I was alone and the lights and heat were off. I tried to calculate how long the warmth sealed inside the bus would last, and this made me drowsy.

When I woke up the bus was freezing, and it was moving. Not forward but slightly, minutely side-to-side. Every window dripped with condensation and in the center of each one a pair of hands pressed against the glass, pushing in, rocking the bus like a cradle.

When I woke up another passenger was poking me in the shoulder with an index finger. She had a malicious grin. The driver waited for me to collect myself and amble up the aisle. It felt like an expedition. I had to use my elbows to shove past several men dressed as devils and witches. They laughed good-naturedly. Someone said, "Happy Halloween, ma'am!"

If I slept at all that night it was intermittent with frantic dreams of trains and bus stations, boarding houses without doors, and neighbors I didn't recognize drifting through.

Nothing was safe. Every drifter stole something: a trunk full of clothes I kept intending to sort; the hummingbirds that gathered around a feeder on the porch in late spring; my mother's silver combs; the Japanese maple in the back yard. When my room was empty except for a sheet on the floor, I lay down and tried to sleep but my mind raced with dates and times from a half-remembered itinerary. I was supposed to be somewhere. It was time to go. Any delay would cause me to miss my connection and then the next one. I tried to stand up but my body clung to inertia. The floor absorbed my full weight. It brought back those times at the end of yoga class when I dozed off while lying flat on my back. The ground held me.

The only thing that got me out of bed and into work the next day was the allure of coffee and Halloween cupcakes supplied by management. They never missed a holiday but as the company's value decreased over the ensuing years the holiday treats would diminish from bakery delicacies to bags of candy purchased in bulk at Costco.

The first call came at nine-thirty. When I heard Garrison Reynolds wheezing I was glad to be so groggy. My sleep deprivation acted as a sedative to take the edge off his words.

"The mailman never came," he told me. He sounded stunned, childlike in the face of something he couldn't explain.

"Yes," I said. "That's because of the snow. You're due for warmer temperatures this weekend, Mr. Reynolds. The ice will melt and you'll probably have your check and the rest of your mail on Monday."

"It's too late now," he said. "They're coming back. You lied to me."

"Mr. Reynolds," I said. "Would you mind putting your wife on the phone?"

"She's gone. She's outside. There should be a newspaper in the driveway. They stole it."

I couldn't tell whether he was telling the truth or describing what he thought was true.

"When Mrs. Reynolds comes back," I said, "will you ask her to give me a call?"

"Comes back?"

"Yes," I said. "Tell her I have some questions. Will you do that?"

"She comes back?"

"Yes."

"They won't stay outside, now," he said. "You fucked that up." Then he hung up the phone.

All day I anticipated another conversation with Reynolds or his wife or both. I wondered, briefly, if Mrs. Reynolds had finally gotten sick of his temper, or his dementia, and left him. But surely a woman who had coped with this man for over forty years wasn't going to abandon him now. Yet I felt a twinge of guilt when Bonnie wished me good night before she left the office for the weekend.

"Happy Halloween!" she said. "Watch out for ghosties and witches and whatchamacallits. I'm dressing as a vampire when I get home. The kids love it."

"You get a lot of trick-or-treaters, in the rain?" I asked.

"Tons! I bought six bags of candy to make sure I don't run out. They get so mad when you run out."

"Do they?"

"Oh, we've got some little devils in my neighborhood," she said. "You know, I wonder if that's what Old Man Reynolds was yelling about. I bet he hates this time of year."

"He doesn't seem very happy, no," I said.

"Is he okay?"

Again I had a twinge of irritation. Bonnie wore a jack-o-lantern button pinned to her coat. When she moved the eyes seemed to glow.

"I'm sure he'll get his check on Monday," I said. "And I can't believe any kids will stop by his house in the snow and ice. When I was a kid we all knew the cranky people on our street, and we stayed away."

"Sure."

"What?" I asked.

"I don't know. Do you think we should call the police?"

"Why?"

"To stop by, and make sure he's okay?"

I considered Bonnie's wide-eyed expression and decided to lie again.

"Sure," I said. "I'll do that."

She waved goodbye even though she was standing right in front of my desk. She was smiling like a child who's just been tucked in after a really good fairy tale. Like most people, Bonnie only wanted to be told everything was fine.

Afternoon crept into dark night. I took the bus home. Opening the front door, I was greeted by the familiar combination of patchouli and mildew. It was a scent that had lingered since my mother occupied the house. There were nights when the hint of patchouli tricked me into thinking I heard her voice, the voices of her friends murmuring in another room. Her lifelong pals with their shoulder-length hair and their poems about the city haunted by spirits. How many hundreds of nights I must have fallen asleep to these whispered tales of loss and longing.

Three children came to my door on Friday night, wearing handmade masks. I couldn't tell what they were supposed to be but I controlled the urge to laugh at their lack of artistic talent. Their parents huddled at the curb wearing hooded rain jackets and sheepish grins. When the children stopped giggling and went away with their chocolate treasures, I tossed the bag of barely touched candy in the garbage and went to bed. Twice I woke up thinking the phone was ringing, only to find the sound had carried over from a dream.

On Saturday I shopped and read magazines. On Sunday the rain stopped for a few hours. Patches of gray and yellow light broke through the clouds. Neighbors appeared on the street, walking dogs or just enjoying the fresh air.

Cable news reported a slight rise in temperatures and the beginning of what they dubbed the Big Thaw. Rain melted what was left of the premature Midwest snow and the rest of the country lost interest.

The following week I worked with hardly a break. Bonnie never transferred any calls and never stopped by to say hello. That month I set a new record for claim processing and felt very pleased with my progress.

Every night I took the bus home, watched an hour of mind-numbing TV, and fell asleep. I dreamed about the bus many times, and when I woke up I had the sense that I'd forgotten something. The more I tried to recall what it was, the more vague my memory became.

In early December several new claims arrived in the mail. One stood out immediately. Before I opened it I stared at the return address for a long time.

Garrison Reynolds, age 73, deceased October 31st. Cause of death was a self-inflicted shotgun wound to the head. His primary beneficiary, his wife, was deceased on October 30th, an apparent heart attack. The account and its remaining funds would go to a secondary beneficiary, a nephew in Chicago.

I completed the paperwork in less than an hour. There were dozens of claims ahead of this one but something compelled me to bump it up and get it off my desk.

I went home early that day. I drank a cup of chamomile tea. Surrounded by the fragrance of patchouli, I lay in bed all night listening to the cold rain dripping from the roof to the damp ground. Sometimes I thought I heard a telephone, distant and isolated, as if it rang in a vacant house down the street.

STRANGE IS THE NIGHT

Rain cut diagonal streaks down the windows of offices and shops all over the city. Where the asphalt had been laid by cheap contractors, puddles overflowed in the potholes, displacing gravel and slowing traffic to less than ten miles an hour. Occasionally a driver would lose patience with his timid compatriots and hit the gas pedal in a panic, only to be stranded without a lane at the next intersection.

By late afternoon, counter to the direction of the storm, dusk began to crawl over the hills and down to the bay. Darkness spread quickly to half a dozen residential neighborhoods where Craftsman houses nestled between modular condos and homeowners competed for a view of urban greenery, although the parks were flooded for most of the winter and spring. There were so many more residents than the city planners ever expected. Street parking had become a vicious contest.

In his cubicle on the second floor of a converted warehouse on 12th Avenue, Pierce regarded the ceiling, listening.

The storm continued with infinite patience. A growl of thunder overhead and Pierce imagined the ceiling cracking open, his oblong, cumbersome body drawn upward, sucked out of his ergonomic chair into the ebony sky. He regained composure with a measured pivot of the chair from left to right and from right to left, willing the dreadful weather away.

A photo occupied the center of his computer screen, a headshot of a young woman. Maybe nineteen, maybe twenty, she swayed and smiled uncertainly at the edges of his memory. Moon face; chestnut bob; an underlying fragrance, a mixture of honey and lemon zest.

"Plump," Pierce said to himself. "Not pleasantly, just plump, a fat kindergartner offering to share candy." Remembering irritated his sense of order.

He glanced at the open envelope and splayed invitation on his desk, an arrival in that morning's mail. Expensively engraved lettering, cream-colored paper with an elaborate seal. The wax had been shaped like a delicate hieroglyph, probably a company logo, now broken in half. A stray bit of the saffron wax had dropped between the C and the V on his keyboard.

Ordinarily Pierce hated these attempts at wooing him with media kits. A week earlier a playwright had mailed him a rubber rodent in a nest of straw with a copy of her seventy-page monologue, *Memoir of a Rat King*. Pierce had tossed the package into the trash. He considered the same fate for the expensive invitation with its wax seal. But the oddly familiar words of the enclosed poem piqued his curiosity.

Song of my soul, my voice is dead...

He had read the lines before. No. Had he heard them spoken? The phrases kept teasing him. If he said them out loud he felt sleepy and warm.

The girl's photo, her insouciant grin, had occupied his computer screen when he'd returned from lunch. No one would own up to playing pranks on Pierce. The girl's face had annoyed him all afternoon. He recollected her scent but not her name. Her face was so much like all the others.

He clicked through several issues of the online edition, scanning his reviews from the previous spring and summer. When he spotted the word "porcine," he stopped.

Well, it was true, wasn't it? At least he hadn't called her "fat." People were so sensitive about everything these days. Who could keep up with the ever-shifting nomenclature?

When Pierce went to school, name-calling had been almost mandatory, certainly expected. Bullying was a required chapter in the adventure of growing up. So his father had reminded Pierce every time he limped home to bury his bruised face in a pillow. But he had toughened up, and that was the point.

No wonder the paper's interns acted like children. They were raised on faint praise and false promises, their education designed to accommodate weakness, delicate bones padded against injury, protected from the world for as long as possible. From pre-school to the first job interview, no one ever told them the truth. Pierce could make them cry just by hiding their personalized coffee cups.

He had known the wrath of the sensitive all too well. He'd lost his chance at a coveted teaching assistant position at Berkeley over an ironic appropriation of the term "pickaninny" in his graduate thesis. The department chair had made an example, rejecting his application, to the satisfaction—in some cases barely concealed glee—of everyone involved. In a final twist, the teaching assignment that would have assured his success went to the young Rhodes Scholar who had accused him of racism.

The name listed in his review and the photo on his screen merged: Molly Mundy, roly-poly, round as a baby and just as free of guile. "Porcine."

If anything, Pierce had been kind. Molly Mundy had been

one of those girls who drive up the coast from Beaverton or Pine Hollow, move in with a houseful of slovenly friends, acquire jobs waiting tables or babysitting, and spend every minute dashing between acting classes and auditions, eyes sparkling, lips parted, betraying a bottomless hunger Pierce found repugnant. Each girl a special snowflake, a thousand snowflakes every year, and despite dozens of fringe theatres and a few equity houses, the city couldn't support their fantasies. There was no film industry to speak of, only a couple of TV series, and very little commercial work, only theatre with its physical demands and non-existent pay.

Eventually all but a few of the snowflakes would drift back home to settle, in every sense. They would gain weight, fry their hair with henna streaks and home perms, and marry men they didn't love, men they wouldn't have glanced at when they'd thought of themselves as ingénues. They would birth another generation of unremarkable girls named Molly, who longed to be famous for some glittering accomplishment beyond their reach. Pierce clicked on the photo and dragged the moon-faced young woman to the trash.

**

All afternoon there had been lulls between the spells of icy rain. Again and again the storm subsided; then came another swell of clouds. In the evening, after rush hour, the dark streets grew sullen beneath the shivering damp.

"In short…" Pierce mumbled, hunched over his computer. His fingers arched and quivered above the keyboard. He was on deadline with another six hundred words to go.

"In *brief*…" Hurley corrected, sidling up to spy over one shoulder. Hurley's gag-inducing aftershave followed, a slowly evaporating shadow.

Pierce regained focus and nodded. Everyone knew Hurley

was the worst editor-in-chief in the paper's history. He had attained a degree of incompetence and self-regard of which legends are constructed. He liked to stride around and sneak up on his writers, offering pearls and threatening extinction.

"In brief…" Pierce corrected the onscreen text. He continued, "Actors ought to use their well-trained bodies to act. They should not reveal their intellectual shortcomings like stained underwear at fundraising summits…"

"Good! Whip the losers into shape!"

Hurley clapped him on the shoulder and strode away in the direction of his office, the only one with a door. Editors and staff writers who had survived the last cut occupied cubicles with peeling walls ranged across one cavernous room. Underlings, mostly interns, divided their cubicles into smaller, shabbier units resembling rabbit hutches. The only remaining senior editor commanded a medium-size cubicle and worked at a lectern to give the illusion of more floor space. All labored under the shadow of the weekly paper's name, painted across the windows of the eastern wall. The paper occupied half of the second floor in a building that housed a healing arts studio, an herbal tea emporium, and a thrift shop.

"Corner of Zen and Mothballs," Pierce quipped whenever someone asked for the address.

He relaxed the muscles across his back as soon as Hurley walked away. He'd escaped torment this time. Hurley of the many backslaps also enjoyed impromptu wrestling matches and headlocks. He was a boy with an indestructible trust fund, a guy's guy who bragged about squandering his education and didn't believe in matching furniture. Behind that lone door lurked a monstrosity of post-modern decor shot through with an odor of moldering jockstraps.

A rumble of thunder brought Pierce to his senses. He typed. He forgot Hurley. Words raced across the screen.

Only two hundred words from his objective, Pierce was

making excellent time when he noticed Ali Franco staring at him from her cubicle across the aisle.

"Problem, Ali?"

Instantly he regretted acknowledging her. The pause was negligible. She must have been biding her time, waiting for an invitation. She strolled the short distance to his desk and stood watching him type.

"Why the heck do you do it?" she asked.

Typically cryptic Ali Franco, with her intuition, her healing blog, her spirit guides and crystal skulls, or were they balls? In the evening she burned aromatherapy candles at her desk. They made the office stink of green tea and wax and another note he couldn't identify, a spice he found irritating. Ali Franco, with all of her woo-woo (or was it voodoo? Or hoodoo?) was unwittingly doomed.

Only a month earlier Pierce had conned Hurley into a drunken ramble across Capitol Hill. The idiot-in-chief confided; he was ditching Franco's column. She didn't know it yet. How about that for intuition? Pierce had to laugh. He was keeping quiet but it was killing him.

"When are you breaking the news?" Pierce had asked.

"Sometime next month." When he wasn't smirking Hurley puffed on a twenty-dollar cigar.

"When the moon is full and the wolf bane blooms at night?" Pierce asked.

They had laughed and laughed.

"What is the subject of your question, Ali?"

Even her name offended him, short for Alice, with the same number of syllables, and pronounced "alley." She had been with the paper forever.

Pierce went on typing. His plan was to meet the word count, let it rest, and see a show. He would come in early next day, freshen things up, and hand over the week's reviews to the proofreader.

Ali Franco was wearing a shapeless gown of the 1970s, something his mother might have worn, a caftan or an afghan. Franco said she "collected" them at flea markets and sometimes the thrift shop downstairs, information that made his skin crawl. Worse, she kept shifting the garment, folding and tucking and then resting in it like a Shar-Pei swaddled in flesh.

Franco said, "Seriously, my friend. Aren't you embarrassed to write like that, at *your* age?"

Pierce raised his eyebrows. "'Seriously?' Aren't you embarrassed to talk like that, at your age?"

She reeked of incense with an under-layer of something. Sweat? Ginger? It made him sneeze if she stood near him for too long.

"Look, I write the way I write, Ali."

Instantly, Pierce decided to skip the performance he'd planned to see. It was a well-made play with a pretty good cast and a respectable director. His review would be a bore.

He was feeling the need to sharpen his knives, to practice his critical skills on a sacrificial lamb. To that end he would give this new company his full attention. The invitation was both pretentious and last minute. The upstarts had the nerve to offer a guest-only preview, basically a dress rehearsal at which the actors would undoubtedly stumble over their lines. It was taking place in a warehouse down the street on the very night the card was delivered to his office. Ridiculous. He would go. The resulting profile of their incompetence might do them good.

"You don't even like theatre anymore, do you?"

Pierce swiveled in his chair to face Ali Franco, who hadn't moved an inch. It was too much, the way she crept around challenging colleagues with her political stand against killing small things with big eyes, and her objection to microwaves and mammograms and some other M thing. His chest burned with a desire to shout, "You're being fired, you hag! Good luck getting another job in your sixties!"

No. He would shake her hand when the time came. It would be worth the wait to see the expression on her face as she marched her box of trinkets and her pictures of kittens and her spellbooks down the hall to the stairs.

"Why would you say that?" Pierce asked. "Of course I like theatre, when it's good. When it isn't good it's like watching someone cook and eat your intestines in front of you. Then having to write about it."

"There are ways to write about it, without doing damage."

"How would you know, Ali? Oh, sorry, I forgot. You wrote a couple of reviews back in the day, when it was just you and the publisher and the production manager keeping the lights on all night. You printed the paper yourselves and delivered it all over the city on your skateboards. What a time that must've been."

"U-Haul trucks, not skateboards. We put together a good paper," she said. "It was honest."

"Then why don't you like my reviews? I always tell the truth."

Pierce went back to work. Franco simply didn't understand his job. He couldn't give people a pat on the back if they were delusional. There were too many untalented artists in the world. Someone had to weed out the weak. Even if Pierce had overlooked their shortcomings, Hurley wouldn't stand for it. Hurley hated theatre, ranked it slightly above circus entertainment, the animal variety.

"Raise the bar on these fucking amateurs," he said, at least once a month. "If I'm going to keep a goddamn theatre section in this paper, it better be entertaining."

This is where Pierce always felt a pinch between his ribs. He had to steady himself. Any sign of fear and Hurley would chase him across the office, mocking his ungainly stride, knocking him to the floor, pinning him there and saying the one word that would destroy him. "Fired."

Sometimes Pierce woke in the morning, shivering with sweat, the word stomping through his head. He would lie in the pale dawn while the city cast jagged shadows across the art deco building where he had lived for twelve years. He would stare at his five hundred square feet of hardwood floors and fluted glass door knobs, and wonder if this studio would be the place where he would die someday, alone, shrouded in Irish linen.

A weekly gutting of theatrical ego granted Pierce two thousand words on pages forty-three and forty-four of the print edition. He wasn't about to let Ali Franco, or anyone else, interfere. Theatre magazines to which he'd once contributed lucrative features had gradually gone out of business. His day job was everything, financially speaking. Those two thousand words were all that separated Pierce from a world of illiterate bloggers, free-content hacks, and people who carried satchels containing sack lunches and the novels they were writing at the public library.

"You could get more people interested in seeing good work," Ali Franco said. "You could encourage artists to practice and mature."

He couldn't believe she was still standing in his cubicle. Staring at him. Resting her hands on her hips, Akimbo Ali.

"Dear woman," he said. "Everyone is interested in seeing good work. Most of the time, there isn't any. What I see on the stage doesn't please me. Since I have a degree in drama from one of the best universities in North America, I think it is safe to say that the work, rather than the critic, is—how do you say—'not good.'"

"You're jaded," she said.

Beyond the eastern window the black sky grated against rooftops and chimneys. Clouds kept shifting, threatening more abuse.

"Why don't you resign honorably, Pierce, while there's still time? You could write whatever you *feel*. Just follow your heart."

Franco's husband had given up a successful career in engineering and retired to a beachfront shop where he painted orcas on pieces of driftwood and sold them to tourists. Ever since he'd been commissioned by the mayor's office to create "an original driftwood," Franco had been urging all of her friends to quit their jobs and follow their hearts.

"My writing sells ads," Pierce said. "Keeping this section of the paper open. Without my acumen and dedication these artists wouldn't be properly reviewed. They would have only the enthusiasm of their friends to gauge their competence. They would live and die without knowing if they have real talent."

As if waiting for this moment, Franco unfolded a scrap of paper. She read out loud, "Astonishingly, in such a minor role, the porcine and barely audible Miss Mundy manages to ruin a production of Ibsen's best known play."

"I knew it!" Pierce said. "You left that photo on my computer, didn't you?"

Franco said nothing.

"I delivered a much-needed antidote to an amateurish approach," Pierce told her. "They were a company of teenagers rehearsing in a garage. If an actor has talent and devotion to craft, he should make a commitment to a decent school."

"For thirty or forty thousand dollars?" Franco asked. "Whatever happened to learning the basics and practicing?"

Arguing was pointless. The woman had to go. The paper's intended demographic was twenty-five to forty. They didn't need herbal tea concoctions, holistic flu remedies, and comforting advice from mom.

"You're forty-six years old!" Franco shouted.

Pierce glanced up and down the row of cubicles. No one

gophered; no one had the nerve.

"Forty-six," Franco repeated. "And writing like a middle-school boy with a grudge." She shook her head and walked away.

"Merciful fucking god," Pierce muttered.

***

By seven o'clock his text had been revised and set aside. Pierce left the office happy to know the next day would be easier than this one. He turned up his collar and ventured across the street.

The nearest café buzzed with fluorescent light, sweating condensation under white awning, a bright bowl of murmuring customers at every hour. Arrivals were announced by a tinkling bell attached to the glass door. Pierce decided an espresso would give him the boost he needed to survive new work by an unknown troupe with nothing to recommend them except an oddly compelling invitation.

The twin suns sink behind the lake...

He felt so tired, sometimes, and unappreciated.

***

After the debacle of his thesis Pierce had wanted very badly to stage his work, to prove his talent. He knew he would starve in New York or L.A., so he retired to his father's house in the Pacific Northwest. Standards were so much lower there. He decided it would make a good launching pad for his plays. Eventually his success here would become so great, New York would come calling.

His father's house was an impressive rambler spread across a hill with a view of Lake Union. Pierce was granted a small room with a private bath in the basement. There he wrote fiercely, madly, in his pajamas and t-shirts, for six years. A housekeeper left his meals on a tray outside the door. On rare occasions he had the run of the upstairs while his father took his trophy wife and children on vacations to Europe and the Caribbean.

Pierce wrote constantly. He seldom attended plays written by his contemporaries, or joined them in debates about the lack of funding and support for new work. Two or three examples of local playwriting confirmed his suspicion that his talent far exceeded their pitiable attempts. Their writing was derivative at best, hackneyed at worst. It was inexplicable how they continued to be produced. There were days, weeks, when the hunger to feel the raw sweetness of success left him jaundiced, sick and exhausted, unable to crawl out of bed, unable to face anyone.

Every theatre company in town rejected his plays, calling them "old-fashioned" and "over-written." Each new coffee date with an A.D. left him shaking, fighting back tears. He couldn't bear to live this way, un-produced, insignificant, while so many people carried on perfectly well without knowing he existed. When he raised the idea of starting his own theatre with a substantial family loan, his father disowned him, sent him packing with five hundred dollars and a one-month bus pass. Pierce made the money last as long as possible, for the thought of menial labor made him swoon with nausea and panic.

This is when a former classmate, Gwen, appeared. Pounding one of her silk-gloved fists against his door at a fleabag motel on Aurora. Black suede pumps neatly sidestepping stray piles of underwear and newspapers. Pursing her lips at the sight of moldy pizza. Offering him a salary to write for a weekly paper.

"Because, darling, I'm moving back to New York where I fucking belong, and I promised my editor a decent replacement."

And her first three choices had turned her down flat.

Pierce would inherit her readership. He could decide on the shows he wanted to cover and the artists he would profile. In short, he was to take over the theatre section, increase its popularity by any means necessary, and make it pay for itself. This was, she warned, a hard sell. Few artists could afford advertising. Theatre people needed discounts, special deals, and trades. They came begging for a mention, however harsh. Pierce said yes, yes, and his career (which would span three editors and five budget cuts) began the following day.

***

The thing he couldn't get over about the photo he'd seen was the young woman's skin. The image had been glowing with internal light. Pierce knew better.

"Porcine" had taxed him. He recalled how he had longed to write "pudgy" or "bloated."

Molly Mundy had come slouching into his cubicle on a Tuesday morning in the summer. She came bearing flyers and postcards—and a puppet, one she'd constructed for him, a puppet *of* him, with a blocky torso and a ghastly expression: tiny round mouth, raised eyebrows imploring, longing without hope. What kind of girl would craft such an awkward gift for a stranger?

She was no opalescent maiden or fairy lit from within. She was doughy and pockmarked. Her hair was uncombed, unwashed, a blunt cut ending at the jaw-line. Crunching bits of hard candy between unbleached yellow teeth. Her warmth was feral. Animal-like, she existed only in the moment, this infant who'd been coddled since birth. Her soft mouth was on a spree, munching a lemon drop and yammering about her boyfriend: a twenty-something prodigy from a family of writers and performers and the founder and A.D. of a theatre she

221

said Pierce really ought to visit and consider reviewing if he wanted to find out what young people were doing all over the city in these tiny venues with no budget just building sets and sewing costumes and painting and rehearsing and selling tickets and really-really being alive in the way organic performance was meant to be instead of polished to the point of death...

"Tell you what," Pierce had interrupted. "Why don't I write a feature about your group? What is it called, again? Crude Motion?" He cringed inside. "Sounds like the sort of thing my editor-in-chief would love."

That same night Molly Mundy had come to visit Pierce at home. She came bearing more gifts, photos of company members in sophomoric poses in makeshift costumes on bare stages with poor lighting.

"Excellent," Pierce said. "These will help readers get a sense of who you are and what you do."

She had come wearing a gossamer dress, empire waist with satin trim and silk wings. Ridiculous and needy as a child, she lingered in the doorway to his studio with her hands clasped in front of her. Giggling at his poster of Hamlet in pajamas. Gulping his wine. ("It has a weird little aftertaste.") Breathlessly describing a "radically re-imagined" production of Ibsen's most frequently produced play. ("So people can really see it, really for the first time.")

Pierce nodded and smiled. When the time was right, when her smile grew lazy and her words began to slur, he pulled Molly Mundy onto his lap and tugged her dress up around her waist. His eyes stayed with hers and she, fairy princess in love with her boy genius, let Pierce put his fingers inside her. The quick brightness in her eyes subsided. He shifted her weight and came without ever unbuttoning his trousers.

"Porcine."

Two weeks later he had summed up her turn as an elderly

housekeeper with one perfect adjective. He knew it was perfect because he never heard from Molly Mundy again. He hoped his assessment of her stage presence had driven the untalented girl back to the trailer park where she belonged.

The boy genius A.D. had fired off a predictable email questioning Pierce and his capacity to judge passionate, ephemeral art. Pierce had run out of energy and patience. He replied, simply, "Eat me." Lowbrow yet effective, and the last time the company or its boy wonder had come to his attention.

***

He pushed open the door of the café. The place was teeming, thanks to the dreary weather. He was about to retreat when a woman in the far corner stood to clear her table. Pierce felt a pang of distress when he realized the woman was Ali Franco and she was crying.

Bastard, he thought. Hurley had done the deed after hours, fired his nemesis and said nothing, depriving Pierce of a pleasure he had anticipated for weeks.

Franco didn't speak, only scooted around him with her face averted and exited the café. He draped his jacket over the chair to reserve the table.

The bell attached to the front door jingled, announcing more customers, this time a couple of Goths in black capes. They regarded the saved spot with disdain. Pierce had broken another unstated rule of the city by claiming a table before placing his order. He sighed with boredom and wondered what else the night would bring.

***

The Tatters Performance Group was supposed to reside in an abandoned warehouse between Pine and Pike. One of the few not yet claimed by developers.

Pierce walked from one corner to the other and back. Two streetlights facing one another across an alley were broken, making it difficult to read the numbers painted on the curb. On his fourth attempt he noticed a small, rain-marked poster taped to a metal door.

TPG

presents

Strange is the Night

Of course! It came to him at last. Chambers' tantalizing mythos must be catnip to these people. When Pierce was in school Alfred Jarry had been all the rage. Now everyone was adapting Chambers' fiction, usually without understanding it. Pierce smiled. The quiver in his stomach might have been joy or indigestion. It would be fun to teach the Tatters Performance Group a lesson.

He pushed open the metal door. After a second the narrow lobby with its plush carpet and brass-plated ticket booth emerged from shadows. Behind the booth's window a dour woman, round-faced and bespectacled, stared out at Pierce.

He noticed a couple of things: Aside from two old women consulting their programs there were no patrons milling about, always a bad sign at these invitation-only events; and his feet were sinking into the dense mush of gold carpeting. He approached the woman in the booth and said, "I'm here to review..."

She cut him off with a ticket stub and a greeting devoid of mirth or expression. "Thank you for joining us tonight, sir. We appreciate your patronage."

Through the window she pushed a manila envelope with the word "Media" printed in the same type as the sign on the front door. A glass of pinot grigio followed.

"Is the box office also the bar?" Pierce said.

"Only for special guests at special events, our finest private reserve," said the woman in the booth. "Complimentary, of course. Enjoy the show."

The carpet was so thick, so deep and spongy, Pierce had to lift his feet purposefully to make his way across the lobby. He felt as if he was goose-stepping but he had no choice. With each movement his feet sank heavily into the marshy substance.

"Strike one," he murmured.

He sipped the wine, found it deliciously bright and tart. The two old women stood nearby, heads inclined together. As he passed them Pierce noticed each wore a pencil skirt with a cashmere sweater set, one in blue and one in violet, with matching brooches, a glittering arc of diamonds forming the letter C. He caught only stray threads of their conversation.

"There, you see, just as I said."

"Cam, there was never a doubt."

"Please."

"I only argued there was no *frisson* if no one identifies with the goddamn protagonist."

"Well, explain the effect of Kabuki, my dear."

"You're off topic. One identifies with a mask, a stereotype, if tradition prepares us for it. You're obfuscating my original point."

"Does it matter whether anyone takes the hero to heart?"

"Oh," said one of the women, eyeing the wine glass Pierce held. "I didn't know they had a liquor license."

He wandered away from the women. He drained his glass. He made a mental note to make a written note about the exceptionally good wine and its questionable legality.

A heavyset woman with chalky gray hair and orthopedic shoes stood next to a curtain separating the lobby from the seating area. She handed Pierce a program. The cover bore the same symbol as the invitation he'd received, a symbol he now recognized as pure fiction, part of the pre-show theatrics, like the two old women in the lobby.

He walked past the usher. She took the empty glass from his hand.

"No drinks in the auditorium," she warned.

Pierce caught a whiff of jonquil-scented powder, and a hint of urine. "Strike two," he said to himself as he entered the theatre.

He noted with dismay only five people occupying seats, scattered as widely as possible in the small space. Including himself and the women in the lobby, they would be an audience of eight, a dismal turnout worth mentioning in his review.

He fumbled his way to an aisle seat in semi-darkness. The scent of dust, decades of it, confirmed his suspicion that this theatre had been handed down from one acting company to another. Dust, as ubiquitous in theatre as the aroma of popcorn at movies, accrued, layer upon layer, over decades.

Nestled in a surprisingly cozy seat, Pierce studied what the usher had so arrogantly called an "auditorium." Forty-nine seats faced a thrust stage without a shred of scenery. In the failing light he opened the program and found it was merely a sheet of paper with the same text he had read on the front door. No cast list. No director was named.

He tore open the media envelope. No production shots, no press release, just another program and an out-of-focus photo. Pierce squinted but he could only make out a soft outline, a blob of light. He stuffed the programs and photo back into the envelope and took another look around.

A woman seated two rows ahead of Pierce glanced back over her shoulder. Before she turned away, quickly facing front again, he was struck by the amount of makeup she was wearing. The colors of her lips and eyes were too well defined, as if tattooed in place.

The feeble house lights blinked off and the room was consumed by darkness. There didn't appear to be an exit sign, a reckless violation of the fire code. A cold rush of night air swept from the back of the stage through the audience. Pierce chuckled. This neophyte company probably thought a tactile approach was revolutionary. Given the quirks and illegalities of the whole affair, his review would write itself. By opening night the building would be condemned.

Following this thought he was aware of a bright amber illumination descending from the flies. He marveled at delicate gold chains and pulleys, crisscrossing beams on a grid, a shimmy of rafters, and the ceiling skewing.

"Marmalade," he mumbled, tongue thumping the roof of his mouth.

Orange-yellow petals spilled from above, lazily looping in air, striking his face and blocking his vision. From the wings, offstage, something rumbled.

***

"How do you do?" Molly said. "Oh, no! We already met at your office, didn't we? Stupid me!"

His hand engulfed hers. Her skin was sticky, warm as candy on a summer sidewalk. Her laugh guttural, trapped in her throat, her left hand opening to reveal a bite-size lozenge.

"More lemon drops?" Pierce said. "No, thank you."

"Marmalade," she said. "So sweet and so tart! Please, try it."

He refused, disgusted by the offer of unwrapped candy from her bare hand. Later he was glad he'd turned it down, after the yellow gore came rushing from her mouth.

"Oh my god, I'm so sorry," she cried, and jumped from his lap. With one hand pulling her dress down into place over her thighs, the other hand wiping vomit from her lips.

Pierce blotted the hardwood floor of his studio with a fist-ful of toilet paper snatched from the bathroom. Disgusting.

"It's this weather," she said. "So warm, and I've been work-ing so many hours, and things have been crazy. Oh, please don't be mad. It isn't you!"

Apologizing to him, with the honey-scented moisture of her pussy still drying on his fingertips. Begging forgiveness for not swooning, for not coming in his hand, for instead vomit-ing on the floor. Asking him to visit the company, watch a rehearsal, join the actors for supper, get drunk with the A.D. and get to know what they were trying to do. Why were these vapid young people always trying to "do" something? Every-thing had been done before they were born.

"Get out," he told her in the flat tone reserved for ingénues he had fucked. "Go."

Prompting the waterworks. Molly Mundy in her rumpled dress and bent wings, blubbering like a child reprimanded on the playground. All sputters and promises.

He had said yes, of course he would see their "radical re-imagining," of course, why not? It was his job to review the show. Don't give it another thought. Really.

And he had seen it. A typical disaster lightened by the young woman's bungled portrayal of an elderly housekeeper in powdered wig and clumsy shoes.

"Porcine." If every person had one word by which they might be destroyed, "porcine" had been Molly Mundy's word.

***

"Marmalade," Pierce mumbled and went silent. His eyes rolled. His tongue no longer knew how to function.

A substance as sticky as resin held him fast, facedown, petals smothering him. He knew saliva quivered on his lower lip but he had no strength to reach up and wipe it away. He groaned in the heat of a hundred lamps. Points of pain, sharp as pins, ran up and down his legs. Hot liquid spilled across his backside.

"That's enough honey. Turn him over," said a voice. "Let him see."

Pierce watched the pale yellow light spinning, arcing around him. When the smell registered he realized the arc was his vomit, an involuntary spasm. Hands pinched his pallid flesh, to hold and to cause damage, using his skin to roll him into position on his back. His vision was limited to a full-length mirror directly above, where he floated, bleeding and naked, smeared with honey, flower petals stuck to his hair and scattered down the length of his trembling body.

In a darkening pocket of his conscious mind he saw his next two thousand words spill across cheap paper, soaking it and disappearing. A blank sheet took its place and filled with a rush of words that sank and faded.

Fat fingers dug at his meaty shoulders, nails scraping bone, grasping for purchase, gripping, peeling. And somewhere in the wings, beyond this pale yellow light dancing over his naked corpus, Molly Mundy waited in her gossamer gown. Giggling. Patient. Hungry.

WATER MAIN

First the vine maples began to shiver, leaves of bright burgundy shot through with translucent veins forming a blood-red wall along the western edge of the park. Alders caught the rhythm and shook loose their amber, ragged leaves onto the yellow grass below. A final ray of sunlight struck the spot where the boy stood afraid to take another step. The sun seemed to roll down the far shoulder of the earth to be consumed by the cold waters of Puget Sound.

That final shimmer lasted only a second; when the boy looked up, night came tumbling down through the clouds. The air was bitterly cold. An underground rumble became a roar with a monstrous echo as it traveled. Bystanders in the park clapped hands to their ears and ran.

"This is what struck me about the grownups and never wore off," the boy said years later when he was a man, when he was a father. "They ran in all directions. Not one of them knew what to do! No one was going to help me. So I ran like hell.

"I heard the ground splitting, the asphalt and the side-walks cracking open. A Volkswagen rolled over in the street. On both sides of me the slopes and hills were rippling. The giant was waking up, stretching his limbs, and shaking loose anything in his path.

"I was running so fast I couldn't breathe, my heartbeat throbbing in my ears and throat. That's when I heard the worst thing, the worst sound you can imagine. Crashing against the ground close behind me I felt his footsteps pounding the earth. The giant was following me. He was chasing me down."

At this point in the story Nancy's father would sometimes wink as if to assure the girl he was much more sensible as an adult. Nancy winked too, anxious to ignore whatever was wrong with her dad, or whatever was still chasing him through his nightmares and into morning. She was forbidden to admit she heard him crying behind closed doors, her mother saying his name over and over until he fell quiet in her arms.

As for the ending to the story, he told a different variation depending upon his most recent dream. In one version he escaped by climbing to the top of a totem pole in the park. In another he ran to a nearby pier and leapt aboard a ship headed to Victoria. He never explained how he got down from the totem pole or returned from British Columbia.

These tacked-on happy endings didn't satisfy Nancy. When she was small and naive enough to believe in the giant, she wanted to know if it tried to shake her father loose from the totem pole. Did it follow him onto the pier, and drown in the bay?

After the age of nine or ten she understood the basic conditions that caused earthquakes. She became curious about the scale of it and the duration. She realized it could only have lasted for a couple of minutes at most, not the amount of time needed for a boy's epic adventure. As she grew up, the facts of the quake were the only parts of the story that interested Nancy. But for her father the childish fantasy of that day and its aftershocks lingered a lifetime—a lifetime being the four decades it took for him to drink himself to death.

A crisp day in autumn not long before Halloween always reminded Nancy of her father and his warnings. Throughout her childhood he had doled them out like candy. In fact, candy was at the top of the list of things she was supposed to avoid, especially holiday treats from strangers. But there were also dire warnings about public toilets, dogs (even on leashes), convenience stores (especially at night), unsupervised children and teens, electrical outlets (during storms), unlit rooms, steep staircases, carnival rides, banquet or buffet food, cocktails on a date, and all weather conditions.

Nancy trudged uphill from the bus stop. When she reached her apartment building she took a deep breath and resisted an urge to kick the jack-o-lanterns piled next to the front door. She wanted to. She wanted to slam her boots right into the crooked mouth of the biggest pumpkin and spread its orange, gooey guts all over the sidewalk.

Jim wasn't waiting for her to get home. He was playing one of his games, the lights from the TV screen sparkling in his otherwise vacant eyes.

"If you don't fix the plumbing by the end of the week," she told him, "I'm calling the manager."

"I'm on it," he said. "I'm all over it."

"What does that mean? I'll bet you haven't done a thing today, have you? Call the manager. Let him send a real plumber this time."

"They'll make us pay a fortune for it. They think this is our fault."

"I don't care, Jim. If you don't fix it by the weekend, I don't know what I'll do."

Vague as it was, this was Nancy's most emphatic threat so far. She had given him more than enough time. Her tender request in July had been followed by earnest pleading in August, sarcasm in September, and then came the October of shouting and angry tears. As they approached Halloween the prospect of one more weekend tiptoeing around an icy puddle to reach the toilet, or changing clothes for work after getting spattered with meat-scented water from the kitchen, made Nancy want to strangle someone. She never drank tap water any more, only bottled. She blamed Jim for the added expense.

He had made a useless promise every week since they leased the place, a spot he'd scoped out for its scenic beauty rather than practicality. Perched halfway up Queen Anne, the steepest hill in the city, the four-story Pacific Willow Arms afforded one quarter of its tenants—those, like Nancy and Jim, facing west and living above the second floor—a panoramic view. Tenants on the east side had to be content with a view of trash dumpsters lining a concrete alley.

"On a clear day we'll be able to watch whales from our living room!" Jim had said the day they moved in. He'd bought a pair of binoculars for each of them and spent hours spying on the bars, cafes, and rooftop gardens down the hill. Clear days, clear enough to see Puget Sound, were unusual. Even in summer they never spotted any ocean life, only massive clouds shaped like whales, gliding morosely parallel to the water.

From the second month of the lease, they'd had plumbing problems. The compact washer-dryer only operated when balanced at one corner by a wine bottle cork. The cold water handle in the bathroom sink was loose; jiggling it prompted a jolting noise from somewhere beneath the wood and porcelain vanity. One day the dishwasher erupted, sending an inch-deep lake of foam across the kitchen floor. Later their basement storage unit flooded, ruining a sofa bed and a trunk full of photo albums and mementos; renters insurance only covered the sofa bed, and the lease agreement left management exempt from responsibility.

"It's probably that water main again," the manager had explained while munching wasabi and seaweed crackers. "That's like a *force majeure*. Happens every few years. You could sue the city for negligence but good luck with that. Ever try fighting a parking ticket? Bureaucracy's gonna outlive all of us."

Recently the garbage disposal seemed to run in reverse, drawing up from the bowels of the Pacific Willow Arms a sulfurous sludge Jim had dubbed "the ick." In less than a week the ick spread beneath the floor, under the living room, to the hall bathroom and lingered until they stopped using the garbage disposal altogether. Nancy was mortified to learn their downstairs neighbor had complained about the smell emanating from his ceiling fan.

"I told him we can't be accountable for natural occurrences or unsanitary personal behavior," the manager said.

Finally, that morning, the shower had come to a stuttering stop. Nancy had toweled dry and dressed for work. All day long she detected a vague underlying funk, a dried layer of sweat trapped between her skin and her clothes. She hated the feeling but she didn't dare cover it with perfume. Nearly everyone at the office was allergic, or claimed to be.

Through a team meeting, an executive tour for the Korean investors, and a couple of video conferences, she kept yearning for a bath—a long, hot, lazy bath with aromatic salts in a tub lit with rose-scented candles. Meanwhile she stank of sweat with a hint of something oily like herring. It seemed as if the day would never end. By the time she stepped off the #8 and began the slow, sweaty ascent to her building—now that she examined it closely, the whole structure of the Pacific Willow Arms appeared to rest uneasily on its carefully graded foundation—she was almost convinced her imaginary bath would be waiting for her because she deserved it.

Instead, as usual, she found Jim slumped in his favorite chair, wearing pajamas and munching a slice of pizza. Cheese stuck to his teeth and he reeked of garlic, anchovies, and onions. Behind him, arranged across the kitchen linoleum, lay a vast array of plumbing tools.

"Why can't you put those on a drop cloth?" Nancy asked while she peeled off her coat.

"What's a drop cloth, again?" he said.

It was a constant source of irritation, this fantasy Jim had of himself as a handyman. His parents had been in construction, his dad a sub-contractor and his mom the company bookkeeper. Jim hated helping his dad with home repairs when he was growing up. Yet ever since his dad passed away he'd been nursing this delusion that he had absorbed the old man's knowledge. Not through practice or study but the way Jim claimed to learn everything—by magic, by osmosis, by picking up signs and clues in the atmosphere.

What he actually picked up were tools. Every time he tackled another section of pipes, he spent hours at Home Depot. When he finally came home he brought wrench sets, clamps, and tube cutters. Then he arranged everything on the floor and spent days in slow motion repairing the most recent trouble area. Within days or even hours of each fix another section would fail, and Jim would start the process all over again with another three-hour trip to Home Depot.

Nancy was sick of it. The leaks and damage now felt like reminders of their incompatibility, as if the place couldn't contain the multitude of differences erupting between them. Her habit of setting aside money from each paycheck was wasted on Jim, who considered earned cash to be instantly expendable. She had no idea how much he spent streaming his latest obsession—a series of poorly produced 1970s cartoons that left Nancy grinding her teeth. The art direction was terrible. All of the characters, both animal and human, were nothing but blobs. Every episode revolved around a different blob getting stuck or lost until his blob friends came to the rescue and all the blobs joined blobby appendages and sang the insipid theme song.

She wondered if she was being mean for not appreciating Jim's idea of fun. Then she blamed him for inciting her guilt and self-criticism. All she wanted was a hot bath or shower and a glass of clean tap water, things she once took for granted and was now beginning to think of as luxuries.

"I'm going for a walk," she said.

She pulled her coat and scarf from the closet and put them back on. She didn't expect him to object. She knew he wouldn't follow, or make sure she was bundled up against the cold, or give her a kiss. Over the past few months he'd grown negligent. They'd stopped taking day trips, stopped having an occasional lunch together. She couldn't remember the last time they'd had sex. He just wasn't interested. He never asked where she was going or how long she would be gone. Most evenings when he wasn't tinkering with the plumbing he sat completely mute, playing the latest versions of his favorite games or staring at his blobby cartoons on TV. In every way, since they'd moved in, Jim had become the opposite of what she wanted. They never talked about getting married, these days. They never talked about anything except the apartment.

She knew all of this. She'd been thinking it through for a long time. Yet she was infuriated when he waved goodbye without a word, without getting up from his chair, and turned his attention back to his game. She yanked the door shut and felt it reverberate in the frame.

A gust of wind spiked with drizzle greeted her when she emerged from the stairwell and stepped outdoors. She tightened her scarf and shivered. Traffic was slower than usual. All of the stores down the hill on Mercer and 1st Avenue were decorated with cobwebs, spiders, witches, and black cats. It only reminded Nancy how much time had gone by, and how much of her life had been wasted on the peculiarities of men she loved.

Not that Jim and her father would have gotten along. Her father would have warned her away from Jim. Her father would have vetoed the slim, soft-spoken young programmer with reddish brown hair hanging down in his eyes. But her father was dead, and before he died he was crazy. All of his paternal advice could be summed up in one word. Don't. Don't trust cab drivers. Don't talk to people on the bus. Don't go anywhere without cash in case a disaster shuts down the electricity and all the ATMs are broken into. Don't tell anyone you carry cash. On and on, all of it based on fear.

She considered walking down to the new bar for a martini. But then she would have to trudge back uphill to get home. The alternative to walking downhill and then up, or uphill and back down, was to turn east and follow Halloran Street alongside her building. There was never much traffic there, thanks to the topography. This was one of the odd areas the early European settlers had failed to conquer by re-grading. The best the city planners could do was to chart around natural inclinations. Landscaping gave way suddenly to rock formations, streets ended abruptly, and a death-defying set of concrete stairs had been laid against the bluff as a grudging accommodation to pedestrians. No one took the stairs unless they were drunk or stupid.

By following Halloran east Nancy would eventually reach another, smaller hill and more exclusive housing protected by low brick walls. But there was a good three blocks of neighborhood before that. She hoped the round trip would give her time to stomp out her anger and prepare for a decent night's sleep.

As soon as she started off she regretted leaving her gloves at home. She had peeled them off and slapped them down on the table in the foyer. The sight of Jim had sent a final electric charge through her veins. In her rage she had forgotten to collect her gloves.

Going back wasn't an option. If Jim turned to her one more time with his dopey, sleepy grin she wasn't sure she could be trusted not to murder him in his sleep. So she clenched her fists, shoved them deep inside her pockets, and pressed on into the soft, icy drizzle.

She took Halloran, crossed the first intersection, and passed the house Jim called Dead Poet's Corner. The 1950s mansion reminded Nancy of a trophy house for some ancient movie star like Doris Day. Its dove-gray walls spread wide from both sides of the front door like welcoming arms. In fact it was a haven, bequeathed to an obscure department of the city as an artists' retreat. At all hours, in all seasons, the lawn was dotted with scruffy bearded men and women with long white hair, most of them wearing loose fitting garments, wandering in a daze or staring at nothing.

"Communing with their muses," Jim had said the first time he and Nancy spotted the house. "Or just waiting for the Man."

"Who's the Man?" Nancy had asked. "You mean, the guy with their drugs?"

"Show some respect for the hippies," Jim had said. "They're a sacred race. This is where they come to die."

She remembered laughing and linking arms with him. They never had silly conversations anymore. She never caught him studying her with an expression of abject devotion. Somehow this year everything between them had dwindled and fallen away.

As she passed Dead Poet's Corner she peeked at the lawn. Tonight a couple walked hand-in-hand there, each step as delicately executed as a Himalayan climbing expedition. Both figures were soft, whisper-thin, with long shawls draping their shoulders and the crocheted hats perched high on their heads giving a tiny shimmy with each movement.

Night was spreading across the neighborhood. Nancy walked on. The sad grace of the couple on the lawn made her shudder but she couldn't say which emotion was stronger, disappointment or dread. She didn't like to think of the future anymore.

In the shadows between streetlamps a pair of sparkling eyes followed her movements. When she reached the darkest point the creature let loose a yowl and pressed its body against her ankle. Nancy tripped and then righted herself, and the cat went galloping across the street.

"Stupid thing," she called after it. "Go home!"

The chill arc of the next streetlamp revealed a three-story house with a yard full of red, yellow, and orange maple leaves, and a cluster of jack-o'-lanterns on the porch. Fussy Victorian trim decorated every surface, and amber light glowed from an attic window.

In the past this would have prompted Jim to tell a story, some awful tale from one of the horror movies he loved. Something about a scar-faced woman hunting children in the dark, or a maniac hiding in the basement.

Nancy winced at the pain these trivial memories conjured. There had been a time when she could tell Jim anything, and he would make a story out of it.

"But what if the giant under the earth was real?" Jim had said, the first time Nancy recounted her father's bedtime story.

"My dad dreamed up a monster to make himself feel less afraid of earthquakes."

"Did it work?" Jim asked. And she laughed bitterly.

"Terrible things happen," she said. "We can't change that. We have to go on living every day, in the real world."

"I don't know," Jim said. "Maybe everyone should be a little bit afraid of the things we can't explain."

In hindsight, Nancy wondered if she should have taken this conversation as a sign of all the differences between herself and Jim. Maybe his strange view of life wasn't healthy. She recalled the most frightening thing her father had ever told her, not long before he died.

"If the giant ever finds you, Nan, don't ask questions. Don't try to reason it out. Don't stop. You run like hell, all the way home."

She wasn't afraid of real things. She was only afraid of her father's nightmares. He was such a fearful man, never at ease. His imagination had poisoned him over the years.

She passed a well-lit house where two children sat in a picture window, gazing out. The drizzle had let up but the air was still damp, the light diffuse. Through the haze Nancy could see the children—a girl dressed as a devil and a boy dressed as a ghost—staring out at her as she walked by.

The elms lining this part of Halloran Street were losing their leaves. She marveled at how the solid trunks in autumn and winter resembled arms; the branches, at mid height, fanned out like fingers.

Jim wasn't a terrible person. She bookmarked this phrase, to use later. She would begin by telling Jim he wasn't a terrible person; he simply wasn't the right person for her. He would be fine after they split up. He made a fair living programming phone apps, he had friends, and he was still young. She would resist the urge to call him childish.

Yet he was childish. Nancy was tired of playing the grownup. She had to manage every aspect of their lives, or risk disappointment. Anything left to his judgment was bound to go wrong. If she let him choose a restaurant they ended up eating pizza at a water-stained table where the kitchen door hit them every time it opened, because Jim was fine with it. If she asked him to locate a comfortable apartment while her team at work crunched a ludicrous number of hours on a big project, they ended up living in a swamp because Jim imagined whale watching from home. Indulging his plan to repair the swamp resulted in misery because Jim didn't see the problem. If she'd left birth control up to him, she would have been pregnant as well as fed up.

He didn't understand how important it was to make plans and follow through, to consider options, and build on what was accomplished. He brought to mind a story she'd read as an undergrad, about an incompetent engineer who bid low to win a contract with the city back in the 1890s. There was an urgent need to stem the spread of cholera following a series of natural disasters that left the downtown flooded. The engineer won his contract and designed a tunnel between the lakes and the bay, to provide a better sewage system. But he disregarded certain geological foundations; his plan was entirely theoretical. He cut corners and hired inexperienced labor. While digging was underway the workers hit an underground lake, causing a rupture that flooded the tunnel and consumed them.

Fortunately Jim's profession didn't require him to lead people into harm's way. But there were other ways to ruin a life. The way Nancy's parents had ruined one another's lives. Slow leaks gradually eroding the ground until the moment when concern and compromise gave way to catastrophe.

A flash of light interrupted Nancy's reverie. She froze with one foot on the curb and the other in the street, and a Mini Cooper whipped past in the wrong lane. In the driver's seat a man wearing a leopard costume and mask glared at her. From the passenger's seat his companion, wearing rabbit ears and whiskers, shouted something Nancy couldn't make out.

She backed up onto the curb and waited, trying to catch her breath. Her impulse was to bolt, to dash home and jump into bed, to let it all out by sobbing herself to sleep. Her father was gone, and Jim was useless. She had to take charge of her life, somehow, without help.

As she turned to head home she noticed a building directly across Halloran. She was surprised to see apartments nestled between the well-tended single-family dwellings. She thought the zoning for such a structure ended at Queen Anne Avenue. But then she remembered Dead Poet's Corner and decided there must be exceptions for old buildings of architectural or historical value.

From where Nancy stood the building resembled bordellos she had seen in photos of the French Quarter in New Orleans, cake-tiered, lined with windows. As she approached, the impression altered. There were no balconies, and the windows were as round as portholes ringed with brass. In the haze she might have been looking at a cruise ship docked at the end of a pier at night. The light on its surface wavered as if it were floating, with greenish waves splashing across the white walls.

A man sat on a folding chair under a square awning at the front door, which was made of brass to match the portholes. The man wore a white shirt with blue trousers and no jacket despite the cold. He was studying his fingernails.

Nancy followed the walkway until she stood directly before him. She glanced at either side of the building but the houses flanking it were in shadow.

"Perambulating on a fine evening," the man said, and looked up at Nancy.

His eyes were a color her mother would have called seafoam green, all the more luminous and startling framed by loose, white tendrils of hair that fell to his shoulders.

"Yes," Nancy said, when she found her voice. "Walking. Just wandering around."

"Such a pity," he said.

"Walking helps me think." She didn't know why she offered an explanation. She told herself she was being extra polite, since she was the one trespassing.

"For a moment you might have been the woman I'm

waiting to see," he replied. "But the time has passed. Time to go indoors."

"Sorry," Nancy said.

It was a sad thought, the man sitting outside waiting for a woman who didn't show up. He was old but she couldn't say whether he might be sixty or eighty.

"And you have no interest, then?"

She didn't know what to say. He couldn't be serious.

"The deposit is very small," he said. "Very cozy here. Private kitchen and bath included of course."

Relief came with a quick exhalation, and then she felt like laughing.

"You have an apartment for rent?" Nancy asked.

"Yes," he said. "Yes. Small, very comfortable for one person, very reasonable rates." He quoted an amount, far less than she was paying for her share of the place with Jim.

"You want to view?" he asked.

"Oh," she said. "Well, I don't know. What if the person you're waiting for shows up, after all?"

"She isn't coming." He shook his head dismissively. "She's lost her appointment here."

The brisk night air made Nancy shiver. She could hear the noise from Queen Anne but it traveled lightly, more music and voices than traffic.

She was curious about the interior of this peculiar building. What could it hurt? She wasn't ready to leave Jim this week but she could report on her expedition. Maybe it was exactly what he needed to shake him up. If she threatened to move out, he would shrug and go back to his video games. He wouldn't take her seriously. But if she came home with a price quote, it might do the trick. At the very least it might scare him into calling a real plumber.

"Yes," she told the man. "I'd like to take a tour."

The hour was well past twilight. All she could see was the

walkway, not Halloran Street beyond. When she turned to face the man again, he was holding open the brass door. She stepped through the rounded archway, impressed once more by the eccentricities of the architect.

"My name is Nancy," she told the man.

"Good," he said. "I'm the manager and I live here. Felix."

"Who designed the building?"

"A man of great means," he said. "Not of this century."

"In the shipping business?"

"No," he said. "Why would you say so?"

"The nautical theme," she replied. But Felix ignored the comment.

Instead of entering a foyer Nancy stood before a narrow, circular stairway with a brass handrail. It crossed her mind that the novelty of such a place could lose its charm after a while. Although she was fit enough to handle the stairs, she didn't imagine the place was up to code in terms of disability access. Her train of thought was interrupted by the sound of Felix pulling the door shut, a whoosh of pistons and a sudden sense of being sealed in.

"Built to keep out cold," he said. He raised one palm toward the stairs. "Please."

"Maybe I should follow you, since I don't know the way," Nancy told him. She was determined not to be silly. Recalling her father's advice about strangers and fast cars and men with long hair, she decided she was perfectly safe taking a brief tour of an apartment three blocks from where she lived. Hers was absurd and useless training, the ignorant advice of an older worldview but also the product of a disturbed mind.

Up and up they climbed. She caught sight of a wide hallway painted bright white with blue baseboards. From her limited perspective it appeared that most of the doors on this level were wide open.

"Do you rent studio space?" Nancy asked. For it occurred

to her that the artists down the street might have living quarters at Dead Poet's Corner, and workspace here.

"No studio," Felix said over his shoulder. He continued up the stairs and Nancy followed.

She saw someone gliding through one of the doors below on the level they were leaving. She couldn't tell if the figure were a man or a woman shuffling sideways and out of sight again. The halting, nervous quality of this motion made Nancy feel queasy, and then ashamed. A practical question occurred to her. If the person she'd seen were disabled, there must be another route through the building. She thought of turning back and descending the stairs but a glance downward brought an unexpected rush of vertigo.

"Excuse me," she said. "Do you mind if we stop at the next floor?"

Above her Felix replied, "Yes, yes, this is where we want to be. At the very next floor."

Nevertheless, when he reached the level above he continued climbing the stairs. This time when Nancy emerged she was sure another figure went scuttling from the hallway to an open door, disappearing before she could determine the reason for his or her shuddering gait.

"Aren't we there yet?" Nancy asked.

"Yes, yes," said Felix. "Very much so."

He stepped off the stairs at the next level and offered one hand to steady her. She touched it for a second but his softly tapered, damp fingers repulsed her. She let go and resisted the urge to wipe her palm on her coat.

"Here we go, then, yes," said Felix. "Come, follow me." He gave no indication he had noticed her disgust and she tried to act as if it hadn't happened.

On this floor the corridor was identical to the ones below but only a few of the doors were open. Wafting through was a distinct odor of boiling cabbage and fried salmon, and the shrill cries of infants. Felix approached a door with no number and unlocked it.

"Oh, yes," he said as though he'd just remembered something important. He knocked briskly on the door, holding it half open and calling out, "Showing these premises now!"

No one answered.

"Good, good," he said. "We're here at the right time. Come in."

He pushed the door open and proceeded inside. A few steps into the dimly lit quarters he beckoned to Nancy to join him.

She leaned in with one foot on the threshold and scanned the room. Filthy rags and soiled clothing lay in piles on the hardwood floor. A closet was sectioned off with a maroon curtain, half open, and the contents appeared to be random— boots, lampshades, inflated beach balls, stacks of vinyl records, some sort of medical equipment with dials, tubes, and funnels.

Felix had reached the opposite side of the room and was still gesturing for Nancy to join him. She might have stepped forward just to be polite if she hadn't noticed the narrow mattress shoved against the wall to her left, covered in stained sheets. It looked as if it had been used by dozens of people and had never been cleaned. Some of the stains were brown and some were black as oil.

"You want to see, yes?" Felix asked. "Come, come, Miss. Come in. Don't be shy."

Nancy backed up a step, and another. "You know what?" she said. "I'll have to ask my boyfriend if he wants to move."

"Come inside and see for yourself," said Felix. He took a step toward her.

The lie made her feel vulnerable and foolish but she didn't care. All she wanted was to get out of there as soon as possible.

"My boyfriend is right outside. He's waiting for me. I'll ask what he thinks." She turned away from Felix, who was still beckoning and moving closer. She heard his voice rising in the background.

"You will be foolish not to take this chance, Miss," he called out. "Don't be childish!"

For a moment she blanked and couldn't figure out where she was in relation to the stairs. She heard a shuffling noise and sensed movement on the floor around her.

She forced herself to look down at three babies crawling in sodden diapers, all of them wailing. Their faces glistened with tears and snot and as they crawled they left wet trails like slugs.

Beyond the open doors came the unmistakable sizzle of a frying pan, and Nancy pictured hotplates with glowing rings. The cabbage and salmon returned in waves, a nauseating, overpowering stench.

She headed for the stairs and started down, fighting dizziness. She descended several steps and stopped, gazing at eye level at another floor full of screaming babies. A large figure emerged from one of the doors. This time she didn't try to decide if it was male or female, gender hardly mattering to a creature without legs, a thick torso shuddering forward on its long, split tail.

The rattle of the stairs coiled beneath her reminded Nancy where she was, or she might have fallen to the floor. She had to reach the brass door before the creatures converged on her. She let instinct guide her body, one foot and then the other landing with a thud on each step, moving robotically and trying not to trip.

As she passed the first floor she saw them coming, more of the crying infants, at least a dozen of them, crawling toward her. She saw them for an instant but it was enough to confirm they were not wearing diapers. Their naked bodies shimmied on the wet trails they left, and their tapered, split ends slid from side to side in the tears and snot.

Nancy stumbled and landed hard, tailbone slamming against the final step. Pain seared her pelvis but she didn't slow down. On all the floors above her the larger creatures were slithering into view, their screams echoing and expanding.

She grabbed the handle of the brass front door with both hands and tugged with all her might. Above her on the last floor she could hear the slobbering of babies, the shrieking of the other creatures, and the voice of Felix calling her back.

"You belong in your room, Miss!"

From every shadow above, the shuddering figures emerged. One of them stretched out and began the descent toward Nancy, walking on its hands and then sliding on its belly down the spiral staircase.

Nancy pounded the brass door with her fists and screamed. She gave the handle another yank and cried out with relief when the pistons let loose with a rush of cold air. She jumped out onto the walkway and began to race through the darkness. She could hear the portholes breaking, the wailing of all the creatures mingling with the rumble of earth beneath her.

She wanted to run all the way home, and she would have, but something more familiar than anything she knew told her to stop in her tracks, or she would never escape.

"Don't try to reason it out. Don't stop."

But she did. She stopped. She let reason flood her mind and body as surely as the creatures pursuing her were flooding the stairwell behind her. Shaking, freezing, with tears running down her face, and more afraid than she had ever been in her life, she turned around.

S.P. Miskowski's debut novel, *Knock Knock*, and first novella, *Delphine Dodd*, were Shirley Jackson Award finalists. Her short stories appear in the magazines *Supernatural Tales, Black Static, Identity Theory*, and *Strange Aeons* as well as in the anthologies *Haunted Nights, The Madness of Dr. Caligari, Little Visible Delight, October Dreams II, Autumn Cthulhu, Cassilda's Song, The Hyde Hotel, Darker Companions: Celebrating 50 Years of Ramsey Campbell*, and *Looming Low*. Her writing has received a Swarthout Award and two National Endowment for the Arts Fellowships. Dim Shores published Miskowski's "Stag in Flight" as a limited edition chapbook with illustrations by Nick Gucker. Her SJA nominated novella, *Muscadines*, is included in the Dunhams Manor Press hardcover series with illustrations by Dave Felton. Her novel, *I Wish I Was Like You*, is available from JournalStone.

S. P. MISKOWSKI

I WISH I WAS
LIKE YOU

CPSIA information can be obtained
at www.ICGtesting.com
Printed in the USA
LVOW11s2110111017
552034LV00002B/481/P